DROWNING

Archer wasn't going anywhere with the case. The women in it were getting to him. The one who had married for money was out to show him how little it now mattered. The one who was being blackmailed didn't care how Archer saved her mockery of a marriage. The young girl was the worst: too innocent to be involved in this sordid tangle. Three beautiful women. They had a way of distracting Archer—even from murder.

THE DROWNING POOL

Don't miss any of the Lew Archer novels, the detective series **The New York Times** called "the finest ever written by an American." Available in Bantam editions where paperbacks are sold:

THE BLUE HAMMER
THE FAR SIDE OF THE DOLLAR
THE GOODBYE LOOK
THE INSTANT ENEMY
THE IVORY GRIN
THE MOVING TARGET
THE WAY SOME PEOPLE DIE

THE DROWNING POOL

ROSS MAC-DONALD

BANTAM BOOKS · TORONTO · NEW YORK · LONDON

*This low-priced Bantam Book
has been completely reset in a type face
designed for easy reading, and was printed
from new plates. It contains the complete
text of the original hard-cover edition.*
NOT ONE WORD HAS BEEN OMITTED.

THE DROWNING POOL

*A Bantam Book / published by arrangement with
Alfred A Knopf, Inc*

PRINTING HISTORY

Knopf edition published August 1950

Bantam edition / October 1970

2nd printing . November 1970	8th printing	December 1973
3rd printing .. February 1971	9th printing	..... July 1975
4th printing ..... March 1971	10th printing	...... July 1975
5th printing ..... March 1971	11th printing	.. August 1975
6th printing . November 1971	12th printing	... January 1976
7th printing . September 1972	13th printing	.... March 1977

14th printing

ISBN 0-553-10910-3

Published simultaneously in the United States and Canada

---

*Bantam Books are published by Bantam Books, Inc. Its trade-
mark, consisting of the words "Bantam Books" and the por-
trayal of a bantam, is registered in the United States Patent
Office and in other countries. Marca Registrada. Bantam
Books, Inc., 666 Fifth Avenue, New York, New York 10019.*

PRINTED IN THE UNITED STATES OF AMERICA

TO TONY

CHAPTER 1

If you didn't look at her face she was less than thirty, quick-bodied and slim as a girl. Her clothing drew attention to the fact: a tailored sharkskin suit and high heels that tensed her nylon-shadowed calves. But there was a pull of worry around her eyes and drawing at her mouth. The eyes were deep blue, with a sort of double vision. They saw you clearly, took you in completely, and at the same time looked beyond you. They had years to look back on, and more things to see in the years than a girl's eyes had. About thirty-five, I thought, and still in the running.

She stood in the doorway without speaking long enough for me to think those things. Her teeth were nibbling the inside of her upper lip, and both of her hands were clutching her black suede bag at the level of her waist. I let the silence stretch out. She had knocked and I had opened the door. Undecided or not, she couldn't expect me to lift her over the threshold. She was a big girl now, and she had come for a reason. Her stance was awkward with urgency.

"Mr. Archer?" she said at last.

"Yes. Will you come in."

"Thank you. Forgive me for hanging back. It must make you feel like a dentist."

1

"Everybody hates detectives and dentists. We hate them back."

"Not really? Actually, I've never been to a dentist." She smiled as if to illustrate the point, and gave me her hand in a free gesture. It was hard and brown. *"Or* a detective."

I placed her in the soft chair by the window. She didn't mind the light. Her hair was its natural brown, without a fleck of gray that I could see. Her face was clear and brown. I wondered if she was clear and brown all over.

"What tooth is bothering you, Mrs. —?"

"Excuse me. My name is Maude Slocum. I always forget my manners when I'm upset."

She was much too apologetic for a woman with that figure, in those clothes. "Look," I said. "I am rhinoceros-skinned and iron-hearted. I've been doing divorce work in L.A. for ten years. If you can tell me anything I haven't heard, I'll donate a week's winnings at Santa Anita to any worthy charity."

"And can you whip your weight in wildcats, Mr. Archer?"

"Wildcats terrify me, but people are worse."

"I know what you mean." The fine white teeth were tugging again at the warm mouth. "I used to think, when I was younger, that people were willing to live and let live—you know? Now I'm not so sure."

"You didn't come here this morning, though, to discuss morals in the abstract. Did you have a specific example in mind?"

She answered after a pause: "Yes. I had a shock yesterday." She looked close into my face, and then beyond. Her eyes were as deep as the sea beyond Catalina. "Someone is trying to destroy me."

"Kill you, you mean?"

"Destroy the things I care about. My husband, my family, my home." The rhythm of her voice faltered and ceased. "It's dreadfully hard to tell you, the thing is so underhanded."

Here we go again, I said to myself. True confession morning, featuring Archer the unfrocked priest. "I should have gone to City College and been a dentist and gone in for something easy and painless like pulling teeth. If you really need my help, you'll have to tell me what with. Did someone send you here?"

"You were recommended. I know a—man who does police work. He said you were honest, and discreet."

"Unusual thing for a cop to say about me. Would you care to mention his name?"

"No, I wouldn't." The very suggestion seemed to alarm her. Her fingers tightened on the black suede bag. "He doesn't know about this."

"Neither do I. I don't expect I ever will." I let a smile go with it, and offered her a cigarette. She puffed on it without relish, but it seemed to relax her a little.

"Damn it." She coughed once over the smoke. "Here I've been up all night, trying to make up my mind, and I still haven't made it up. No one knows, you see. It's hard to bring myself to tell anyone else. One acquires the habit of silence, after sixteen years."

"Sixteen years? I thought it happened yesterday."

She colored. "Oh, it did. I was simply thinking of how long I'd been married. This has a good deal to do with my marriage."

"So I gather. I'm good at guessing-games."

"I'm sorry. I don't mean to offend you or insult you." Her contriteness was unexpected in a woman of her class. It didn't go with hundred-dollar suits. "It isn't that I think you'll spread it around, or try to blackmail me—"

"Is somebody else trying to blackmail you?"

The question startled her so that she jumped. She recrossed her legs and leaned forward in the chair. "I don't know. I haven't any idea."

"Then we're even." I took an envelope out of the top drawer of my desk, opened it, and began to read the mimeographed enclosure. It informed me that the chances were one in three that I'd enter a hospital within the year, that I couldn't afford to be unprotected by health insurance, and that he who hesitates is lost. "He who hesitates is lost," I said aloud.

"You're making fun of me, Mr. Archer. But just what is the arrangement? If you take the case, you'll naturally be governed by my interests. But if you don't, and I've told you about this thing, can I trust you to forget it?"

I let my irritation show in my voice, and this time I didn't smile, or even grimace. "Let's both forget it. You're wasting my time, Mrs. Slocum."

"I know I am." There was self-disgust in her tone, more than there should have been. "This thing has been a physical blow to me, a blow from behind." Then she spoke with sudden decision, and opened her bag with taut white fingers: "I suppose I must let you see it. I can't just go home now and sit and wait for another one."

I looked at the letter she handed me. It was short and to the point, without heading or signature:

Dear Mr. Slocum:
Lilies that fester smell far worse than weeds. Can you possibly enjoy playing the role of a complaisant cuckold? Or are you strangely unaware of your wife's amorous activities?

The message was typed on a sheet of cheap white typing paper that had been folded to the size of a small envelope. "Is there an envelope to go with this?"

"Yes." She rummaged in her purse, and handed me a crumpled white envelope, which was addressed to James Slocum, Esq., Trail Road, Nopal Valley, California. The postmark was clear: Quinto, Calif., July 18.

"This is Wednesday," I said. "It was mailed Monday. Do you know people in Quinto?"

"Everybody." She managed a strained smile. "It's only a few miles from Nopal Valley, where we live. But I haven't the faintest notion who could have sent it."

"Or why?"

"I have enemies, I suppose. Most people have."

"I take it your husband hasn't seen it. James Slocum *is* your husband?"

"Yes. He hasn't seen it. He was busy in Quinto when it came. I usually bicycle down to the mailbox, anyway."

"Is he in business in Quinto?"

"Not in business. He's very active in the Quinto Players—it's a semi-professional theatrical group. They're rehearsing every afternoon this week—"

I cut her short: "Do you usually read your husband's mail?"

"Yes, I do. We read each other's—I hardly expected to be cross-questioned, Mr. Archer."

"One more question. Is the allegation true?"

The blood coursed under the clear skin of her face, and her eyes brightened. "I can't be expected to answer that."

"All right. You wouldn't be here if it weren't true."

"On the contrary," she said.

"And you want me to find out who sent the letter, and prosecute him or her?"

"Oh, no." She wasn't clever. "I simply want it stopped. I can't stand guard over the mailbox to intercept his mail, and I can't stand the strain of waiting and wondering—"

"Besides, the next note might be handed to him personally. Would it matter so much if he read it?"

"It would matter terribly."

"Why? Is he violently jealous?"

"Not at all, he's a very quiet man."

"And you're in love with him?"

"I married him," she said. "I haven't regretted it."

"If your marriage is a good one, you don't have to worry about a poison-pen or two." I tossed the letter on the desk-top between us, and looked into her face.

Her mouth and eyes were tormented. "It would be the last straw. I have a daughter who is still in school. I simply won't permit this thing to happen."

"What thing?"

"A breakup and divorce," she answered harshly.

"Is that what it means if your husband gets one of

those?" I pointed my cigarette at the scrap of white paper.

"I'm afraid it does, Mr. Archer. I could cope with James, perhaps, but he'd take it to his mother, and *she'd* hire detectives."

"Could they find grounds for divorce? Is there evidence against you?"

"There must be," she said bitterly. "Someone knows." Her entire body moved slightly, twitched like a worm on a hook. For the moment she loathed her sex. "This is very painful for me."

"I know," I said. "My wife divorced me last year. Extreme mental cruelty."

"I think you might be capable of it." There was gentle malice in her voice; then her mood changed again: "Please don't imagine I take divorce lightly. It's the last thing I want."

"On account of your daughter, you say?"

She considered that. "Ultimately, yes. I was the child of a divorced couple myself, and I suffered for it. There are other reasons, too. My mother-in-law would like it much too well."

"What sort of a woman is she? Could she have sent the letter?"

The question caught her off guard, and she had to think again. "No. I'm sure she didn't. She'd act much more directly. She's a very strong-minded woman. As I told you, I haven't the slightest idea who sent it."

"Anybody in Quinto then. Population about twenty-five thousand, isn't it? Or anybody who passed through Quinto on Monday. It's a pretty tough setup."

"But you will try to help me?" She wasn't too much of a lady to arrange herself appealingly in the chair, and dramatize the plea. There was a chance that she wasn't a lady at all.

"It will take time, and I can't promise any results. Are you fairly well-heeled, Mrs. Slocum?"

"Surely you don't reserve your services exclusively for the wealthy." She looked around at the plain, small, square office.

"I don't spend money on front, but I charge fifty dollars a day, and expenses. It will cost you four or five hundred a week, and with what I've got to go on it may take all summer."

She swallowed her dismay. "Frankly, I'm not well off. There's money in the family, but James and I don't have it. All we have is the income from a hundred thousand."

"Thirty-five hundred."

"Less. James's mother controls the money. We live with her, you see. I do have a little money that I've saved, though, for Cathy's education. I can pay you five hundred dollars."

"I can't guarantee anything in a week, or a month for that matter."

"I have to do something."

"I have an idea why. The person who wrote that letter probably knows something more definite, and you're afraid of the next letter."

She didn't answer.

"It would help if you'd let me know what there is to be known."

Her eyes met mine levelly and coldly. "I don't see the necessity for me to confess adultery, or for you to assume that there is anything to confess."

"Oh hell," I said. "If I have to work in a vacuum, I'll waste my time."

"You'll be paid for it."

"You'll waste your money, then."

"I don't care." She opened her purse again and counted ten twenties onto the desk-top. "There. I want you to do what you can. Do you know Nopal Valley?"

"I've been through it, and I know Quinto slightly. What does your husband do with the Quinto Players?"

"He's an actor, or thinks he is. You mustn't try to talk to him."

"You'll have to let me do it my own way, or I might as well sit in my office and read a book. How can I get in touch with you?"

"You can phone me at home. Nopal Valley is in the Quinto book. Under Mrs. Olivia Slocum."

She stood up and I followed her to the door. I noticed for the first time that the back of the handsome suit was sun-faded. There was a faint line around the bottom of the skirt where the hem had been changed. I felt sorry for the woman, and I liked her pretty well.

"I'll drive up this morning," I said. "Better watch the mailbox."

When she had gone, I sat down behind the desk and looked at the unpolished top. The letter and the twenties were side by side upon it. Sex and money: the forked root of evil. Mrs. Slocum's neglected cigarette was smouldering in the ash-tray, marked with lipstick like a faint rim of blood. It stank, and I crushed it out. The letter went into my breastpocket, the twenties into my billfold.

In the street when I went down the heat was mounting toward ninety. In the sky the sun was mounting toward noon.

CHAPTER 2

An hour north of Santa Monica a sign informed me:
YOU ARE ENTERING QUINTO, JEWEL OF THE SEA. SPEED
25 MILES. I slowed down and began to look for a
motor court. The white cottages of the Motel del
Mar looked clean and well-shaded, and I turned into
the gravel apron in front of the U-shaped enclosure.
A thin woman in a linen smock came out of the
door marked OFFICE before I could stop the car. She
danced towards me smiling a dazed and arty smile.

"Did you wish accommodation, sir?"

"I did. I still do."

She tittered and touched her fading hair, which
was drawn tightly back from her sharp face in a bun.
"You're travelling alone?"

"Yes. I may stay for a few days."

She blinked her eyes roguishly, wagging her head.
"Don't stay too long, or the charm of Quinto will
capture you. It's the Jewel of the Sea, you know.
You'll want to stay forever and ever. We've a very
nice single at seven."

"May I look at it?"

"Of course. I believe that you'll find it delightful."

She showed me a knotty pine room with a bed, a
table, and two chairs. The floor and furniture shone
with polishing wax. There was a Rivera reproduction

9

on one wall, its saffrons repeated by a vase of fresh
marigolds on the mantel over the fireplace. Below the
western window the sea glimmered.

She turned to me like a musician from his piano.
"Well?"

"I find it delightful," I said.

"If you'll just come up and register, I'll have Henry
fill the carafe with ice water. We *do* try to make you
comfortable, you see."

I followed her back to the office, feeling a little
uncomfortable at her willingness to tie herself in
knots, and signed my full name in the register, Lew
A. Archer, with my Los Angeles address.

"I see you're from Los Angeles," she said, taking my
money.

"Temporarily. As a matter of fact, I'd like to settle
here."

"Would you really?" she gushed. "Do you hear that,
Henry? The gentleman here would like to settle in
Quinto."

A tired-looking man half-turned from his desk at
the back of the room, and grunted.

"Oh, but you'd love it," she said. "The sea. The
mountains. The clear, cool air. The nights. Henry and
I are awfully glad we decided to buy this place. And
it's full every night in the summer, no-vacancy sign
up long before it's dark. Henry and I make quite a
game out of it, don't we, Henry?"

Henry grunted again.

"Are there many ways to make a living here?"

"Why, there are the stores, and real estate, all sorts
of things. No industry, of course, the Council won't
permit it. After all, look what happened to Nopal
Valley when they let the oil wells in."

"What happened to Nopal Valley?"

"It was ruined, absolutely ruined. Great hordes of
low-class people, Mexicans and dirty oil crews, came
in from gosh knows where, and simply blighted the
town. We can't let it happen here."

"Absolutely not," I said with a phoniness she had no
ear to catch. "Quinto must remain a natural beauty

spot and cultural centre. I've heard quite a lot about
the Quinto Players, by the way."

"Now have you really, Mr. Archer?" Her voice sank
to a simpering whisper: "You're not a Hollywood per-
sonage, are you?"

"Not exactly." I left the question open. "I've done a
good deal of work in and about Hollywood." Peeping
on fleabag hotel rooms, untying marital knots, blackmailing blackmailers out of business. Dirty, heavy, hot
work on occasion.

She narrowed her eyes and pressed her lips together as if she understood me. "I sensed you were from
Hollywood. Of course you'll be wanting to see the new
play this weekend. Mr. Marvell wrote it himself—he's
a very brilliant man—and he's directing it, too. Rita
Treadwith, a very dear friend of mine, is helping with
the costumes, and she says it has great possibilities:
movies, Broadway, anything."

"Yes," I said. "I've had reports of it. Where's the
theater they're rehearsing in?"

"Right off the highway in the center of town. Just
turn right at the courthouse, and you'll see the sign:
Quinto Theatre."

"Thank you," I said, and went out. The screen door
slammed a second time before I reached my car, and
Henry came plodding toward me across the gravel. He
was leathery and lean, beaten and parched by long
summers. He came up so close to me that I could
smell him.

"Listen, friend, you mean it what you said about
settling down here?" He looked behind him to make
sure that his wife was out of earshot, and spat in the
gravel. "I got an income proposition if you're interested. Ten thousand down and the rest out of earn-
ings. Fifty thousand for the works, that's twelve good
cottages and the good will."

"You want to sell this place? To me?"

"You'll never get a better at the price."

"I thought you were mad about Quinto."

He shot a contemptuous yellow glance at the door
of the office. "That's what *she* thinks. Thinks, hell.

She lets the Chamber of Commerce do her thinking for her. I got a chance for a liquor license in Nopal."

"Money in Nopal, I hear."

"You can say it again. The Valley's lousy with money since they struck oil, and there's no spenders like oilmen. Easy come, easy go."

"I'm sorry," I said. "I'm not interested."

"That's O.K., I just thought I'd raise the question. *She* won't let me put up a sign, or list the god-damn place." He plodded back to the office.

The men and women in the streets had the rumpled, sun-worshipping look of people on holiday. Many of them were very young or very old, and most of the former wore bathing-suits. The white Spanish buildings seemed unreal, a stage-setting painted upon the solid blue sky. To the left at the bottom of the cross-streets the placid sea rose up like a flat blue wall.

I parked in front of a restaurant near the courthouse and went in for a cold lunch. The waitress had a red-checked apron that matched the tablecloth, and a complexion that matched the coffee. I tipped her very lightly, and walked around the block to the Quinto Theatre. It was two o'clock by my watch, time for the rehearsal to be under way. If the play was scheduled for the week end, they'd be running the whole thing through by Wednesday.

The theatre stood back from the street in a plot of yellowing grass: a massive windowless box of a building with its stucco scabbing off in patches to show the aged plaster. Two weather-pocked plaster pillars supported the roof of the portico. On each of the pillars a playbill announced the World Premiere of *The Ironist,* a New Play by Francis Marvell. On the wall beside the box office there was a layout of photographs mounted on a large sheet of blue cardboard. Miss Jeanette Dermott as Clara: a young blonde with luminous dreaming eyes. Mrs. Leigh Galloway as The Wife: a hard-faced woman smiling professionally, her bright teeth ready to eat an imaginary audience.

The third of the glossy trio interested me. It was a man in his late thirties, with light hair waving over a pale and noble brow. The eyes were large and sorrowful, the mouth small and sensitive. The picture had been taken in three-quarters face to show the profile, which was very fine. Mr. James Slocum, the caption said, as "The Ironist." If the picture could be believed, Mr. James Slocum's pan was a maiden's dream. Not mine.

A prewar Packard sedan drew up to the curb in front of the theatre, and a young man got out. His long legs were tightly encased in a pair of faded levis, his heavy shoulders bulged in a flowered Hawaiian shirt. The levis and the shirt didn't go with the black chauffeur's cap on his head. He must have been conscious of the cap, because he tossed it on the front seat of the Packard before he came up the walk. The glistening dark hair frothed on his head in tight curls. He looked at me from eyes that were paled by the deep tan of his face. Another maiden's dream. They pastured in herds in the California resorts.

Dream Two opened the heavy door to my left, and it swung shut behind him. I waited a minute and followed him into the lobby. It was small and close and dimly lit by the red glow of the Exit lamps. The young man had disappeared, but there was a murmur of voices beyond a further door. I crossed the lobby and entered the main auditorium. It was blacked out except for the stage, where there were lights and people. I sat down in an aisle seat in the back row, and wondered what the hell I was doing there.

The set had been erected, an English drawing-room with period furniture, but the players were not yet in costume. James Slocum, looking as pretty as his picture, in a yellow turtleneck sweater, shared the stage with the blonde girl, in slacks. They were talking at each other in center stage.

"Roderick," the girl was saying, "have you honestly

been aware of my love for you, and never breathed a word of it to me?"

"Why should I have?" Slocum shrugged his shoulders in weary amusement. "You were content to love, and I was content to be loved. Naturally, I did my best to encourage you."

"You encouraged me?" She overdid the surprise, and her voice screeched slightly. "But I never knew."

"I took care that you should not, until you had passed the narrow line that lies between admiration and passion. But I was always ready with a match for your cigarette, a compliment for your gown, a touch of the hand at parting." He moved his hand in the air, and unconsciously underlined the corn.

"But your wife! What of her? It seems incredible that you should deliberately lead me on to the dark edge of adultery."

"Dark, my dear? On the contrary, passion is radiant with the radiance of a thousand suns, luminous as the dayspring, shot through with rainbow splendors!" He spoke the words as if he meant them, in a ringing voice which held only a trace of reediness. "Beside the love that we may have—shall have—the legal mating of the married is the coupling of frightened rabbits in a hutch."

"Roderick, I hate and fear and adore you," the girl announced. She cast herself at his feet like a ballerina.

He gave her both his hands and lifted her to her feet. "I adore to be adored," he answered lightly. Clinch.

A thin figure had been pacing nervously in the orchestra pit, silhouetted against the reflection of the footlights. Now he vaulted onto the stage in a single antelope bound, and circled the mugging pair like a referee.

"Very fine," he said. "Very fine, indeed. You've caught my intention beautifully, both of you. But would it be possible, Miss Dermott, to bring out just a shade more emphatically the contrast between *hate and fear* on the one hand, and *adore* on the other?

After all, that's the very keynote of the first act: the ambivalence of Clara's response to the Ironist, externalizing the ambivalence of his attitude to love and life. Would you take it again from 'rabbits in a hutch'?"

"Of course, Mr. Marvell."

Which made him the author of the play, as I'd suspected. It was the kind of play that only a mother or an actor could love, the kind of stuff that parodied itself. Phony sophistication with a high gloss, and no insides at all.

I turned my attention to the darkened auditorium, which seemed larger than it was because it was almost empty. A few people were clustered in the first rows, silently watching the actors rehash their tripe. The rest of the plywood seats were unoccupied, except for a couple a few rows ahead of me. As my eyes became used to the dim light, I could make out a boy and a girl, their heads leaning close together. At least the boy was leaning toward her; the girl sat straight in the seat. When he raised his arm and placed it along the back, she moved to the next seat.

I saw his face as he leaned sideways to speak to her: Dream Two. "God damn you," he said. "You treat me as if I was dirt. I think I'm getting someplace with you, and then you crawl into your little igloo and slam the door in my face."

"Igloos don't have doors, you crawl in through a tunnel." Her voice was soft and prim.

"That's another thing." He was trying to whisper, but anger jerked at his vocal cords and made the words uneven. "You think you're so damn superior, the big brain. I could tell you things you never even heard of."

"I don't care to hear of them. I'm very interested in the play, Mr. Reavis, and I wish you'd leave me alone."

"*Mr.* Reavis! What makes you so bloody formal all of a sudden. You were hot enough last night when I took you home, but now it's '*Mr.* Reavis'."

"I was not! And I won't be talked to like that."

"That's what you think. You can't play around with me, do you understand? I'm big stuff, and I got ideas, and there's plenty of women I can have if I want them, see?"

"I know you're irresistible, Mr. Reavis. My failure to respond is unquestionably pathological."

"Two-bit words don't mean nothing," he cried in frustration and fury. "I'll show you something that does mean something."

Before she could move again, he was crouching in front of her, holding her down in her seat. She let out a stifled squawk and beat his face with closed hands. But he found her mouth and held on, with one of his large hands on either side of her head. I could hear their breath whistling, the seat creaking under the weight of their struggling bodies. I stayed where I was. They knew each other better than I knew them, and nothing could happen to her where they were.

He released her finally, but stayed bending over her, with something hopeful in the arch of his shoulders.

"Dirt!" she said. "You dirt."

The words hit him hard, a spatter of mud in the face. "You can't call me that!" He had forgotten about whispering. His hands were groping for her shoulders, or her neck.

I was halfway out of my seat when the overhead lights came on. The dialogue on the stage had ceased, and everyone in the theatre was running up the aisle, with Marvell at their head. He was a flaxen-haired man in Harris tweeds and a dither. The trace of an English accent fogged his voice:

"Really! What on earth is happening here?" He sounded like a spinster schoolteacher who has caught a pupil in the act.

The boy had scrambled to his feet and half-turned, leaning over the back of the seat. There was shamed awkwardness in his movements, but danger, too. His muscles were strained taut, and his eyes were black ice.

Slocum stepped forward and laid his hand on Marvell's shoulder. "Let me handle this, Francis." He turned to the girl, who was sitting tense in her seat. "Now, Cathy, what's been going on?"

"Nothing, father." Her voice was demure again. "We were sitting here talking, and Pat got mad, that's all."

"He was kissing you," Slocum said. "I saw you from the stage. You'd better wipe your face, and I'll talk to you later."

Her hand flew up to her mouth. "Yes, father," she said between her fingers. She was a pretty girl, much younger than I'd thought from the words she used. The auburn hair blossomed at the back of her neck into curls that were alive with copper glints.

The boy looked down at her head, and back to her father. "No," he said. "She had nothing to do with it. I tried to kiss her, and she wouldn't let me."

"You admit that, do you, Reavis?"

The boy walked up to Slocum, and dwarfed him. With his thin shoulder-blades projecting under the yellow sweater, it was Slocum who looked like the youngster. He stood where he was, unbending and outraged.

"Why shouldn't I admit it?" Reavis said. "There's no law against kissing a girl—"

Slocum spoke in deliberate cold fury: "Where my young daughter is concerned, certain things are impossible and inconceivable and"—he groped for a word and found it—"foul. No lout of a chauffeur—"

"I won't always be a chauffeur—"

"You're quite right. You're not one now."

"I suppose you mean I'm fired." His tone was flat and scornful.

"Absolutely."

"Why, you poor damn ninny, you can't fire me. You never paid my wages, anyway. Not that I want your friggin' job. You can stick it."

The two men were facing each other, so close they were almost touching. The rest of the people in the aisle surged forward around them. Marvell insinuated himself between them, and laid a graceful hand on Reavis's chest. "That will be about enough of that." He

omitted the "my man" tag, but it was implied. "I
advise you to get out of here before I summon the
police."

"For calling a phony's bluff?" Reavis tried to laugh,
and almost succeeded. "I'd of walked out months ago
if it wasn't for Cathy. The little buzzard's doing me a
favor."

The girl Cathy got out of her seat, her eyes bright
with tears about to spill. "Go away, Pat. You mustn't
say these dreadful things to father."

"You heard her, Reavis." Slocum was flushed in the
neck and white around the mouth. "Get out of here,
and don't come back. We'll send your things to you."

The tension was leaking out of the situation as
Reavis, its center, gradually relaxed. He knew that he
was beaten, and his shoulders showed it. He turned to
look at Cathy, and she wouldn't meet his eyes. Before
the focus of attention could shift to me, I slid out of
my $7.70 seat and into the lobby.

The photograph of the Ironist on the portico was
staring unblinkingly into the afternoon sun. The
offstage drama in Quinto, I told it silently, was better
than the kind they rehearsed. It didn't answer; it was
lost in a dream of its own loveliness.

CHAPTER 3

I found a phone booth in a drugstore down the block. There was no James Slocum in the Nopal Valley section of the directory, but there was a Mrs. Olivia Slocum, presumably his mother. I made the ten-cent toll call and got a cracked dry voice which could have belonged to man or woman:

"The Slocum residence."

"Mrs. James Slocum, please."

There was a click on the line: "All right, Mrs. Strang. I'll take it on my extension."

Mrs. Strang grunted and went off the line.

"Archer speaking," I said. "I'm in Quinto."

"I hoped you would call. Yes?"

"Look here, Mrs. Slocum, I'm practically handcuffed. I can't ask questions, or I'll start talk where there isn't any. I have no lead and no contacts. Isn't there some way I can meet your family—your husband, at least?"

"But he has nothing to do with it. You'll only rouse suspicion."

"Not necessarily. If I float around without an explanation, I'll rouse suspicion for sure. And I won't find anything out if I can't talk to anybody."

"You sound discouraged," she said.

"I was never encouraged, I told you that. Operating

19

in a vacuum, I don't stand much chance of helping you. Even a list of suspects—"

"But there are none. I can't name a single person. Is the case really so hopeless?"

"Unless I get a lucky break, like somebody running up to me in the street and confessing. This is a very intimate business, there's nothing overt in it like the ordinary divorce setup, and I need to get closer to your life."

Very softly, she said: "Are you proposing to spy on me, Mr. Archer?"

"Hardly. I'm working for you. But I need a center to work from, and you and your family are it. I got a look at your husband and daughter just now, but a look is not enough."

"I specifically instructed you not to approach my husband."

Her moods were hard to follow and match. I changed mine: "If you don't let me handle the thing my own way, I'll have to drop it. I'll mail you your money."

In the silence that followed, I could hear her tapping with a pencil on the base of the telephone. "No," she said finally. "I want you to do what you can. If you have any reasonable suggestion—"

"It's not very reasonable, but it should do. Do you have any friends in Hollywood? Picture people?"

Another silence. "There's Mildred Fleming, she's a secretary in one of the studios. I had lunch with her today."

"Which studio?"

"Warner's, I think."

"All right. You told her how good the play is. She has a boy-friend who works for an agent who deals in literary properties. Me."

"I see," she answered slowly. "Yes, that's reasonable enough. Actually, it will fit in very well. A few of James's friends are coming in for cocktails. If you could be here at five?"

"I'll come early."

"Very well, Mr. Archer." She gave me directions, and hung up.

My shirt was dank from sitting in the steaming booth. I drove back to my motel, changed to shorts and went down to the beach for a swim. The blue-green swells were heaving slowly beyond the surf. Further out, a few white sails leaned across the horizon, curved sharp like wings in the wind, but motionless in the distance. I met a wave head-on as it broke and took the cold shock running. My feet kicked out behind me and I swam straight out for a quarter of a mile. There the kelp-beds stopped me, a tangled barrier of brown and yellow tubes and bulbs floating low in the water. I hated the touch of underwater life.

I turned on my back and floated, looking up at the sky, nothing around me but cool clear Pacific, nothing in my eyes but long blue space. It was as close as I ever got to cleanliness and freedom, as far as I ever got from all the people. They had jerrybuilt the beaches from San Diego to the Golden Gate, bulldozed super-highways through the mountains, cut down a thousand years of redwood growth, and built an urban wilderness in the desert. They couldn't touch the ocean. They poured their sewage into it, but it couldn't be tainted.

There was nothing wrong with Southern California that a rise in the ocean level wouldn't cure. Except that there were too many Ararats, and I was no Noah. The sky was flat and empty, and the water was chilling me. I swam to the kelp-bed and plunged down through it. It was cold and clammy like the bowels of fear. I came up gasping and sprinted to shore with a barracuda terror nipping at my heels.

A wave thrust me up on the beach, where a cold late afternoon wind took over, armed with small needles of sand. I wasn't a noble savage after all.

I was still chilly a half-hour later, crossing the pass to Nopal Valley. Even at its summit the highway was wide and new, rebuilt with somebody's money. I could smell the source of the money when I slid down into the valley on the other side. It stank like rotten eggs.

The oil wells from which the sulphur gas rose crowded the slopes on both sides of the town. I could see them from the highway as I drove in: the latticed triangles of the derricks where trees had grown, the oil-pumps nodding and clanking where cattle had grazed. Since 'thirty-nine or 'forty, when I had seen it last, the town had grown enormously, like a tumor. It had thrust out shoots in all directions: blocks of match-box houses in raw new housing developments and the real estate shacks to go with them, a half-mile gauntlet of one-story buildings along the highway: veterinarians, chiropractors, beauty shops, marketerias, restaurants, bars, liquor stores. There was a new four-story hotel, a white frame gospel tabernacle, a bowling alley wide enough to house a B-36. The main street had been transformed by glass brick, plastic, neon. A quiet town in a sunny valley had hit the jackpot hard, and didn't know what to do with itself at all.

More had changed than the face of the buildings, or the number and make of the cars. The people were different and there were too many of them. Crowds of men whose faces were marked by sun and work and boredom walked in the streets and in and out of the bars, looking for fun or trouble. Very few women showed on the main street. The blue-shirted cop on the main corner wore his holster on the front of his hip, with the flap unbuttoned and the gun-butt showing.

Trail Road turned off to the right on the far side of the town, and climbed through the oil fields to a gently sloping mesa which overlooked the valley. As it climbed it dwindled down to a narrow blacktop looping up the side of the sunbaked hill. The mountains rose sheer in front of the nose of my car, starkly shadowed by the declining light. A long, low house half-hidden by giant oaks sat in the middle of the mesa, as indigenous as a boulder. Before I reached it I had to stop and open a gate which barred the road.

On either side of it a six-foot cyclone fence topped by strands of barbed wire stretched out of sight.

The road inside the gate was freshly gravelled, and sentineled by twin rows of young palms. There were a couple of cars parked in the circular drive that curved around in front of the house. One was the old Packard sedan I had seen in front of the Quinto Theatre. I left my car beside it and crossed the terraced lawn, dodging the rainbowed spray from a sprinkling system.

The house was built of adobe brick the color of the earth, pressed down to the earth by a heavy red tile roof, and massive as a fortress. A deep veranda ran along its front. I climbed the low concrete steps. A woman in a red sweater and slacks was curled like a scarlet snake in one corner of a green canvas porch swing. Her head was bent over a book, and red harlequin spectacles gave her shadowed face a look of queer concentration. The concentration was real; she gave no sign of hearing me or seeing me until I spoke:

"Excuse me. I'm looking for Mrs. Slocum."

"Excuse *me*." She looked up in real surprise, her eyes refocusing like a sleeper's, and flicked the spectacles off. It was Cathy Slocum; I hadn't recognized her until then. The glasses and the look they gave her had added ten years to her age, and the shape of her body was misleading. It was one of those female bodies that bloomed very young. Her eyes were large and deep like her mother's, and she had better lines. I could understand the chauffeur's passion for her. But she was very young.

"My name is Archer," I said.

She gave me a long, cool look, but didn't know me. "I'm Cathy Slocum. Is it mother or grandmother you want to see?"

"Mother. She asked me to the party."

"It's not her party," she said under her breath to herself. A spoiled-little-girl look made two black vertical lines between her eyebrows. Then she remembered me, and smoothed them out, and asked me very sweetly: "Are you a friend of mother's, Mr. Archer?"

"A friend of a friend's. Would you like my Bertillon measurements?"

She was clever enough to get it, and young enough to blush. "I'm sorry, I didn't mean to be rude—we see so few strangers." Which might account for her interest in a rough-talking chauffeur named Reavis. "Mother's just come up from the pool, and she's dressing, and father hasn't come home. Would you care to sit down?"

"Thank you." I followed the tall fine body to the swing, amused by the fact that it contained an adolescent who had to be reminded of her manners. Not a usual adolescent, though. The book in her hand, when she laid it down on the cushion between us, turned out to be a book on psychoanalysis by Karen Horney.

She began to make conversation, swinging the spectacles back and forth by one end: "Father's rehearsing a play in Quinto, that's what the party's about. He's really a very fine actor, you know." She said it a little defensively.

"I know. Much better than the play."

"Have you seen the play?"

"I caught a scene of it this afternoon."

"And what did you think of it? Isn't it well written?"

"Well enough," I said, without enthusiasm.

"But what do you really think of it?"

Her look was so candid and girlish that I told her. "They should jack up the title and build a new play under it and change the title. If what I saw was a fair sample."

"But everyone who's seen it thinks it's a masterpiece. Are you interested in the theatre, Mr. Archer?"

"Do you mean do I know what I'm talking about? Probably not. I work for a man in Hollywood who deals in literary properties. He sent me up to look at it."

"Oh," she said. "Hollywood. Father says it's much too literary for Hollywood, and it's not written to a formula. Mr. Marvell plans to take it to Broadway. Their standards are much subtler, don't you think?"

"Much. Who is Mr. Marvell? I know he's author-director of the play . . ."

"He's an English poet. He went to Oxford, and his uncle's a lord. He's a good friend of father's, and father likes his poetry and I tried to read some of it but I couldn't understand it. It's awfully difficult and symbolic, like Dylan Thomas."

The name rang no bell. "Is your father going along, when Marvell takes the play to New York?"

"Oh, no." The swinging spectacles described a full circle and struck against her knee with an audible tap. She put them on again. They lengthened and aged her face, and gave it piquancy. "Father's just helping Francis out. He's putting it on to try and get some backing. Father has no histrionic ambitions, though he is a really fine actor, don't you think?"

A mediocre amateur, I thought. I said: "No question about it." When the girl mentioned her father, as she frequently did, her mouth went flower-soft and her hands were still.

But when he mounted the veranda a few minutes later, with Marvell skipping beside him up the steps, she looked at James Slocum as if she were afraid of him. Her fingers interlaced and strained against each other. I noticed that the nails were bitten stubby.

"Hello, father." The words left her mouth ajar, and the tip of her tongue moved along her upper lip.

He walked toward us purposefully, a middle-sized, thin-chested man who should have had a Greek torso to support his startling head. "I've been wanting to talk to you, Cathy." The sensitive mouth was stern. "I expected you to wait for me at the theatre."

"Yes, father." She turned to me. "Do you know my father, Mr. Archer?"

I stood up and said hello. He looked me over with his sad brown eyes, and gave me a limp hand as an afterthought. "Francis," he said to the blond man at his shoulder: "See if you and Archer can find a drink for yourselves. I'd like to have a moment with Cathy here."

"Right." Marvell touched me in the small of the back, ushering me to the front door. Cathy watched us go. Her father stood looking down at her with one hand on his hip, the other at his chin, in an actorish pose.

We entered a living-room as dim and cool as a cave. The windows were few and small, masked by venetian blinds which laid horizontal bars across the light. The barred light fell on a floor of black oak, partly covered with faded Persian rugs. The furniture was heavy and old: a rosewood concert grand at the far end of the room, carved elaborately to nineteenth-century taste, stiff-backed chairs of mahogany, a tap-estried divan in front of the deep fireplace. The beams that supported the time-stained plaster ceiling were black oak like the floor. A chandelier of yellow-ing crystal hung down from the central beam like a misshaped stalactite.

"Queer old place, what?" Marvell said to me. "Well, what shall it be, old boy? A Scotch and soda?"

"Fine."

"I expect I'll have to look you up some ice."

"Don't bother."

"No bother at all. I know where everything is." He trotted away, his light hair flying in the wind of his own motion. For the nephew of a lord, he was very obliging. I myself was the nephew of my late Uncle Jake, who once went fifteen rounds with Gunboat Smith, to no decision.

I tried to remember what my Uncle Jake looked like. I could remember the smell of him, compounded of bay rum, hair oil, strong clean masculine sweat and good tobacco, and the taste of the dark chocolate cigarettes he brought me the day my father took me to San Francisco for the first time; but I couldn't remember his face. My mother never kept his pictures, because she was ashamed to have a professional fighter in the family.

The murmur of voices drew me to a window which

opened outward onto the veranda. I sat down in a straight chair against the wall, hidden from outside by the heavy drapes and the half-closed blind. Cathy and her father were talking on the swing.

"I didn't see him afterwards," she said tensely. "I walked out and got in the car and drove myself home. He wasn't even in sight."

"But I know he drove you home. I saw his cap on the front seat of the car just now."

"He must have left it before. I swear I didn't see him after."

"How can I believe you, Cathy?" The man's voice held genuine torment. "You've lied to me before, about him, too. You promised me you'd have nothing to do with him, or any other man, until you were older."

"But I didn't! I didn't do anything wrong."

"You let him kiss you."

"He made me. I tried to get away." A trace of hysteria came into her voice like a thin entering wedge.

"You must have encouraged him in some way. A man doesn't act like that without a reason, surely. Think about it, Cathy, didn't you do or say something which might have led him on?" He was trying to be cool and fair, the impersonal cross-examiner, but hurt and rage buzzed like blundering insects in his tone.

"Led him on, father. That's a hideous thing to say." The onset of sobbing rocked her words.

"Darling," he said. "Poor darling." The swing creaked as he leaned toward her, and the sobs were smothered. "I didn't mean to hurt you, Cathy, you know that. It's simply because I love you that I'm so concerned about this—this ugly thing."

"I love you too, father." The words were muffled, probably by his shoulder.

"I wish I could believe that," he said gently.

"But I do, father, I do. I think you're the best man in the world."

There was something queer about the conversation,

made stranger still by the girl's extreme urgency. They could have been two lovers, of the same age.

"Oh, Cathy," he said brokenly. "What am I going to do about you?"

A third voice entered the colloquy: "What are you trying to do to her, James?" It was Maude Slocum's voice, and it was cold with anger.

"This is no affair of yours," he answered.

"I should think it is. She is my daughter, you know."

"I'm well aware of that, my dear. It doesn't necessarily follow that she can't have a good, decent life."

"She won't have if you go on like this, stirring her up and torturing her nerves."

"For heaven's sake, mother." Cathy spoke as if the older woman were the child. "The way you talk about me, you'd think I was a bone for two dogs to fight over. Why can't you treat me like a human being?"

"I try to, Cathy. You'll never listen to me. I know something about these things—" She faltered.

"If you know so much, why don't you put them into practice? There've been nothing but scenes in this family since I was old enough to talk, and I'm sick of it."

The girl's footsteps crossed the veranda, and the elder Slocums were silent. A full minute passed before the woman said, in a voice I barely recognized: "Leave her alone, James. I'm warning you."

The throaty whisper made the short hairs prickle at the back of my neck.

CHAPTER 4

I moved to the center of the room and leafed through a *Theatre Arts* magazine that was lying on a table. In a little while Marvell came back with a bowl of ice, glasses, Scotch, and soda, clinking together on a myrtlewood tray. "Excuse the delay, old man. The housekeeper's busy making canapes, and gave me absolutely no help at all. Do you like it strong?"

"I'll pour my own, thanks." I made a tall highball with plenty of soda. It was still early, a few minutes after five by my watch.

Marvell made himself a short one and took it in two gulps, his Adam's apple bobbing like a soft egg caught in his throat. "The Slocums aren't inhospitable," he said, "but they're nearly always late. One has to fend for oneself. Cathy informs me you're a literary agent?"

"Of a kind. I work for a man who buys fiction if he thinks it has movie possibilities. Then he tries to interest a producer, or make a package deal with a star."

"I see. Would I know the gentleman's name?"

"Probably not. I'm not allowed to use his name, anyway, because it's worth money. It bids up prices." I was improvising, but I knew twenty men in the game, and some of them operated like that.

He leaned back in his chair and hitched one thin knee over the other. His legs were pale and hairless above the drooping socks. His pale blond gaze seemed lashless. "You don't seriously think my play is cinematic material? I've sought a rather difficult beauty, you know."

I dipped my embarrassment in whiskey and soda, and waited for it to dissolve. It stayed where it was, a smiling mask on my face. "I never make snap decisions. I'm paid to keep tabs on the summer theaters, and that's what I do. There's a lot of young acting-talent floating around. In any case, I'll have to see all of your play before I can make a report."

"I noticed you there this afternoon," he said. "What *did* happen before that frightful scene between Cathy and her father?"

"I wouldn't know. I was watching the play."

He got up for another drink, moving sideways across the room like a shying horse. "The girl's quite a problem," he said over his shoulder. "Poor dear James is positively hag-ridden by his womenfolk. A less responsible man would simply decamp."

"Why?"

"They bleed him emotionally." He smiled palely over his second drink. "His mother began it when he was a very small boy, and it's gone on for so many years that he actually doesn't know he's being imposed upon. Now his wife and daughter are carrying on the good work. They're wasting the dear man's emotional substance."

He realized then that he was talking too much, and changed the subject abruptly: "I've often wondered why his mother chooses to live on a barren slope like this. She could live anywhere, you know, absolutely anywhere. But she *chooses* to wither away in this dreadful sun."

"Some people like it," I said. "I'm a native Californian myself."

"But don't you ever weary of the soul-destroying monotony of the weather?"

Only of phonies, I thought. Of the soul-destroying

monotony of phonies I wearied something awful. But I explained, for the hundredth time, that Southern California had two seasons, like any Mediterranean climate, and that people who couldn't tell the difference lacked one or more of the five senses.

"Oh, quite, quite," he told me, and poured himself another stiff drink, while I was still sipping the dregs of my first. The whisky didn't seem to affect him at all. He was an aging Peter Pan, glib, bland and eccentric, and all I had really found out was that he was fond of James Slocum. Everything he said and did was so stylized that I couldn't get at his center, or even guess where it was.

I was glad when Maude Slocum came into the room, her straight white smile gleaming in the amber light from the windows. She had left her emotions on the veranda, and seemed in control of herself. But her eyes looked past me, and far beyond the room.

"Hello, Francis." He half rose from his chair, and slumped back into it. "You really must forgive me, Mr. Archer, I'm a most unsatisfactory hostess—"

"On the contrary." She was dressed to attract attention in a black-and-white striped linen dress with a plunging neckline and a very close waist. I gave her attention.

"Francis," she said sweetly, "would you see if you can find James for me? He's somewhere out front."

"Right, darling." Marvell seemed pleased with the excuse to get away, and trotted out of the room. Nearly every family of a certain class had at least one hanger-on like him, dutiful and useless and untied. But unless Maude Slocum and he were very smooth actors, Marvell wasn't the apex of her triangle.

I offered to make her a drink but she poured her own, straight. She wrinkled her nose over the glass. "I hate Scotch, but James so loves to make the cocktails himself. Well, Mr. Archer, have you been probing the household secrets, rattling the family skeletons and so on?" The question was humorously put, but she wanted an answer.

I glanced at the open window and answered in a lower tone: "Hardly. I've had some talk with Marvell, and some with Cathy. No light. No skeletons." But there was electric tension in the house.

"I hope you don't think Francis—?"

"I don't think about him, I don't understand him."

"He's simple enough, I should think—a perfectly nice boy. His income's been cut off by the British government, and he's trying desperately to stay in the United States. His family's the fox-hunting sort, he can't abide them." The chattering stopped abruptly, and her voice went shy: "What do you think of Cathy?"

"She's a bright kid. How old?"

"Nearly sixteen. Isn't she lovely, though?"

"Lovely," I said, wondering what ailed the woman. Almost a total stranger, I was being asked to approve of herself and her daughter. Her insecurity went further back than the letter she had given me. Some guilt or fear was drawing her backward steadily, so that she had to enthuse and emote and be admired in order to stay in the same place.

"Loveliness runs in the family, doesn't it?" I said. "Which reminds me, I'd like to meet your mother-in-law."

"I don't understand why—"

"I'm trying to get a picture, and she's a central figure in it, isn't she? Put it this way. You're not so worried about who sent the first letter—that's safe in my pocket—as you are about the possible effects of a second letter. If I can't stop the letters at their source, I might be able to circumvent their effects."

"How?"

"I don't know. The main thing is that your husband, and your daughter, and your mother-in-law, shouldn't take the letters seriously. Your husband might divorce you, your daughter might despise you—"

"Don't say that." She set down her glass peremptorily on the coffee-table between us.

I went on evenly: "Your mother-in-law might cut off your income. I've been thinking, if I launched a poison-pen campaign against the whole family, and made a lot of different accusations, the one that hurts could get lost in the shuffle, couldn't it?"

"God no! I couldn't stand it, none of us could." The violence of her reaction was surprising. Her whole body heaved in the zebra-striped dress, and her breasts pressed together like round clenched fists in the V of her neckline.

"I was only playing with the idea. It needs refining, but there's something there."

"No, it's horrible. It would cover us all with filth to hide one thing."

"All right," I said, "all right. To get back to your mother-in-law, she's the one that would break you, isn't she? I mean it's her money that runs the house?"

"It's really James's, too. She handles the income in her lifetime, but his father's will requires her to provide for him. Her idea of providing is three hundred a month, a little more than she pays the cook."

"Could she afford to pay more?"

"If she wanted to. She has income from half a million, and this property is worth a couple of million. But she refuses to sell an acre of it."

"A couple of million? I didn't realize it was that big."

"There's oil under it," she said bitterly. "As far as Olivia is concerned, the oil can stay in the ground until we all dry up and blow away."

"I take it there's no love lost between you and your mother-in-law."

She shrugged her shoulders. "I gave up trying long ago. She's never forgiven me for marrying James. He was her pampered darling, and I married him young."

"Three hundred a month isn't exactly pampering, not if she has a couple of million in capital assets."

"It's the same as he got in college." The details of her grievances poured out, as if she'd been waiting for a long time to borrow somebody's ear. "She never increased it even when Cathy was born. For a while before the war we managed to live on it in a house of our own. Then prices went up, and we came home to mama."

I put the important question as tactfully as I could: "And what does James do?"

"Nothing. He was never encouraged to think of making a living. He was her only son, and she wanted him around. That's the idea of the allowance, of course. She's got him."

Her eyes were looking past me at a flat desert of time that stretched backward and forward as far as she could see. It occurred to me for an instant that I'd be doing her a favor if I showed her mother-in-law the letter in my pocket, and broke up the family for good. It was even possible that that was her own unconscious wish, the motive behind her original indiscretion. But I wasn't even certain that there had been an indiscretion, and she would never talk. After sixteen years of waiting for her share, and planning for her daughter, she was going to wait for the end.

She rose suddenly. "I'll take you to meet Olivia, if you must. She's always in the garden in the late afternoon."

The garden had fieldstone walls higher than my head. Inside, the flowers broke the light into almost every shade of the spectrum, and held it glowing. The sun was nearly down behind the western mountains and the light was fading, but Mrs. Slocum's flowers burned brightly on as if with fires of their own. There were fuchsias, pansies, tuberous begonias, great shaggy dahlias like separate pink suns. Olivia Slocum was working among them with a pair of shears, when we came up to the gate. Of indeterminate shape and size in a faded linen dress and a wide straw hat, she was bent far over among the blooms.

Her daughter-in-law called to her, with a slight nagging tone in her voice: "Mother! You shouldn't be straining yourself like that. You know what the doctor said."

"What did the doctor say?" I asked her under my breath.

"She has a heart condition—when it's convenient."

Olivia Slocum straightened up and came toward us, removing her earth-stained gloves. Her face was handsome in a soft, vague, sun-flecked way, and she was much younger than I'd expected. I'd imagined her as a thin and sour old lady pushing seventy, with gnarled hands grasping the reins she held on other people's lives. But she wasn't over fifty-five at most, and she carried her age easily. The three generations of Slocum women were a little too close for comfort.

"Don't be ridiculous, my dear," she said to Maude. "The doctor says mild exercise is beneficial to me. Anyway, I love to garden in the cool of the day."

"Well, as long as you don't overtire yourself." The younger woman's voice was grudging, and I suspected that the two never agreed on anything. "This is Mr. Archer, mother. He came up from Hollywood to see Francis's play."

"How nice. And have you seen it, Mr. Archer? I've heard James is quite distinguished in the leading role."

"He's very accomplished." The lie came easier as I repeated it, but it still left a bad taste on my tongue.

With a queer look at me, Maude excused herself and went back to the house. Mrs. Slocum raised both arms to take off her woven straw hat. She held the pose a moment too long, and turned her head so that I could see her profile. Vanity was her trouble; she was fixed on her own lost beauty, and couldn't grow old or let her son grow up. The hat came off after the long moment. Her hair was dyed bright red, and combed over her forehead in straight bangs.

"James is one of the most versatile people in the world," she said. "I brought him up to take a creative interest in everything, and I must say he's justified my faith. Of course you know him only as an actor, but he paints quite passably, and he has a beautiful tenor voice as well. He's even taken to writing verse lately. Francis has been a great stimulus to him."

"A brilliant man," I said. I had to say something to stem her flow of words.

"Francis? Oh, yes. But he doesn't have a tithe of James's energy. It would be a boon to him if he could rouse some Hollywood interest in his play. He's been urging me to back it, but naturally I can't afford to speculate in that sort of thing. I presume that you're connected with the studios, Mr. Archer?"

"Indirectly." I didn't want to get involved in explanations. She chattered like a parrot, but her eyes were shrewd. To change the subject, I said: "As a matter of fact, I'd like to get out of Hollywood. It's ulcer territory. A quiet life in the country would suit me fine, if I could get a piece of property in a place like this."

"A place like this, Mr. Archer?" She spoke guardedly, and her green eyes veiled themselves like a parrot's eyes.

Her reaction surprised me, but I blundered on: "I've never seen a place I'd rather live in."

"I see, Maude sicked you on me." Her voice was unfriendly and harsh. "If you represent the Pareco people, I must ask you to leave my property at once."

"Pareco?" It was the name of a gasoline. My only connection with it was that I used it in my car occasionally. I told her that.

She looked closely into my face, and apparently decided I wasn't lying. "The Pacific Refinery Company has been trying to get control of my property. For years they've been laying siege to me, and it's made me a little suspicious of strangers, especially when they express an interest in real estate."

"My interest is entirely personal," I said.

"I'm sorry if I've maligned you, Mr. Archer. The events of the last few years have embittered me, I'm afraid. I love this valley. When my husband and I first saw it, more than thirty years ago, it seemed our earthly paradise, our valley of the sun. When we could afford to, we bought this lovely old house and the hills around it, and when he retired we came here to live. My husband is buried here—he was older than I—and I intend to die here myself. Do I sound sentimental?"

"No." Her feeling for the place was stronger than sentimentality, and a little frightening. Her heavy body leaning on the gate was monumental in the evening light. "I can understand your attachment to a place like this."

"I am a part of it," she continued throatily. "They've ruined the town and desecrated the rest of the valley, but they shan't touch my mesa. I told them that, though they'll never take no for an answer. I told them that the mountains would be here long after they were gone. They didn't know what I was talking about." She rolled a cold green eye in my direction: "I believe you understand me, Mr. Archer. You're very sympathetic."

I muttered some kind of an affirmative. I understood a part of her feeling all right. A friend of mine who lectured in economics at UCLA would call it the *mystique* of property. What I failed to understand was the power of her obsession. Perhaps it was explained by the fact that she felt besieged, with her daughter-in-law a fifth column in the house.

"I sometimes feel that the mountains are my sisters—" She cut herself off short, as if she'd suddenly realized that she was going off the deep end. I was thinking that she had enough ego to equip a dictator and leave enough over for a couple of gauleiters. Perhaps she noticed the change in my expression.

"I know you're wanting to go to the party," she said, and gave me her hand briefly. "It was nice of you to come and talk to an old woman like me."

I started back to the house through an aisle of tall Italian cypress. It opened on a lawn in which a small swimming-pool was sunk, its filter system masked by a cypress hedge. At the far end a burlap-covered springboard stuck out over the water. The water in the pool was so still it seemed solid, a polished surface reflecting the trees, the distant mountains, and the sky. I looked up at the sky to the west, where the sun had dipped behind the mountains. The clouds were writhing with red fire, as if the sun had plunged in the invisible sea and set it flaming. Only the mountains stood out dark and firm against the conflagration of the sky.

CHAPTER 5

The sound of an approaching motor stopped me at the corner of the veranda. There were several more cars on the apron of the drive: a Jaguar roadster, a fishtail Cadillac, an ancient Rolls with wire wheels and a long, square British nose. Another car came into sight between the lines of palms, a quiet black machine with a red searchlight mounted on the front. I watched it being parked. A police car in that company seemed as out of place as a Sherman tank at a horse show.

A man got out of the black car and came up the flagstone walk which ascended the terraces in front of the house. He was tall and thick, a bifurcated chunk of muscle that moved with unexpected speed and silence. Even in slacks and a sports jacket, with a silk shirt open at the neck, he had the authority of a uniform, the bearing of a cop or a veteran soldier. Shadowed eyes, cragged nose, wide mouth, long jaw; his face was a relief map of all the male passions. Short hair the color of faded straw bristled on his head and sprouted from the shirt-opening at the base of his heavy red neck.

I moved a step to show myself and said: "Good evening."

"Good evening." He bit the words off with clean

39

white teeth, smiling automatically, then mounted the
steps to the veranda.

He glanced around as though he were ill at ease,
before knocking on the door. I watched him over the
veranda railing, and our eyes met for a meaningless
instant. I was about to speak again—something about
the weather—when I noticed Cathy curled in the
porch swing as she'd been an hour before. She was
leaning forward, watching the man intently.

His eyes shifted to her, and he took a step toward
her. "Cathy? How are you, Cathy?" Hesitant and un-
certain, the tone of a man talking to a child he didn't
know.

Her only answer was a clucking deep in her throat.
With a slow boldness she rose from the swing and
walked toward him in silence. Past him and down the
steps and around the far corner of the veranda, without once turning her head. He pivoted on his heels
and half-raised one hand, which stayed forgotten in
the air until she was out of sight. The large hand,
open and futile, curled into a fist. He turned to the
door and struck it twice as if it had a human face.

I climbed the steps behind him while he was waiting. "Fine weather we're having," I said.

He looked at me without hearing what I said or
seeing my face. "Yeah."

Maude Slocum opened the door and took us in in a
single swift glance. "Ralph?" she said to the other
man. "I wasn't expecting you."

"I met James downtown today, and he asked me to
come over for a drink." His heavy voice was apologetic.

"Come in then," she said, without graciousness.
"Since James invited you."

"Not if I'm not wanted," he answered sullenly.

"Oh, come in, Ralph. It would look rather strange if
you came to the door and went away again. And
what would James say to me?"

"What does he usually say?"

"Nothing, nothing at all." If they had a joke between them, it didn't fit my wave length. "Come in and *have* your drink, Ralph."

"You twisted my arm," he said wryly, and passed her in the doorway. Almost imperceptibly, her body arched away from his. Hatred or some other feeling had drawn her as tight as a bowstring.

She remained in the doorway and moved her hips so that she blocked my way. "Please go away, Mr. Archer. Pretty please?" She tried to make it pleasant and light, but failed.

"You *are* kind of inhospitable, aren't you? Apart from the curious fact that you hired me to come up here."

"I'm sorry. I'm afraid a situation is developing, and I simply couldn't stand the extra strain of having you around."

"And here was I, thinking I was a welcome addition to any group gathering. You lacerate my ego, Mrs. Slocum."

"It's no laughing matter," she told me sharply. "I don't lie very well. So I avoid situations in which lying is necessary."

"Then who's the large character with the thirst?"

"One of James's friends. I don't see the point of these questions."

"Does James have many policeman friends? I didn't think he was the type."

"Do you know Ralph Knudson?" Surprise made her face look longer.

"I've seen the pattern they're made from." Five years on the Long Beach force were in my record. "What's a tough cop doing at an arty party in the hills?"

"You'll have to ask James—but not now. He takes peculiar fancies to people." She wasn't a competent liar. "Of course, Mr. Knudson isn't an ordinary policeman. He's the Chief of Police in town, and I understand he has a rather distinguished record."

"But you don't really want him at your parties, is that it? I used to be a cop, and I'm still one in a way. I've felt that kind of snobbery myself."

"I'm not a snob!" she said fiercely. Apparently I'd touched something she valued. "My parents were ordinary people, and I've always hated snobs. But why I should be defending myself to you!"

"Then let me come in for a drink. I promise to be very suave and smooth."

"You're so terribly persistent—as if I didn't have enough to contend with. What makes you so persistent?"

"Curiosity, I guess. I'm getting interested in the case. It's quite an interesting setup you've got here; I've never seen a fishline with more tangles."

"I suppose you realize I can dismiss you, if you continue to make yourself completely obnoxious."

"You won't."

"And why won't I?"

"I think you're expecting trouble. You said yourself that something was building up. I can feel it in the air. And it's possible your policeman friend didn't come up here for fun."

"Don't be melodramatic. And he isn't my friend. Frankly, Mr. Archer, I've never had to deal with a more difficult—employee, than you."

I didn't like the word. "It might help you," I said, "if you thought of me as an independent contractor. In this case I'm expected to build a house without going near the lot." Or perhaps demolish a house, but I didn't add that.

She looked at me steadily for twenty or thirty seconds. Finally a smile touched her generous mouth and parted it. "You know, I think I rather like you, damn it. Very well, come in and meet the wonderful people, and I'll buy you a drink."

"You talked me into it."

I got my drink and lost my hostess in the same motion, as soon as we entered the big living-room. Ralph Knudson, the big man who was no friend of hers, caught her eye as she handed me my glass. She went to him. Her husband and Francis Marvell were sitting on the piano bench with their heads together, leafing through a thick volume of music. I looked

around at the rest of the wonderful people. Mrs.
Galway, the amateur actress, with the professional
smile clicking off and on like a white electric sign. A
bald-headed man in white flannels setting off his mahogany tan, who daintily smoked a small brown ciga-
rillo in a long green-gold holder. A fat man with a
cropped gray head, in a tweed suit with padded
shoulders, who turned out to be a woman when she
moved her nyloned legs. A woman leaning awkwardly on the arm of the chair beside her, with a dark
long tragic face and an ugly body. A youth who
moved gracefully about the room, pouring drinks for
everybody and smoothing the receding hair at his
temples. A round little woman who tinkled on and
on, whose bracelets and earrings tinkled when her
voice paused.

I listened to them talk. Existentialism, they said.
Henry Miller and Truman Capote and Henry Moore.
André Gide and Anais Nin and Djuna Barnes. And
sex—hard-boiled, poached, coddled, shirred, and
fried easy over in sweet, fresh creamery butter. Sex
solo, in duet, trio, quartet; for all-male chorus; for
choir and symphony; and played on the harpsichord
in three-fourths time. And Albert Schweitzer and the
dignity of everything that lives.

The fat man who had been listening to the tinkling
woman closed his face against her and became ab-
sorbed in his drink. She looked around brightly and
gaily like a bird, saw me, and picked up her drink. It
was short and green. She sat down on a hassock by
my chair, crossed her plump ankles, so that I could
see the tininess of her feet, and tinkled:

"I *so* love creme de menthe; it's *such* a pretty
drink, and I always drink it when I wear my emer-
alds." She bobbed her birdlike head, and the earrings
swung. They were the right color, but almost too big
to be real.

"I always eat oyster stew when I wear my pearls," I
said.

Her laughter had the same quality as her voice, and

was an octave higher. I decided not to make her laugh, if possible.

"You're Mr. Archer, aren't you? I've heard such interesting things about you. My daughter's on the stage in New York, you know. Her father's constantly urging her to come home, because of course it costs him a great deal of money, but I tell him, after all, a girl is only young once. Don't you agree?"

"Some people manage it twice. If they live long enough."

I meant it as an insult, but she thought it was funny, and made me the curious gift of her laughter again. "You must have heard of Felice. She dances under the name of Felicia France. Leonard Lyons has mentioned her several times. Mr. Marvell thinks she has dramatic talent, too; he'd love to have her play the ingénue in his play. But Felice has given her heart and soul to the dance. She has a very, very beautiful body, dear child. I had a lovely body myself at one time, really utterly lovely." Meditatively, she fingered herself, like a butcher testing meat which had hung too long.

I looked away, anywhere, and saw James Slocum standing up by the piano. Marvell struck a few opening chords, and Slocum began to sing, in a thin sweet tenor, the *Ballad of Barbara Allen*. The trickle of melody gradually filled the room like clear water, and the bubbling chatter subsided. Slocum's face was untroubled and radiant, a boy tenor's. Everyone in the room was watching it before the song ended, and he knew it, and wanted it that way. He was Peter Pan, caught out of time. His song had killed the crocodile with the ticking clock in its belly.

"Quite utterly lovely," the emerald earrings tinkled. "It always reminds me of Scotland for some reason. Edinburgh is really one of my favorite places in the world. What is your favorite place in the whole wide world, Mr. Archer?"

"Ten feet underwater at La Jolla, watching the fish through a face-glass."

"Are fish so terribly fascinating?"

"They have some pleasant qualities. You don't have to look at them unless you want to. And they can't talk."

Below her bird-brained laughter, and drowning it out, a heavy male voice said clearly: "That was very nice, James. Now why don't you and Marvell sing a duet?"

It was Ralph Knudson. Most of the eyes in the room shifted to him, and wavered away again. His thick face was bulging with blood and malice. Maude Slocum was standing beside him, facing her husband. Slocum stood where he was, his face as white as snow. Marvell was motionless, his eyes fixed on the keyboard and his back to the room. Short of homicidal violence, the atmosphere around the piano was as ugly as I had ever seen.

Maude Slocum walked through it, moving easily from Knudson to her husband, and touched him on the arm. He drew away from her, and she persisted.

"That would be nice, James," she said simply and quietly, "if only Francis had a voice like yours. But why don't you sing by yourself? I'll accompany you."

She took Marvell's place at the bench, and played while her husband sang. Knudson watched them, smiling like a tiger. I felt like going for a long drive by myself.

CHAPTER 6

The fire in the sky had died, leaving long wisps of cloud like streaks of ashes livid against the night. All I could see of the mountains was their giant shadowed forms shouldering the faintly lighted sky. A few lights sprinkled their flanks, and a car's headlights inched down into the other side of the valley and were lost in darkness. Then the night was so still that motion seemed impossible, all of us insects caught in the final amber. I moved and broke the spell, feeling my way down the dew-slick terraces beside the flagstone walk.

I closed a contact when I took hold of the left doorhandle of my convertible. The headlights and dashlights came on with a click. My right hand moved by reflex under my coat for a gun that wasn't there. Then I saw the girl's hand on the switch, the girl's face like a ghost's leaning towards me.

"It's only me, Mr. Archer. Cathy." There was night in her voice, in her eyes, night caught like mist in her hair. In a soft wool coat buttoned up to her soft chin, she was one of the girls I had watched from a distance in high school and never been able to touch; the girls with oil or gold or free-flowing real-estate money dissolved in their blood like blueing. She was also young enough to be my daughter.

"What do you think you're doing?"

"Nothing." She settled back in the seat and I slid under the wheel. "I just turned on the lights for you. I'm sorry if I startled you, I didn't mean to."

"Why pick on my car? You've got one of your own."

"Two. But father took the keys. Besides, I like your car. The seat is very comfortable. May I ride along with you?" She gave her voice a wheedling little-girl inflection.

"Where to?"

"Anywhere you're going. Quinto? Please, Mr. Archer?"

"I don't think so. You're a little young to be running around nights by yourself."

"It's not late, and I'd be with you."

"Even with me," I said. "You'd better go back to the house, Cathy."

"I won't. I hate those people. I'll stay out here all night."

"Not with me you won't. I'm leaving now."

"You won't take me along?" Her clenched hand vibrated on my forearm. There was a note in her voice that hurt my ears like the screech of chalk on a wet blackboard. The smell of her hair was as clean and strange as the redheaded girl's who sat ahead of me in senior year.

"I'm not a nursemaid," I said harshly. "And your parents wouldn't like it. If something's bothering you, take it up with your mother."

"*Her!*" She pulled away from me and sat stonily, her eyes on the lighted house.

I got out and opened the door on her side. "Good night."

She didn't move, even to look at me.

"Do you get out under your own power, or do I lift you out by the nape of the neck?"

She turned on me like a cat, her eyes distended: "You wouldn't dare touch me."

She was right. I took a few steps toward the house, my heels grinding angrily in the gravel, and she was out of the car and after me. "Please don't call them.

I'm afraid of them. That Knudson man—" She was standing on the margin of the car's light, her face bleached white by it and her eyes stained inky black.

"What about him?"

"Mother always wants me to make up to him. I don't know if she wants me to marry him, or what. I can't tell father, or father would kill him. I don't know what to do."

"I'm sorry, Cathy, you're not my baby." I moved to touch her shoulder, but she drew back as if I carried disease. "Why don't you get the cook to make you some hot milk and put you to bed? Things usually look better in the morning."

"Better in the morning," she repeated, with toneless, empty irony.

She was still standing tense and straight, with her hands clenched at her sides, when I started to back the car. The white beam swerved as I turned, and left her in darkness.

I stopped at the gate, but it was open, and I went on through. A few hundred yards beyond it a tall man appeared in the road, lifting his thumb for a ride. I was passing him up when I caught a glimpse of his face: Pat Reavis. I barked to a quick stop and he came running.

"Thanks very much, sir." He smelled strongly of whisky, but he didn't look drunk. "Your dashboard clock working?"

I compared the lighted dial with my watch. Both indicated twenty-three minutes after eight. "Seems to be."

"It's later than I thought, then. God, I sure hate walking. I walked enough in the Marines to last me the rest of my life. My own car's in the garage, front end smashed."

"Where did you do all the walking?"

"One place and another. I landed on Guadal with Carlson's Raiders, for one. But we won't go into that. You know the Slocums?"

To get him talking, I said: "Anybody who is anybody knows the Slocums."

"Yeah, sure," he answered in the same tone. "All that class. What the Slocums need is an equalizer." But he said it in a good-humored way. "You trying to sell them something?"

"Life insurance." I was tired of the farce of pretending to be interested in Marvell's play.

"No kidding? That's a laugh." He laughed to prove it.

"People die," I said. "Is it so funny?"

"I bet you ten to one you didn't sell any, and you never will. The old lady's worth more dead than she is alive already, and the rest of them don't have one nickel to clink against another."

"I don't get it. I heard they were good prospects, well-heeled."

"Sure, the old lady's sitting on a couple of million bucks in oil, but she won't sell or lease. Slocum and his wife can't wait for her to bump. The day she bumps, they'll be down at the travel bureau buying tickets for a de luxe round-the-world cruise. The oil under the ground's their life insurance, so you can stop wasting your time."

"I appreciate the tip. My name is Archer."

"Reavis," he said. "Pat Reavis."

"You seem to know the Slocums pretty well."

"Too damn well. I been their chauffeur for the last six months. No more, though. The bastards fired me."

"Why?"

"How the hell do I know. I guess they just got sick of looking at my pan. I got sick enough looking at theirs."

"That's a nice-looking kid they got, though. What was her name?"

"Cathy."

But he gave me a quick look, and I dropped the subject. "The wife has her points, too," I offered.

"She had it once, I guess. No more. She's turning into another bitch like the old lady. A bunch of women go sour like milk when they got no man around to tell them where to get off."

"There's Slocum, isn't there?"

"I said a man." He snorted. "Hell, I'm talking too much."

The car went over the little ridge that marked the edge of the mesa. The headlights swept empty blackness and dipped down into the valley. There were a few islands of brightness on either side of the road where night crews were working to bring in new wells. Further down the slope, aluminum-painted oil tanks lay under searchlights like a row of thick huge silver dollars in a kitty. At the foot of the hill the lights of the town began, white and scattered on the outskirts, crowded and crawling with color in the business section, where they cast a fiery glow above the buildings.

The traffic in the main street was heavy and unpredictable. Fenderless jalopies threatened my fenders. Hot rods built low to the ground and stacked with gin-mill cowboys roamed the neon trails with their mufflers off. A man in a custom-made Buick stopped in my path abruptly to kiss a woman in the seat beside him, and drove on with her mouth attached to the side of his neck. Eats, Drinks, Beer, Liquor, the signs announced: Antonio's, Bill's, Helen's, The Boots and Saddle. Little knots of men formed on the sidewalk, jabbered and laughed and gesticulated, and broke apart under the pull of the bars.

Reavis was feeling that pull, his eyes were glistening with it. "Anywhere along here," he said impatiently. "And thanks a million."

I angled into the first empty parking space and turned off the lights and ignition. He looked at me with one long leg out the door. "You staying in town tonight?"

"I've got a room in Quinto. Right now I could use a drink."

"You and me both, friend. Come on, I'll show you the best place in town. Better lock your car."

We walked back a block and turned into Antonio's. It was a single large room, high-ceilinged and deep, with restaurant booths along one wall and a fifty-foot bar to the left. At the far end a fry cook worked in a cloud of steam. We found two empty stools near him. Everything in the place looked as if it had been there for a long time, but it was well-kept. The cigarette butts on the floor were new, the scarred mahogany surface of the bar was clean and polished. Reavis rested his arms on it as if it belonged to him. The sleeves of his gaudy shirt were rolled up, and his forearms looked as heavy and hard as the wood under them.

"Nice place," I said. "What are you drinking?"

His answer surprised me: "Uh-uh. This is on me. You treat me like a gentleman, I treat you like a gentleman, see?"

He turned and smiled wide, full in my face, and I had my first chance to study him. The teeth were white, the black eyes frank and boyish, the lines of the features firm and clean. Reavis had quantities of raw charm. But underneath it there was something lacking. I could talk to him all night and never find his core, because he had never found it.

He offered the smile too long; something for sale. I put a cigarette in my mouth. "Hell, you just lost your job. I'll buy the drinks."

"There are plenty of jobs," he said. "But buy 'em if you want. I drink Bushmill's Irish whisky myself."

I was reaching for a match when a lighter flicked under my nose and lit my cigarette. The bartender had approached us noiselessly, a middle-sized man with a smooth hairless head and a lean ascetic face. "Good evening, Pat," he said without expression, replacing the lighter in the pocket of his white jacket. "What are you gentlemen drinking?"

"Bushmill's for him. A whisky sour for me."

He nodded and moved away, narrow-hipped and poised as a ballet-dancer.

"Tony's a cold-blooded bastard," Reavis said. "He'll take your money for six months and then cut you off with a cup of coffee if he thinks you're eighty-six. Now I'm not Jesus Christ—"

"Excuse my mistake."

"You're a right gee, Lew." He smiled the big raw

smile again, but he got to first names too quickly. "What do you say we pull the rag and have ourselves a time? I got me a neat blonde stashed over at Helen's. Gretchen can find you a playmate. The night's still young."

"Younger than I am."

"What's the trouble, you married or something?"

"Not at present. I have to hit the road early tomorrow."

"Aw, come on, man. Have a couple of drinks and you'll feel better. This is a wide-open town."

When our drinks arrived he took his quickly and went out through a swinging door marked Gents. The bartender watched me sip my whisky sour.

"Good?"

"Very good. You didn't spend your apprenticeship in Nopal."

He smiled bleakly, as a monk might smile over the memory of an ecstasy. "No. I began at fourteen in the great hotels of Milan. I graduated before twenty-one to the Italian Line." His accent was French, softened by a trace of native Italian.

"All that training so you can mix 'em for a gang of oilfield winos."

"Nopal Valley is a fine place to make money. I bought this place for thirty-five thousand and in one year paid off the mortgage. Five years and I can retire."

"In Italy?"

"Where else? You are a friend of Pat Reavis?"

"Never saw him before."

"Be careful then," dryly and quietly. "He is a very pleasant boy most of the time, but he can be very unpleasant." He tapped the side of his lean skull. "There is something wrong with Pat: he has no limit. He will do anything, if he is drunk or angry. And he is a liar."

"Have you had trouble with him?"

"Not me, no. I don't have trouble with anybody." I could see why in his face. He had the authority of a man who had seen everything and not been changed by it.

"I don't have much trouble myself," I said, "but thanks."

"You are welcome."

Reavis came back and draped a ponderous arm over my shoulder. "How you doing, Lew boy? Feeling younger now?"

"Not young enough to carry extra weight." I moved, and his arm dropped away.

"What's the matter, Lew?" He looked at the bartender, who was watching us. "Tony been running me down as usual? Never believe a dago, Lew. You wouldn't let a dago spoil the beginning of a beautiful friendship."

"I like Italians very much," I said.

The bartender said slowly and clearly. "I was telling the gentleman that you are a liar, Pat."

Reavis sat and took it. The lips drew back from his fine white teeth, but he didn't say a word. I put a cigarette in my mouth. The lighter flicked under my nose before I could reach for a match.

Normally I objected to being waited on. But when a man was perfect in his role it was a pleasure to see him walk through it.

"Two more of the same," I said to his slim impassive back as he walked away.

Reavis looked at me like a grateful dog. Which I was observing for rabies.

CHAPTER 7

Two more drinks, which I paid for, restored Reavis's opinion of himself and the use of his tongue. He told me how he was promoted in the field on Guadalcanal, to become the youngest captain in the whole Pacific. How the OSS heard of his prowess and gave him a hush-hush assignment tracking down spies and saboteurs. How the *Saturday Evening Post* offered him several thousand dollars for an article about his personal experiences, but he was sworn to secrecy and besides he had other sources of income. He told me he could walk a city block on his hands, and frequently did. He was going through an interminable list of the female friends he had served and sent on their way rejoicing, when someone came up behind me and tapped my shoulder.

A dirty gray fedora, dirty-gray eyes, a long probing nose with a slightly bulbous tip, a lipless mouth like the wrinkle formed by a scar. His face was lopsided in the bar mirror and still looked lopsided when I turned. The corners of his mouth had tobacco-juice stains.

"Lewis Archer?"

"Right."

"I found your car down the street and I figured

you were in one of the places along here. I'm Franks, Detective-Sergeant."

"Parking trouble? I didn't see any signs."

The scar tore open and showed some yellow teeth. It seemed that Detective-Sergeant Franks registered amusement in this way. "Death trouble, Mr. Archer. The Chief phoned down and said to pick you up."

"Mrs. Slocum," I said, and I realized I'd liked her pretty well. Too often the human ones were the ones that got in the way.

"Now how would you know it was the old lady—"

"It's not the young Mrs. Slocum then—James Slocum's wife?"

"Naw, the old lady," he said, as if that could be taken for granted.

"What happened to her?"

"Don't you know? I thought maybe you'd know. The Chief says you're the last one that seen her alive." He averted his face coyly and spat on the floor.

I got up suddenly. His hand went to his right hip and stayed there. "What happened to her?" I said.

"The old girl got drowned. They found her in the swimming-pool a little while ago. Maybe she jumped in for fun, or maybe somebody pushed her. You don't go swimming at night with all your clothes on. Not if you can't swim a stroke and got a weak heart in the bargain. The Chief says it looks like murder."

I glanced at Reavis, and saw that his stool was unoccupied. The door marked Gents was oscillating slightly on its hinges. I moved for it and pushed it wide. At the far end of the passage the shadow of a big man moved in an open doorway and disappeared. Simultaneously a gun went off behind me and something jarred the door under my hand. A spent slug dropped to the floor at my feet among a shower of slivers. I picked it up and turned to face Franks, tossing the slug from hand to hand because it was hot. He advanced crabwise, with a service .45 steady in his hand.

"You coming peaceable, or do I shoot to maim this time?" The people in the room had formed a group behind him, a heaving body with twenty staring heads. Antonio, still and scornful, watched from behind the bar.

"Trigger-happy, Sergeant? Who gave you a gun with real live shells in it?"

"Hands up, you, and watch your lip."

I tossed him the piece of lead and put my hands on my head. My hair was thinner than it used to be. He caught the slug in his left hand and dropped it in the coat-pocket of his shiny blue umpire suit. "Now march, you."

He circled me cautiously, and the crowd made way for us. When I opened the door a small shiny object whizzed past my head and rang on the sidewalk. It took me a minute to realize what it was: the fifty-cent piece I had left on the bar as a tip for Antonio. Then I began to get angry.

When Franks unsnapped the handcuffs from his belt, I was ready to fight him for them. He saw that, and didn't insist. Instead, he put me in the front seat of the police car, beside the uniformed driver, and sat in the back where he could watch me.

"The siren, Kenny," he said. "The Chief wants him there in a hurry."

A fool in an official job, with guns and gadgets to play with, could cause a lot of disturbance. The siren purred, growled, whooped, screeched and ululated like a mountain lion as we went up the hill. I didn't say a word. Detective-Sergeant Franks wouldn't know an explanation if it bit him in the leg and called him brother.

His Chief was another story. He had set up a temporary office in the kitchen and was questioning the witnesses one by one, while a uniformed policeman took notes in shorthand. When the sergeant took me in to him, Knudson was talking to Francis Marvell. The authority I had noticed in his bearing had flared up in the emergency, like a slow fire doused with gasoline. The opaque eyes and the thick face were full of life and power. Homicide was his dish.

"Archer?" The heavy voice was crisp.

"This is him, Chief." Sergeant Franks was staying close to me, still with his hand on his gun.

"I'd like to congratulate the sergeant," I said. "He only needed one shot to bring me in. And I'm a witness in a murder, and you know how serious that is."

"Murder?" Marvell spread his hands on the red plastic-topped table and pushed himself to his feet. His jaw moved down and up silently before more words came out. "I understood it was an accident."

"That's what we're trying to find out," Knudson snapped. "Sit down." He used the same tone on Franks: "What's this about shooting?"

"He tried to escape, so I fired a warning shot."

"Yeah," I said. "I made a wild break for freedom."

He whirled on me: "If you didn't try to escape, why did you go for the door?"

"I needed a breath of fresh air, Sergeant. Now I need another one."

"Break it up," Knudson cut in. "Franks, you go out and help Winowsky with his photographic equipment. You, Archer, sit down and I'll be with you shortly."

I sat down in a straightbacked kitchen chair on the other side of the room and lit a cigarette. It tasted bitter. A large wooden tray of what had been hors d'oeuvres stood on the tiled sink beside me: the remains of anchovies, a little earthenware crock half full of caviar. I helped myself to some caviar on a cracker. Mrs. Slocum had lived well.

Marvell said: "You didn't tell me she was murdered. You permitted me to think it was an accident." He sounded badly shaken. His yellow hair was wet, but the water that glistened on his forehead came from his own pores.

"They're no deader when they're murdered. In any case, we don't know if she was."

"Murder is such a perfectly dreadful thought." His blurred gaze wandered around the room and skipped past me. "It was bad enough when I found the poor woman's body. Now I simply know I shan't sleep a wink tonight."

"Take it easy, Mr. Marvell. You did exactly the right thing and you should be feeling more than satisfied with yourself." Knudson's rippling bass was gentle and bland. "One thing I don't quite understand, though, and that is why you decided to take a swim all by yourself after dark."

"I don't entirely understand it myself," Marvell answered slowly. "It was one of those half-conscious motivations, I believe. I'd just stepped outside for a bit to smell the jasmine, and I was strolling in the loggia, when I thought I heard a splash from the swimming-pool. It had no sinister connotations, you know, nothing like that; I must have thought that someone else was taking a dip, and I decided to join them. I'm always one for fun and games, you see—"

"I see."

"Well, first I went down to the pool to see who it was—"

"Right after you heard the splash?"

"No, not immediately. It took a little while for the idea to grow on me—"

"And meanwhile the splashing continued?"

"I believe it did. Yes, I think it must have. By the time I got down there, however—it's quite a piece from the house—"

"Nearly a hundred yards. By the time you got down there?"

"It was perfectly silent again, and perfectly dark. Naturally I was a little surprised to find that the lights weren't on. I stood by the pool for a moment, wondering what had happened, and then I made out this round dark object. It was a large straw hat floating upside down in the water, and when I realized that I became alarmed. I switched on the underwater lights, and saw her. She was lying face down at the bottom of the pool, her hair swirling round her head, her skirt billowing, her arms spread out. It was ghastly." The water from his pores had made bright marks along his cheeks and formed a single clear droplet at the point of his chin. He brushed it away with the back of a nervous hand.

"Then you went in after her," Knudson stated.

"Yes. I took off my clothes, all but my underthings, and brought her to the surface. I found I couldn't raise her onto the side, so I pulled her to the shallow end and got her out there. She was terribly hard to handle. I'd thought that dead people were stiff, but she seemed loose all over. Like soft rubber." A second droplet formed.

"It was then that you raised the alarm?"

"Yes. I should have done before, but all I could think of was to get that poor dear woman out of the cold water."

"You did just fine, Mr. Marvell. A minute or two didn't make any difference, anyway. Now I want you to think carefully before you answer this: how much time elapsed between the initial splash and the alarm? It was twenty to nine when you called for help. You see, I'm trying to fix the time of death."

"I understand that. It's very hard to say how long it was, impossible in fact. I was lost in the beauty of the night, you know, and I wasn't consciously taking note of time, or of what I heard. It might have been ten minutes, or it might have been twenty, I really couldn't say."

"Well, think about it some more, and let me know if you can set it more definitely. You're perfectly certain, by the way, that you didn't see anybody else at all at the pool, or while you were back of the house?"

"As certain as I can be, yes. Now if you'll excuse me—"

"Of course. And thank you."

Marvell left the room in a nervous sidewise movement, stroking his hair with his hand.

"Jesus," Knudson said as he stood up. "He never saw a stiff before, let alone touched one, and it hit him in the middle. It takes guts to dive for a cadaver at night, though. You get all of that, Eddie?"

"All but the gestures." The man in uniform stroked himself elaborately from hairline to nape.

"Okay, take a little walk while I talk to Archer here." He crossed the room and stood above me with fists on hips until the door had closed. I put some caviar on a cracker and ate it daintily, in two bites.

"Have some?"

He didn't answer that. "Just who the hell are you, anyway?"

I took out my wallet and showed him the photostat of my license. "Now ask me what the hell I'm doing here. Unfortunately my chronic aphasia has taken a bad turn for the worse. It always goes like that when a dumb cop takes a shot at me."

He wagged his stubbled head good-humoredly. "Forget Franks, eh? I can't help it if he's a ward-heeler in the Mayor's party, and the Mayor is *ex officio* on the Police Commission. Can I?"

"You could put him on a desk, or issue him blanks."

"Yeah. You're a fast talker, Archer, but you needn't get your back up. Maude Slocum told me about you."

"How much?"

"Enough. The less said about that the better. Right?" His mind was quick and cold, out of place in his big, full-blooded body. I could almost see it turning a leaf and writing a new heading at the top of a clean page. "So far as she knew, you were the last one to talk to the old lady before she died. Exactly when did you see her?"

"Just before sunset. That would be a few minutes after seven."

"A couple of minutes before. It's earlier here on account of the mountains. You talked to her in the garden, I believe? If you'll tell me now exactly what was said—" He went to the door and called his short-hand writer, who took his position at the kitchen table. I told him what was said.

"Nothing much there, eh?" He sounded disappointed. "No sign of suicidal impulse? Or illness? She had a pretty bad heart, the doctor says."

"Nothing that I could put my finger on. She

seemed a little screwy to me, but nearly everyone does. What's the physical evidence?"

"Everything external points to drowning. That's the presumption, anyway, when you find a corpse in water—though how the hell she got there I can't say. About the body, we'll know more tomorrow. The Coroner's ordering an autopsy and an inquest."

"What's the assumption in the meantime? Fell, or got pushed?"

"Fell, but I'm handling it as homicide until I know for sure. Old ladies do fall into swimming-pools, I guess."

"She wasn't so old."

"I know. And there's no good reason why she should go near the pool, let alone into it. She never used it. It was built for her husband's arthritis years ago. She was forbidden the water, on account of her heart, and she was afraid of it, anyway."

"Not without reason."

"No." His thick, square-nailed fingers drummed on the hard tabletop. "I tried a reconstruction from the condition of the lawn around the pool. The trouble was, when Marvell yelled for help, everybody came running. They trampled out any traces there might have been."

"One thing, if it's murder, you'll have most of your suspects accounted for. The people at the party."

"It's not that simple." To the man with the note-book he said, "Don't bother with this," and turned back to me: "They had a buffet lunch in the dining-room, and at the time it happened the guests were moving in and out. Even Marvell could have pushed her in, then fished her out himself."

"Why pick on Marvell?"

"Figure it out. He wants money to take his play east. He's very close to Slocum. Now Slocum has money."

"You're skipping Slocum, aren't you?"

His face twisted sourly. "James is a mother's boy. He wouldn't touch a hair of his mother's head."

"And Maude Slocum?"

"I'm skipping her, too." His mind flicked another page, and started a new heading: "Assuming she was murdered, there's a possibility it was an outside job. A woman like that makes lots of enemies."

"Like Pareco," I said.

He grunted: "Huh?"

"The Pacific Refining Company."

"Oh. Yeah. Only the oil companies don't go in for murder any more. Not for a little matter like an oil lease. I meant to ask you, you didn't see any strangers around the place?"

This was the question I'd been waiting for, and wondering how to answer. Reavis was the logical suspect: on the spot, drunk, and with a grievance. The only trouble was that when I picked him up, he hadn't looked or talked or acted like a man who had just committed a crime. And the timing was wrong. But if the police were looking for a quick and easy out, they could probably send him to the gas chamber on circumstantial evidence. I'd seen it happen before, in the L.A. jungle, and I had to be sure about the Nopal Valley police. I decided that Knudson could be trusted, but I kept one card face down. I didn't tell him that when I picked Reavis up a mile or more from the house, it was exactly 8:23 by my dashboard clock and my wristwatch. It was Reavis who had called attention to the time, and that could mean that Reavis was trying to use me for a phony alibi. I hated to be used.

Knudson didn't like the delay, but he kept his temper. "All right. So you gave this boy a lift from outside the gate sometime after eight. You realize we don't know when she was killed, and probably never will know. Marvell's evidence is inconclusive. In his first account he didn't even mention the splash he heard, or thinks he heard. Did Reavis have murder on his mind?"

"Not unless he enjoys it. He was in a good mood."

"What sort of a boy is he? I've seen him around, but never talked to him."

"There's nothing wrong with him a pre-frontal

lobotomy wouldn't fix. He'd steal his widowed mother's rent-money to play the ponies, but I don't see him pushing her into the water. Psychopath, maybe, but not extreme. He takes it out in talking."

He leaned toward me, as wide as the tabletop. "You like the boy? Is that why you let him slip away from Franks?"

"I lose my well-oiled precision when a slug just misses my kidneys. I don't like Reavis at all, but some people do." I pitched him a curve, low, on the outside: "Cathy Slocum likes him pretty well."

His face swelled up with blood, and he leaned closer. "You're a liar. Cathy doesn't mess with trash like that."

"Take it easy, Knudson." I stood up. "Ask her father about it, if you like."

The life went out of his face and left it stupid. "What goes on here?" he said to himself. Then he remembered me, and the shorthand man.

He took the notebook out of the man's hands, and ripped out the last page of pencilled shorthand. "All right, Eddie, take a rest." And to me: "What are you going to do? Help us find Reavis?"

"I'll talk to Mrs. Slocum."

"Do that. She's in the front sitting-room with her husband. It's across the hall from the living-room."

I said: "I'm not a liar."

"What?" He stood up slowly. He was no taller than I was, but he was wide and powerful. His thick body dominated the room even though the mind behind his pale blue eyes was turned elsewhere.

"I'm not a liar," I said.

The eyes focused on me, cold with hostility. "All right," he said after a time. "You're not a liar." He sat down at the table again, with his shoulders slumped like a padded coat on an inadequate hanger.

CHAPTER 8

Passing the open door of the living-room, I caught a glimpse of the people waiting inside. Voices were subdued, faces white and strained. Nobody seemed to be drinking, and all the gay conversation had run out. The party was a group hangover, the dim old room the ancestral cave of death. A policeman in a blue shirt sat hunched in a chair by the door, studying the visored cap on his knee as if it were the face of a dear friend.

The door of the sitting-room across the hall was locked. I was about to knock on it, when a man on the other side uttered a four-letter word. It sounded incongruous in his high tenor. He was answered by a woman's voice, rapid and low, too low to penetrate the heavy door and let me hear her words. The only sounds I could make out plainly were the sobbing gasps that punctuated the sentences.

I moved to the next door on that side and entered the dark room beyond it. The light from the hall made crouched shadows of the chairs along the wall and gleamed among the silver and dishes that cluttered the buffet. There was still a little light in the room when I closed the door behind me: a thin shining under the old-fashioned sliding doors that separated the dining-room from the sitting-room. I crossed the room quietly and lay down by the sliding doors. Maude Slocum's voice slid under them:

"I've stopped trying. For years I did my best for you. It didn't take. Now I'm giving up."

"You never tried," her husband answered, flatly and bitterly. "You've lived in my house, and eaten my bread, and never made the slightest attempt to help me. If I'm a personal failure, as you say, the failure is certainly yours as well as mine."

"Your mother's house," she taunted him. "Your mother's bread—a very unleavened loaf."

"Leave Mother out of it!"

"How can I leave her out?" Now her voice was purring smoothly, in control of itself and of the situation. "She's been the central figure in my married life. You had your chance to make a clean break with her when we were married, but you hadn't the courage to take it."

"I had no real chance, Maude." The actorish voice wobbled under the burden of self-pity. "I was too young to get married. I was dependent on her—I hadn't even finished school. There weren't many jobs in those days, either, and you were in a hurry to be married—"

"*I* was in a hurry? You begged me with tears in your voice to marry you. You said your immortal soul depended on it."

"I know, I thought it did." The simple words held echoes of despair. "You wanted to marry me, too. You had your reasons."

"You're damned right I had my reasons, with a child in my belly and nobody else to turn to. I suppose I should have been the true-hearted little woman and swallowed my pride and gone away somewhere." Her voice sank to an acid whisper: "That's what your mother wanted, wasn't it?"

"You were never little, Maude."

She laughed unpleasantly. "Neither was Mother, was she? Her lap was always big enough for you."

"I know how you feel about me, Maude."

"You can't. I have no feeling at all. You're a perfect blank as far as I'm concerned."

"Very well." He struggled to keep his voice steady. "But now that Mother's dead, I'd think you'd be a little kinder to—her memory. She was always good to Cathy. She had to go without things herself to send Cathy to school and dress her properly—"

"I admit that. What you don't understand is the fact that I'm thinking about myself. I put Cathy first, of course. I love her, and I want the best of everything for her. But that doesn't mean I'm ready for the shelf. I'm a woman as well as a mother. I'm only thirty-five."

"That's rather late to start all over again."

"Right now I feel as if I haven't started—that I've been saving myself for fifteen years. I won't keep much longer. I'm going rotten inside."

"Your version at the moment. This is the chance you've been waiting for. If Mother hadn't died, you'd have been perfectly willing to go on as before."

"I'm afraid you don't know what you're talking about."

"Approximately as before, then. I know that something's been happening to you since you made that trip to Chicago."

"What about that trip to Chicago?" A threat tightened her voice like an unused muscle.

"I haven't asked you any questions about it. I don't intend to. I do know that you'd changed when you came back that spring. You had more life—"

She cut him short contemptuously: "You're well advised not to ask questions, James. I could ask questions, too, about Francis, for instance. Only, I know the answers."

He was silent for a time. I could hear one of them breathing. Finally, he sighed. "Well, we're getting nowhere. What do you want?"

"I'll tell you what I want. Half of everything you have, and that includes half of this property now."

"*Now!* Mother's death has been exceedingly convenient for you, hasn't it? If I didn't know you, Maude, I'd believe that you killed Mother yourself."

"I won't pretend I'm sorry that it happened. As soon as this unpleasantness is over with, and you've agreed to a settlement, I'm going to court."

"I'll make a settlement," he said thinly. "You've waited long enough for your share of the property. Now you can have it."

"And Cathy," she insisted. "Don't forget Cathy."

"I have not forgotten her. Cathy is staying with me."

"So she can live *à trois* with you and Francis? I think not."

He spoke with great effort: "Francis doesn't enter into the picture."

"Francis or someone like him. I know your penchant, James."

"No." The word exploded from his lips. "Cathy is all I want."

"I know what you want. You want a healthy life so you can twine around it like a vine. You tried it with me, but I tore you loose, and you shan't twist yourself around Cathy. I'm moving out of here, and taking her with me."

"No. No." The second word trailed off in a painful whimper. "You mustn't leave me alone."

"You have your friends," she said with irony.

"Don't leave me, Maude. I'm afraid to be left alone. I need you both, much more than you believe." His voice was quite unmanned, a hysterical boy's.

"You've neglected me for fifteen years," she said. "When I've finally got my chance to go, you insist I have to stay."

"You must stay. It's your duty to stay with me. I can't be left alone."

"Be a man," she said. "I can't have any feeling for a whining jellyfish."

"You used to love me—"

"Did I?"

"You wanted to be my wife and look after me."

"That was a long time ago. I can't remember."

I heard breath drawn in, feet moving quickly on the floor. "Whore!" he cried in a harsh choking voice. "You're a horrible cold woman, and I hate you."

"It chills a woman off," she said clearly and firmly, "being married to a fairy."

"Horrible. Woman." The caesura between the words was marked by a blow on flesh. Then something bony, his knees perhaps, bumped unevenly on the floor. "Forgive me," he said, "forgive me."

"You struck me." Her voice was blank with shock. "You hurt me."

"I didn't mean it. Forgive me. I love you, Maude. Please stay with me." A retching sob tore through his babbling and lengthened rhythmically. For a long time there was nothing but the sound of the man's crying.

Then she began to comfort him, in a gentle lulling voice. "Be quiet, Jimmie. Dear Jimmie. I'll stay with you. We'll have a good life yet, won't we, my dear?"

I staggered slightly when I got to my feet. I felt as if I'd been listening in on a microphone built into the walls of hell. I passed the closed door of the sitting-room without breaking my stride, and went out onto the lawn. The sky was black and moving. Long gray clouds streamed across the mountains to the sea, flowing like a river over the jagged edge of the world.

I was halfway across the lawn to the drive when I remembered that my car was parked on the street in Nopal Valley. I went around to the back of the house and found the kitchen empty except for the house-keeper. Mrs. Strang was an elderly woman with a long, soft face and fading hair. She was cooking something in a saucepan on the stove.

She jumped sideways at the sound of my footsteps. "Heavens! You frightened me."

"I'm sorry. I'm Archer, a friend of Mrs. Slocum's."

"Oh yes, you phoned, I remember." Her lips were trembling and blue.

I said: "Is Cathy all right?"

"Yes, she's all right. I'm making her some hot milk

to put her to sleep. The poor child needs her rest after all these terrible things happening."

In a way I felt responsible for Cathy, if only because there was nobody else to feel responsible. Her parents were completely involved in their private war, negotiating their little armistice. Probably it had always been like that.

"You'll take good care of Cathy?" I said to Mrs. Strang.

She answered me with pride: "I always have, Mr. Archer. She's very well worth it, you know. Some of her teachers think she is a genius."

"This place is lousy with geniuses, isn't it?"

I left before I got into an argument. From the kitchen door, I saw a white flash splatter the darkness below the garages like a brushful of whitewash. They were still taking pictures around the pool.

Knudson was there with three members of his department, directing a series of measurements. Near them the body lay under a blanket, waiting patiently to be taken away. The underwater lights of the pool were on, so that the water was a pale emerald depth with a luminous and restless surface filming it.

When he saw me Knudson moved away from his group and lifted his chin at an angle. When I was near enough to hear his low voice: "What did she say? Co-operate with us?"

"I didn't see her. She was locked in the room with her husband."

His nostrils flared in a private nasal sneer, not intended for me. "I've got our radio cars out looking for Reavis. You could be a help, since you know him to see."

"It's a little off my beat, isn't it?"

"You be the judge of that." His shoulders rose and fell in a muscular slow-motion shrug. "It seems to me there's a certain responsibility—?"

"Maybe so. Can you get me a lift into town? *Not* with Franks."

"Sure." He turned to the photographer, who was

kneeling by the body. "Just about finished, Winow-sky?"

"Yeah." He threw back the blanket. "A couple more shots of the stiff. I want to do her justice, my professional honor demands it."

"You take Mr. Archer into town with you."

"Yeah."

He stood over the body in a crouching position and flashed the bulb attached to the top of his camera. The white magnesium light drew the dead face from the shadows and projected it against the night. The freckles grew like acne on the lime-white skin. Bulbous and white, like deepsea life, the foam bulged from the nostrils and gaping mouth. The open green eyes gazed up in blank amazement at the dark sky moving between the darker mountains.

"Once more," the photographer said, and stepped across the body. "Now watch the birdie."

The white light flashed again on the unmoving face.

CHAPTER 9

The building was pink stucco, big and new and ugly. It had a side entrance with "Romp Room" lettered above it in red neon. The wall was blind except for the door and a couple of round screened ventilators. I could hear the noise of the romping from the outside: the double-time beat of a band, the shuffling of many feet. When I pulled the heavy door open, the noise blasted my ears.

Most of it came from the platform at the rear end of the room, where a group of young men in white flannels were maltreating a piano, a guitar, a trombone, a trumpet, drums. The piano tinkled and boomed, the trombone brayed, the trumpet squawked and screeched. The guitar bit chunks from the chromatic scale and spat them out in rapid fire without chewing them. The drummer hit everything he had, drums, traps, cymbals, stamped on the floor, beat the rungs of his chair, banged the chrome rod that supported the microphone. The Furious Five, it said on his biggest drum.

The rest of the noise came from the booths that lined three walls of the room, and from the dance-floor in the middle where twenty or thirty couples whirled in the smoke. The hight titter of drunk and flattered women, the animal sounds of drunk and eager men. Babel with a wild jazz obbligato.

A big henna redhead in a shotsilk blouse was making drinks at a service bar near the door. Her torso jiggled in the blouse like a giant soft-boiled egg with the shell removed. The waitresses came and went in an antlike stream, and all the whiskies came from the same bottle. In an interval between waitresses, I went up to the bar. The big woman smashed an empty bottle under it and straightened up, breathing hard.

"I'm Helen," she said with a rubber-lipped public smile. "You want a drink, you find a seat and I send a waitress to you."

"Thanks, I'm looking for Pat."

"Pat who? Does she work here?"

"He's a man. Young, big, with curly dark hair."

"Friend, I got troubles of my own. Don't you go away mad, though. Try the waitresses if you want." She took a deep breath when she finished, and the egg swelled up almost to her chin.

"Two bombs, beer chasers," a waitress said behind me.

I asked her: "Is Gretchen here?"

"Gretchen Keck, you mean?" The waitress jerked a flat thumb at a tall girl on the dance floor. "That's her, the blonde in the blue dress."

I waited till the music stopped, and crossed to an empty booth. Some of the couples stayed where they were in the center of the room, arms locked, face to face. A Mexican boy in blue jeans and a white shirt stood with the tall blonde. Gretchen was as light as the boy was dark, with a fair skin and a pull-taffy pompadour that made her taller than he was. They couldn't stand still. Their hips, pressed flat together, moved in a slow weaving round and round until the music started and quickened their beat.

While she danced on a dime by herself, he moved in a circle about her, turkey strutting, flapping his arms like a rooster, leaping and stamping. He moved his head and neck in the horizontal plane, Balinese fashion, danced squatting on his heels like a Cossack, invented new gyrations of the hips, body and feet jerked by separate rhythms. She stood where she was, her movements slightly mimicking his, and his circle tightened about her. They came together again, their bodies shaken and snaked through their length by an impossible shimmy. Then she was still on his arched breast, and her arms fell loose. He held her, and the music went on without them.

In the booth behind me, a woman called in *bracero* Spanish upon the Mother of God to witness her justifiable act of violence. She thrust herself out of her seat, a gaunt Mexican girl with hair like fresh-poured tar. From her clenched right fist, a four-inch knife-blade projected upward. I moved, bracing one hand on the seat and pivoting. My left toe caught her instep and she fell hard, face down. The spring-knife struck the floor and clattered out of her reach. At its signal the dark boy and the blonde girl sprang apart, so suddenly that the girl staggered on her high heels. The boy looked at the knife on the floor and the woman struggling to her knees. His eyes watered and his bronze face took on a greenish patina.

Slouching and woebegone, without a backward look, he went to the woman and tried awkwardly to help her rise. She spat out words in Spanish that sounded like a string of cheap firecrackers. Her worn black satin dress was coated with dust. Half of her sallow pitted face was grimy. She began to weep. He put his arms around her and said, "Please, I am sorry." They went out together. The music stopped.

A heavy middle-aged man in a fake policeman's uniform appeared from nowhere. He picked up the knife, broke it across his knee, and dropped the blade and handle in the pocket of his blue coat. He came to my booth, stepping lightly as if he was walking on eggs. His shoes were slit and mis-shapen across the base of the toes.

"Nice work, son," he said. "They flare up so fast sometimes I can't keep track of 'em."

"Knife-play disturbs my drinking."

His red-rimmed eyes peered from a face that was gullied by time. "New in these parts, ain't you?"

"Yeah," I answered, though I felt as if I'd been in Nopal Valley for days. "Speaking of my drinking, I haven't been doing any."

He signalled to a waitress. "We'll fix that." She set down a trayful of empty glasses grained with the leavings of foam. "What'll it be?"

"A bottle of beer." I distrusted the bar whisky. "Ask Gretchen what she's drinking, and if she'll have one with me."

The drink and Gretchen arrived simultaneously. "Helen says no charge," the waitress said. "Your drinks are on the house. Or anything."

"Food?"

"Not this late. The kitchen's closed."

"What, then?"

The waitress set my beer down hard so that it foamed, and went away without answering.

Gretchen giggled, not unpleasantly, as she slid into the seat across from me. "Helen's got rooms upstairs. She says there's too many men in this burg, and somebody has to do something to take the pressure off." She sipped her drink, rum coke, and winked grotesquely over the rim of the glass. Her eyes were naïve and clear, the color of cornflowers. Not even the lascivious red mouth constructed with lipstick over her own could spoil her freshness.

"I'm a very low-pressure type myself."

She looked me over carefully, did everything but feel the texture of the material my coat was made of. "Maybe. You don't have the upstairs look, I admit. You can move, though, brother."

"Forget it."

"I wish I could. I never get scared when something happens, it always come over me later. I wake up in the middle of the night and get the screaming mee-mies. God damn that babe to hell."

"She's there already."

"Yeah, I know what you mean. These Spanish babes

take things so hard, it's getting so a girl can't have any fun any more."

"You do all right," I said. "If Pat can be believed."

She blushed, and her eyes brightened. "You know Pat?"

"He was my buddy," I said, almost gagging on the word. "In the Marines."

"He really *was* in the Marines, then?" She seemed surprised and pleased, and was sharper than I thought.

"Sure. We were on Guadal together." I felt just a little like a pander.

"Maybe you can tell me." She bit her lower lip and got lipstick on her teeth. Even her front teeth were bad. "Is it true what he says, that he's a secret agent or something?"

"In the war?"

"Now. He says him being a chauffeur is only a blind, that he's some kind of an undercover man."

"I wouldn't know."

"He tells so many stories, half the time I don't know what to believe. Pat's a swell joe, though," she added defensively. "He's got a good brain, and he'll go far."

I agreed, as heartily as I could. "Yeah, a good guy. I was hoping to see him tonight. There's a business opportunity in our organization, and he could get in on the ground floor."

"A business opportunity?" The words had a magical four-color advertisement quality, and she repeated them with respect. The cornflower eyes saw Gretchen in an apron freshly laundered in the new Bendix, cooking for Reavis in the tiled kitchen of a new one-bedroom G.I. house in the suburbs of what city? "In L.A.?"

"Yeah."

"He might be at my place. He waits for me in the trailer sometimes."

"Can you leave now?"

"Why not? I'm a freelance." The patter went on like a record she'd forgotten to turn off, but her thoughts were far ahead, on Gretchen in a new phase: attractive young wife of rising young executive Reavis.

She stroked the fender of my car as if it was an animal she could win by affection. I wanted to say, forget him. He'll never stay long with any woman or pay his debts to any man. I said: "We're doing good business these days. We can use a boy like Pat."

"If I could help to get him a real good job—" she said. The rest of it was silent but unmistakable: he'd marry me. Maybe.

A few blocks off the main street I turned, as she directed, down a road lined with large old houses. The eroded asphalt rattled the tools in the trunk of the car. It was one of those streets that had once been the best in town. The houses were Victorian mansions, their gables and carved cornices grotesque against the sky. Now they were light-housekeeping apartments and boarding houses, wearing remnants of sleazy grandeur.

We went up an alley between two of them, to a yard oppressed by the black shadows of oaks. There was a trailer under the trees, on the far side of the yard. In the light of the headlights I could see that its metal side was peeling and rusting like an abandoned billboard. The littered yard gave off an odor of garbage.

"That's our trailer there." The girl was trying to be brisk, but there was a strain of anxiety rising in her voice. "No lights, though," she added, when I switched off the headlights and the engine.

"He wouldn't be waiting in the dark?"

"He might have gone to sleep. Sometimes he goes to sleep here." She was on the defensive again, describing the habits of a large and troublesome pet whom she happened to love.

"You said 'our trailer,' by the way. Yours and Pat's?"

"No sir, he just visits me. I got a bunkmate name of Jane, but she's never home nights. She works in an all-night hamburger up the line."

Her face was a pale blur, swallowed completely then by the shadow of the oaks. Their sharp dry leaves crackled under our feet. The door of the trailer was unlocked. She went in and turned on a light in the ceiling.

"He isn't here." She sounded disappointed. "Do you want to come in?"

"Thanks." I stepped up from the concrete block that served as a doorstep. The top of the door was so low I had to duck my head.

The little room contained a sink and butane stove at the end nearest the door, two narrow built-in bunks covered with identical cheap red cotton spreads, a built-in plywood dresser at the far end cluttered with cosmetics and bobbypins and true-romance comic-books, and above it a warped, dirty mirror reflecting a blurred distorted version of the girl's room, the girl, and me.

The man in the mirror was big and flat-bodied, and lean-faced. One of his gray eyes was larger than the other, and it swelled and wavered like the eye of conscience: the other eye was little, hard and shrewd. I stood still for an instant, caught by my own distorted face, and the room reversed itself like a trick drawing in a psychological test. For an instant I was the man in the mirror, the shadow-figure without a life of his own who peered with one large eye and one small eye through dirty glass at the dirty lives of people in a very dirty world.

"It's kind of cramped," she said, trying to be cheerful, "but we call it home sweet home."

She reached past me and closed the door. In the close air, the smell of spilled rancid grease from the stove and the sick-sweet odor of dime-store perfume from the dresser were carrying on an old feud. I wasn't rooting for either. "Cozy," I said.

"Sit down, sir," she said with forced gaiety. "I'm out of rum and cokes, but I got some muscatel."

"Thanks, not on top of beer."

I sat on the edge of one of the red-covered bunks. The movements of the man in the mirror had the quickness and precision of youth, but none of youth's enthusiasm. Now his forehead was bulbous like a cartooned intellectual's, his mouth little and prim and cruel. To hell with him.

"We could have a little party if you want," she said uncertainly. Standing in the full glare of the light, she looked like a painted rubber doll, made with real human hair, that wasn't quite new any more.

"I don't want."

"Okay, only you don't have to be insulting about it, do you?" She meant to say it in a kidding way, but it came out wrong. She was embarrassed, and worried.

She tried again: "I guess you're pretty anxious to see Pat, eh? He might be down in his place in L.A., you know. He don't usually go down in the middle of the week, but a couple of times he did."

"I didn't know he had a place in L.A."

"A little place, a one-room apartment. He took me down one week end to see it. Gee, wouldn't that be funny if you came all the way up here to find him and he was down in L.A. all the time."

"That would be a scream. You know where it is, so I can look him up tomorrow?"

"He won't be there tomorrow. He's got to be back on the job, at Slocum's."

I let her think that. "Too bad. I have to get back to L.A. tonight. Maybe you can give me his address."

"I don't have the number, but I could find it again." Her eyes flickered dully, as if she hoped to promote something. She sat down on the bunk opposite me, so close that our knees touched. A pair of nylons hanging from a towel-rack above the bed tickled the back of my neck. "I'd do anything I could to help," she said.

"Yeah, I appreciate that. Does the place have a name?"

"Graham Court, something like that. It's on one of the little side streets off North Madison, between Hollywood and L.A."

"And no phone?"

"Not that I know of."

"Thanks again." I stood up. She rose like my shadow, and we were jammed in the narrow aisle between the beds. I tried to move past her to the door, and felt the touch of her round thighs.

"I kind of like you, Mister. If there was anything I could do?"

Her breasts were pointed like a dilemma. I pushed on past. The man in the mirror was watching me with one eye as cold as death. "How old are you, Gretchen?" I asked her from the doorway.

She didn't follow me to the door. "None of your business. A hundred years, about. By the calendar, seventeen."

Seventeen, a year or two older than Cathy. And they had Reavis in common. "Why don't you go home to your mother?"

She laughed: paper tearing in an echo chamber. "Back to Hamtramck? She left me at Stanislaus Welfare when she got her first divorce. I been on my own since 1946."

"How are you doing, Gretchen?"

"Like you said, I'm doing all right."

"Do you want a lift back to Helen's?"

"No thank you, sir. I got enough money to live on for a week. Now that you know where I live, come and see me sometime."

The old words started an echo that lasted fifty miles. The night was murmurous with the voices of girls who threw their youth away and got the screaming meemies at three or four a.m.

CHAPTER 10

I stopped at a lunch-bar east of the cemetery on Santa Monica Boulevard, for a sandwich and coffee and a look at the telephone book. It hung by a chain from the pay telephone on the wall beside the front window. A Graham Court on Laredo Lane was listed. I dialed the number and watched the sidewalk roamers. The young hepcats high on music or weed, the middle-aged men on the town, the tourists waiting for something to fulfill their fantasies, the hopeful floozies and the despairing ones, the quick, light, ageless grifters walked the long Hollywood beat on the other side of the plate glass. The sign above the window was red on one side, green on the other, so that they passed from ruddy youth to sickly age as they crossed my segment of sidewalk, from green youth to apoplexy.

A dim voice answered on the twelfth ring. Pat Reavis didn't live at Graham Court, he never had, goodnight.

The counterman slid a thin white sandwich and a cup of thick brown coffee across the black lucite bar. He had pink butterfly ears. The rest of him was still in the larval stage.

"I couldn't help hearing," he said moistly. "You're looking for a contact, I know a good number to call."

"Write it in blood on a piece of rag-content paper and eat it with your breakfast."

"Huh?" he said. "Blood?"

"What makes you think that sex is the important thing in life?"

He laughed through his nose. "Name another."

"Money."

"Sure, but what does a guy want money for, answer me that."

"So he can retire to a lamasery in Tibet." I showed him a Special Deputy badge which I'd saved from a wartime case on the Pedro docks. "Pimping will get you a couple of years up north."

"Jesus." His face underwent a sudden and shocking change. Old age ran crooked fingers over it, and held it crooked. "I was only kidding, I didn't mean nothing, I don't know any number. Honest to God."

His whine followed me onto the sidewalk. The closing door shut it off. I was in an unpleasant mood.

Laredo Lane was one of the little lost stucco-and-frame streets between the two big boulevards. Its street lights, one to a block, spaced long patches of gloom. There were occasional houselights where after-midnight parties were going on. I caught fragments of music and laughter, glimpses of dancing couples in the windows as I drove past. Some of the dancers were black, some white; some had brown Indian faces. Most of the small marginal houses were dark behind closed blinds. One entire block was empty, its broken row of concrete foundations bared by an old fire.

I felt like a lonely cat, an aging tom ridden by obscure rage, looking for torn-ear trouble. I clipped that pitch off short and threw it away. Night streets were my territory, and would be till I rolled in the last gutter.

The letters GRAHAM COURT were cut in the front of a rectangular metal box lit from inside by an electric bulb. Nailed to the post which supported the sign was a piece of white-painted board on which an unsteady hand had lettered VACANCY. The NO was hidden by a weathered cardboard flap. I parked two hundred feet past the sign and left my engine running. The exhaust made little blue puffs like pipe-smoke in the chilling air.

The Court was a row of decaying shacks bent around a strip of withering grass. A worn gravel drive brought the world to their broken-down doorsteps, if the world was interested. A few of the shacks leaked light through chinks in their warped frame sides. The building marked Office, which was nearest the street, was closed and dark. It looked abandoned, as if the proprietor had given up for good. Over my head a red-flowering eucalyptus moved in a wind as soft as night-time breathing, and dropped its thin small petals to the ground. I picked one off the sidewalk for no good reason and ground it to red powder between my fingers.

I was deciding between the direct approach and a long dull wait in the car, when the door of one of the cottages opened, halfway down the row. It dropped a yellow plank of light across the grass. A man's shadow moved in it, and then the light went out. I walked on up the street, away from my car. After an interval, quick footsteps followed me.

I turned up the walk of an unlighted house, casually and with a sort of reluctance, to give the impression that I belonged there. My long vague shadow merged with the shadows of bushes, and I knew that no more than my outline would be visible to the man behind me. A car was parked in the driveway beside the house, and I moved out of sight behind it. The footsteps on the sidewalk went by without a pause.

At the corner, the man crossed under the streetlight. It was Reavis, walking with an eager swagger, chin up and shoulders held back consciously as if he was pied-piping a bevy of girls at broad noon. When he had turned the corner, I ran back to my car and drove it around the block in time to shut off the lights and see the one-man parade cross the next intersection.

I took no chances. Because he knew my car, I

locked it and left it parked where it was. I let him stay nearly a block ahead and used whatever cover was convenient: trees, hedges, parked cars. He never looked back; he moved like a man whose conscience was clear, or lacking. When he got to Sunset, he turned left. I crossed the boulevard and closed the distance between us. He had on a hounds-tooth suit in clashing black and tan. I could practically hear the suit across the wide traffic-humming thoroughfare.

Reavis headed for a taxi stand, where several cabs stood in line along the curb. I expected him to take one, and was set to follow him in another. Instead, he sat down on the bench at the bus-stop, crossed his legs, and lit a cigarette. I went a few yards up the cross-street and watched him from the shadow of the building on the corner. Off to my left, the tall apartment hotels stood against a sky whose moving reddish color was like the inside of closed eyelids. The late night traffic flowed between me and Reavis at a steady thirty-five to forty.

A long black car nosed out of the stream and into the red curb where Reavis was sitting. He stood up and flipped his cigarette away. A man in a dark gray livery got out of the chauffeur's seat and opened the back door for him. I was halfway across the street, in the thin aisle of safety between the moving lanes, when the limousine got under way again. I opened the door of the first cab in the line and told the driver to follow it.

"Double fare?" he said above the starting roar of his motor.

"Sure thing. And an extra buck for the license number."

The cab left the curb in a jet-propelled takeoff that threw me back in the seat, and went up to fifty in second. Cutting in and out of traffic, it gained on the black limousine.

"Don't pull up on him too fast. Drop back when you get the number."

He slowed a bit, but gradually narrowed the space

between the two cars. "The number is 23P708," he said after a while. "You tailing the guy or what?"

"This is a game I play."

"Okay, I was only asking a natural question."

"I don't know the answer." That ended our conversation. I wrote the number inside a match-folder and slipped it into my watch-pocket.

The black car drew into the curb unexpectedly, dropped Reavis, and pulled away again. He swaggered across the sidewalk under a sign which spelled out Hunt Club. The leather-padded door swung to behind him.

"Let me out here," I said to the driver. "Park as near as you can and wait for me."

He raised his right hand and brushed the ball of his thumb back and forth across the first two fingers. "Show me a little green first, eh?"

I handed him a five.

He looked at the bill and turned to look at me over the back of the seat. His face was Sicilian, black-eyed, sharp-nosed. "This wouldn't be a heist or nothing like that?"

I told him: "I'm a private cop. There won't be any trouble." I hoped there wouldn't.

Dennis's Hunt Club was dim and chilly and crowded. Indirect lights shone with discretion on polished brass and wood, on polished pates and highly polished faces. The photographs that lined the panelled walls were signed by all the big names and the names that had once been big. Dennis himself was near the door, a gray-haired man wearing undertaker's clothes, clown's nose, financier's mouth. He was talking with an air of elegant condescension to one of the names that had once been big. The fading name glanced at me from under his fine plucked eyebrows. No competition. He registered relief and condescension.

The place was built on two levels, so that the bar commanded a view of the dining-room. It was nearly two o'clock. The bar was doing a rush-hour business before the curfew knelled. I found an empty stool, ordered a Guinness stout for energy, and looked around me.

The hounds-tooth suit was raising its visual din in the middle of the dining-room. Reavis, his back to me, was at a table with a woman and a man. The man leaned across his four-inch steak in Reavis's direction, a blue dinner-jacket constricting his heavy shoulders. The wide neck that grew through his soft white collar supported an enormous head, covered with skin as pink and smooth as a baby's. Pinkish hair lay in thin ringlets on the massive scalp. The eyes were half-closed, listening: bright slits of intelligence in the great soft, chewing face.

The third at the table was a young ash blonde, wearing a gown of white pleated chiffon and the beauty to outshine it. When she inclined her head, her short bright hair swung forward, framing her features chastely like a wimple. Her features were fine.

She was trying to hear what the men were talking about. The big face looked at her and opened its eyes a little wider and didn't like what it saw. A babyish petulance drove a wedge between the invisible eyebrows and plucked at the munching mouth, which spoke to her. The woman rose and moved in the direction of the bar. People noticed her. She slid onto the empty stool beside me, and was served before I was. The bartender called her by name, "Mrs. Kilbourne," and would have tugged at his forelock if he'd had one. Her drink was straight bourbon.

Finally the bartender brought me my stout, foaming in a chilled copper mug. "Last call, sir."

"This will do."

I stole a look at the woman, to confirm my first impression. Her atmosphere was like pure oxygen; if you breathed it deep it could make you dizzy and gay, or poison you. Her eyes were melancholy under heavy lashes, her cheeks faintly hollowed as if she had been feeding on her own beauty. Her flesh had that quality of excess drawn fine, which men would turn and follow in the street.

Her hands fumbled with the diamond clasp of a

gold lamé bag, and groped inside. "God damn and blast it," she said. Her voice was level and low.

"Trouble?" I said it not too hopefully.

She didn't turn, or even move her eyes. I thought it was a brush-off, and didn't especially mind, since I'd asked for it. But she answered after a while, in the same flat level tone: "Night after night after night, the run-around. If I had taxi fare I'd walk out on him."

"Be glad to help."

She turned and looked at me—the kind of look that made me wish I was younger and handsomer and worth a million, and assured me that I wasn't. "Who are you?"

"Unknown admirer. For the last five minutes, that is."

"Thank you, Unknown Admirer." She smiled and raised her eyebrows. Her smile was like an arrow. "Are you sure it isn't father of five?"

"Vox populi," I said, "vox dei. I also have a fleet of taxis at my disposal."

"It's funny, but I really have. My husband has, anyway. And I don't have taxi fare."

"I have a taxi waiting. You can have it."

"Such sweetness, and self-denial to boot. So many unknown admirers want to be known."

"Kidding aside."

"Forget it, I was talking. I haven't the guts to do anything else *but* talk."

She glanced at her table, and the large head jerked peremptorily, beckoning her. Downing her drink, she left the bar and went back to the table. The large head called for its check in a rich, carrying voice.

The bartender spread his arms and addressed the people at the bar: "Sorry now, good people, it's time to close now, you know."

"Who's the Palomino?" I asked him quietly.

"Mrs. Kilbourne, you mean?"

"Yeah, who's she?"

"Mrs. *Walter* Kilbourne," he stated with finality. "That's Walter Kilbourne with her." The name had connotations of money for me, but I couldn't place it definitely.

I was waiting in the taxi across the street when they appeared on the sidewalk. Simultaneously, the limousine drew up to the curb. Kilbourne's legs were small for his giant torso. As they crossed the sidewalk, his great head moved level with his wife's. This time Reavis sat up front with the chauffeur.

My driver said: "You want to play tag some more?"

"Might as well, it's barely two o'clock."

"Some guys," he grumbled, "got a very peculiar sense of humor."

He made a U-turn at the corner and came back fast. The traffic had thinned, and it was easy to keep the widely spaced red tail-lights in sight. In the center of the Strip, the black car pulled into the curb again. The blonde woman and her husband got out and entered The Flamenco. Reavis stayed where he was, beside the chauffeur. The black car U-turned suddenly, and passed us going in the opposite direction.

My driver had doubled-parked a hundred yards short of The Flamenco. He slammed the gear-shift savagely into low and wrestled with the steering wheel. "How long does this go on?"

"We'll have to wait and see."

"I usually get myself a bite and java round about two o'clock."

"Yeah, it's sure hell. Murder certainly breaks up a man's schedule."

The speedometer needle jumped ten miles, as if it was attached directly to his heartbeat. "Did you say murder?"

"Right."

"Somebody get it, or somebody going to get it?"

"Somebody got it."

"I don't like messing with killings."

"Nobody does. Just keep that car in sight, and vary your distance."

The black car stopped with a blaze of brake-lights at the Cahuenga stoplight, and my driver made a mistake. Before it turned left, he pulled up close to it. Reavis looked back, his eyes wide and black in our headlights, and spoke to the chauffeur. I cursed under my breath, and hoped that he was discussing the beauty of the night.

He wasn't. Once the limousine got onto the Freeway, it began to move at the speed it was built for. Our speedometer needle moved up to eighty and stayed there like the hand of a stopped clock. The tail-lights disappeared around a curve and were gone when we rounded the next curve on whining tires.

"Sorry," the driver said, his head and body rigid over the wheel. "That Caddie can hold a hundred from here to San Francisco. Anyway, it probably turned off on Lankershim."

CHAPTER 11

Graham Court had changed in the hour or so since I had seen it last. The place had the same abandoned ugliness, the same foul-breathed atmosphere of people living desperately on their uppers, but these things had lost a part of their reality. By stepping out of it into a limousine which took him into the company of Mrs. Kilbourne, Reavis had given the place a new dimension: the possibility that there was more behind the thin warped walls than drinking and poverty, copulation and despair. For Reavis, at least, Graham Court was a place where anything could happen: the low-life set where actors played at being poor for a thousand dollars a day; the slum where the handsome prince lived incognito.

In the first cottage, a woman sighed mournfully in her sleep, and a man's blurred growl instructed her to shut her big loud yap. A radio chirped like a frenzied cricket in the shack at the front of the row, where someone was listening to an all-night disc-jockey or had forgotten to turn it off. Reavis's was the third from the street on the left. The door opened at the first try with an ordinary passkey. I closed it behind me and found the light-switch beside it.

The room precipitated out of darkness and enclosed me in a dingy wallboard cube. The light was a paper-shaded bulb in a hanging double socket, drawn sideways by a cord which ran to a nail in the wall and down the wall to a two-burner electric plate. There were dark crumbs on the oilcloth-covered table beside the burner, and some of them were moving. A chest of drawers sagged against the opposite wall, its veneer flaked like crackleware. Its top, indented with charred cigarette burns, held a bottle of barbershop hair-oil and a pair of military brushes in a pigskin case initialed P.M.R.

I went through the drawers and found two laundered shirts, two pairs of cotton socks in brilliant patterns, a change of underclothes, a cardboard box bearing a Sheik label and a colored picture of the Sheik himself, a blue silk ribbon signifying second place in Junior Field and Track at Camp Mackenzie, wherever that was, in 1931; and a carton of cardboard matchfolders. The carton was nearly full, and each of the folders bore the legend, printed in gold on black: Compliments of Patrick "Pat" Reavis. The bottom drawer contained dirty clothes, including the Hawaiian shirt.

An iron bed in the left-hand corner of the room opposite the door took up about a quarter of the floor space. It was covered with a U.S. Navy blanket. The pictures on the wall above the bed seemed to go with the blanket. They were photographs of nude women, both glossy prints and cutouts, perhaps a dozen of each. Gretchen Keck was among them, the face above the soft young body set in a smiling tetany of embarrassment. The pictures in the drawer of the table by the bed were more unusual. They included a set of the Herculaneum murals, which did not mean that Reavis was an amateur archaeologist. There was nobody there that I knew. Opposite the bed a faded green curtain, hung from a curved iron pipe, enclosed a sink and toilet and a portable shower stall sheathed with rusting metal. A pool of dirty water spread across the rotting linoleum and darkened the hem of the curtain.

Without getting down on my knees, I reached far

under the bed and brought out a cardboard suitcase with scuffed leather corners. It was locked, but the cheap clasp loosened when I gave the lid a sharp upward kick with my heel. I dragged it under the light and wrenched it open. Beneath a mouldy smelling tangle of dirty shirts and socks, the bottom of the suitcase was lined with disordered papers. Most of them were personal letters written in unformed hands and signed with girls' names or nicknames; exceedingly personal letters. I sampled one which began: "My Dearest Darling: You drove me just wild the other night," and ended: "Now that I know what love is all about, my Dearest Darling, you won't go away and leave me—write and say you won't." Another, in a different hand, began: "Dear Mister Reavis," and ended: "I love you pashunitly with all my haert."

There were official discharge papers which stated that one Patrick Murphy Ryan, born in Bear Lake County, Kentucky, on February 12, 1921, had enlisted in the U.S. Marine Corps on June 23, 1942, in San Antonio, Texas, and been discharged in San Diego in December of the same year, dishonorably. Ryan's civilian experience was listed as agriculturalist, garage mechanic, and oil well maintenance apprentice, and his preferred occupation as commercial airplane pilot. There was a copy of an application for National Service Life Insurance in the amount of two thousand dollars, made out by the same Patrick Ryan, and dated July 2, 1942. It requested that the policy be mailed to Elaine Ryan Cassidy, R.R. 2, Bear Lake, Kentucky. She could be his mother, his sister, or his ex-wife.

The name Elaine appeared again, this time with a different surname, on a torn and empty envelope crumpled in a corner of the suitcase. The envelope was addressed to Mr. Patrick Ryan, Graham Court, Los Angeles, and postmarked Las Vegas, July 10, that year. The return address was scribbled across the ripped flap: Mrs. Elaine Schneider, Rush apts., Las Vegas, Nev. If this was the same Elaine who had been sent Pat's insurance policy, she was one woman he trusted. And Las Vegas wasn't far, as the buzzard flies. I memorized the address.

I was going through the bundle of letters, looking for the one that matched the empty envelope, when a breeze blew light and cold on the back of my neck. I picked up one of the letters and straightened slowly without turning, as if to have light to read by; then slowly turned with the letter in my hands. The door was ajar a few inches, pure darkness beyond.

I reached for the light-switch. The step I took threw me a little off balance. A hand came through the aperture, pushing it wider, and closed on my wrist: fingers like curled white sausages, speckled with short black bristles. It pulled me further off balance and my head slammed against the wall. The wallboard crunched. A second hand closed on my arm and began to bend it around the edge of the door. I set one foot against the door-jamb and brought the hands into the room. The hands, then the arms, then the shoulders. When the whole man came, he brought the door along with him. It fell against the green curtain with very little noise.

His nose and brows were brown fungus growing on a thick stump of face. Small eyes like shiny black beetles lived in it. They burrowed out of sight when I struck at them with my free hand, and reappeared again. I hurt my hand on the thick chin. The head rolled away with the punch and came back grinning at me.

He turned suddenly, raised his arms and swung me off balance. His fingers ground on my wristbones. His heavy shoulders labored. I would not turn in to his hold. His coat split up the back with a sharp report. I twisted my hand free, joined both hands under his chin, and set my knee in the small of his back. Gradually he straightened, came over backwards and down. The floor cracked against the back of his head, then the ceiling fell on the back of mine.

I came to, lying face down in darkness. The surface under my face seemed to be vibrating, and the same vibration beat savagely at the base of my skull. When

I opened my mouth I tasted dusty cloth. Something heavy and hard pressed down on the small of my back. I tried to move and found that my shoulders and hips were tightly enclosed on both sides. My hands were tied together, pressed hard into my stomach. Coffin fear took me by the back of the neck and shook me. When the shaking subsided my head was clearer and more painful. I was on the floor of a moving car, wedged face down between the front and back seats.

The wheels bumped and slid across two sets of car tracks. I raised my head from the floor.

"Take it easy, buster," a man's voice said. One heavy object was removed from the small of my back and placed on the nape of my neck.

I said: "Take your feet off me."

The foot on my neck shifted, pressing my face into the floor. "Or what will you do, buster? Nothing? That's what I thought."

I lay still, trying to memorize pitch, tone, inflection, so that I would not mistake them if I ever heard them again. The voice was soft and liquid in the way that molasses is liquid, with a fruity tremor of vanity running through it. A voice like the stuff cheap barbers put on your hair before you can stop them.

It said: "That's right, buster, you can do your talking later. And you will."

More car tracks. A left turn. Pitted city pavement. Another turn. The blood was roaring angrily in my ears. Then there was no sound but the roaring of my blood. The feet were lifted, a car door opened. I struggled upright to my knees and tore at my bound wrists with my teeth. They were bound with wire.

"Now take it *easy*. This is a gun I have at your back. Don't you feel it?"

I felt it. I took it easy.

"Backwards out of the car, buster. Don't raise a hullabaloo or you'll take another ride and never know it. Now you can stand up and let me look at you. Frankly, you look like hell."

I looked at him, first at the steady black gun. He

was slender and tall, pinched at the waist by over-elaborate tailoring, heavily padded at the shoulders. The hair on top of his head was thick and black and glossy, but it didn't match the gray hair over his ears. I said: "You're showing a little middle-aged sag yourself."

He nicked me under the chin with the front sight of his gun. My head snapped back and I fell against the open door of the car, slamming it shut. The sound rang out along the deserted street. I didn't know where I was, but I had the Glendale feeling: end of the line. No lights went on in any of the dark houses. Nothing happened at all, except that the man pressed his gun to my sternum and made threats like cello music into my face.

The other man leaned out of the front window. A little blood flowed from a cut over his right beetle. "You're sure you can handle this screw?"

"It will be a pleasure," the tall man said to both of us.

"Don't mark him up unless he asks for it. We just want to get his story and put him on ice for a while."

"How long?"

"You'll hear in the morning."

"I'm not a baby-sitter," the tall man grumbled. "What about your place, Mell?"

"I'm going on a trip. Goodnight sweetheart." The car went away.

"Quick march," the tall man said.

"Goosestep, or plain?"

He put one heel on my instep and his weight on the heel. His eyes were dark and small. They picked up the light of a distant streetlamp and reflected it like a cat's.

I said: "You're very active for an elderly man."

"Cut the comical chatter," he said throatily. "I never killed a man, but by Jesus—"

"I have, Amy. He kicked me in the head when I was down."

"Stop calling me Amy." He backed away and held

the gun higher. Without it he was nothing. But he had it.

I quick-marched up the cracked and slanting concrete to the porch. It was cavernous and sunken, a place of shadows. He kept his eyes and gun on me while he fumbled for his key-ring and snapped back the lock. A woman's voice spoke from the shadows then:

"Is it you, Rico? I've been waiting for you."

He turned catlike from the door, shifting his gun from me to the darkness behind me. "Who is it?" His voice was jangled.

I leaned on the balls of my feet, ready to move. The gun came back to me. The key-ring forgotten in the lock.

"It's me, Rico," the voice from the shadows said. "Mavis."

"Mrs. Kilbourne!" Amazement raked his face, and his voice choked. "What are you doing here?"

"Mavis to you, tall and handsome. I haven't been out by myself for a long time. But I haven't forgotten how you looked at me."

She moved out of the shadows past me as if I wasn't there, immaculate in a high-shouldered ermine jacket. Her left hand was behind her with the forefinger extended. It curled and straightened, pointed at the floor.

"Be careful, Mrs. Kilbourne." The man's voice was wretched, straining to repress an impossible hope. "Please go home, Mrs. Kilbourne."

"Won't you call me Mavis?" She brushed the side of his face with a white-gloved hand. "I call you Rico. I think of you when I'm lying in bed at night. Aren't you ever going to give me a break?"

"Sure I will, baby, only be careful. I'm holding a gun—"

"Well, put it away," she said with coy petulance. She pushed the gun to one side and leaned heavily on him, her arms around his shoulders, mouth on mouth.

For an instant the gun wavered. He was still, enclosed by her in a white and perfumed dream. I raised my doubled fists and brought them down. Something snapped in his hand. The gun rattled on the floor. The woman went down after it, scurrying on her knees, and Rico went after her. My arms looped over his head, hugged him and lifted him. I held him suspended by the neck until his hands stopped scratching at me and dragged on the floor. Then I let him fall on his face.

CHAPTER 12

The woman stood up with the gun. She held it in a gingerly way, as if it were a reptile. "You catch on quickly, Archer. That is your name, isn't it?"

"Unknown admirer," I said. "I didn't realize I had this fantastic power over women."

"Didn't you? I knew when I saw you you were for me. Then I heard my husband telling them to bring you here. I came. What else could I do?" Her hands made a pretty gesture, spoilt by the gun.

"Unlike Rico," I said, "I'm allergic to ham." I looked down at the man at my feet. His toupee was twisted sideways, so that the straight white line of the part ran from ear to ear. It was funny, and I laughed.

She thought I was laughing at her. "Don't you dare to laugh at me," she said in a blind white rage. "I'll kill you if you do."

"Not if you hold the gun that way. You'll sprain your wrist and shoot a hole in the roof. Now put it away and kiss your boyfriend goodnight and I'll take you home. I suppose I should thank you, too? Mavis."

"You'll do as I say," but her heart wasn't in what she said.

"I'll do as I think best. You hadn't the guts to tackle Rico alone, and I'm a tougher proposition than Rico."

She dropped the gun in her coat pocket and

clasped her white silk hands below her bosom.
"You're right. I need your help. How did you know?"

"You didn't go to all this trouble for fun. Unwire my
hands."

She slipped off the gloves. Her fingers unwound
the thin steel wire. The man on the floor rolled onto
his side, the breath whistling tinnily in his throat.
"What can we do with him?" she said.

"What do you want to do with him? Keep him out
of mischief, or get him into mischief?"

A smile brushed her lips. "Keep him out, of course."

"Give me the wire." My fingers were nearly numb,
pierced by shooting pains from returning circulation,
but they worked. I turned the tall man onto his back,
doubled up his knees, and wired his wrists together
behind his thighs.

The girl opened the door, and I dragged him over
the threshold by the shoulders. "Now what?"

"There's a closet here." She closed the front door
and switched on the light.

"Is that safe?"

"He lives here by himself."

"You seem to have cased the joint."

She touched a finger to her mouth and glanced at
the man on the floor. His eyes were open, glaring up
at her. Their whites were suffused with blood. His
hair had fallen off entirely, so that his skull looked
naked. The toupee lay on the floor like a small black
animal, an infant skunk. Its master's voice came thin
between purplish lips:

"I'm going to make bad trouble for you, lady."

"You're in it now." To me: "Put Tall and Handsome
in the closet, will you?"

I put him in under a dirty raincoat, with a muddy
pair of rubbers under his head. "Make a noise and I'll
plug the cracks around the door." He was still.

I shut the closet door and looked around me. The
lofty hallway belonged to an old house which had
been converted into an office. The parquetry floor
was covered with rubber matting, except at the edges
where the pattern showed. The walls had been paint-

ed grey over the wallpaper. A carved staircase loomed at the rear of the hall like the spine of an extinct saurian. To my left, the frosted glass pane of a door bore a sign in neat black lettering: HENRY MURAT, ELECTRONICS AND PLASTICS LABORATORY.

The woman was bent over the lock of this door, trying one key after another from the keyring. It opened with a click. She stepped through and pressed a wall-switch. Fluorescent lights blinked on. I followed her into a small office furnished in green metal and chrome. A bare desk, some chairs, a filing cabinet, a small safe with a phony dial that opened with a key. A framed diploma on the wall above the desk announced that Henry Murat had been awarded the degree of Master of Electronic Science. I had never heard of the school.

She knelt in front of the safe, fumbling with the keys. After a few attempts she looked around at me. Her face was bloodless in the cruel light, almost as white as her coat. "I can't, my hands are shaky. Will you open it?"

"This is burglary. I hate to commit two burglaries in one night."

She rose and came towards me, holding out the keys. "Please. You must. There's something of mine in there. I'll do anything."

"That shouldn't be necessary: I told you I'm not Rico. But I like to know what I'm doing. What's in there?"

"My life," she said.

"More histrionics, Mavis?"

"Please. It's true. I'll never have another chance."

"At what?"

"Pictures of me." She forced the words out. "I never authorized them. They were taken without my knowledge."

"Blackmail."

"Call it that, but it's worse. I can't even kill myself, Archer."

She looked half dead at the moment. I took the keys with one hand and patted her arm with the other. "Why should you think of it, kid? You have everything."

"Nothing," she said.

The key to the safe was easy to pick out. It was made of brass, cut long and flat. I turned it in the keyhole under the dial, pressed the chrome handle, and pulled the heavy door open. I opened a couple of drawers filled with bills, old letters, invoices. "What am I looking for?"

"A roll of film. I think it's in a can."

There was a flat aluminum can on the upper shelf, the kind that was sometimes used for 16 mm. movies. I peeled off the tape that sealed the edges, and pulled off the lid. It contained a few hundred feet of film rolled in a flat cylinder. I held the end frame up to the light: it was Mavis flat on her back in a brilliant sun, with a towel over her hips.

"No. You wouldn't dare." She snatched the film from my hands and hugged it to her.

"Don't get excited," I said. "I've seen a human body before."

She didn't hear me. She threw the film on the linoleum floor and huddled over it. For a moment I didn't know what she was doing. Then I saw the gold lighter in her hand. It flicked open and made sparks, but didn't light.

I kicked the film out of her reach, picked it up, replaced it in the can. She cried out and flung herself at me. Her gloved hands beat on my chest.

I dropped the can in my pocket and took her wrists. "That stuff explodes sometimes. You'll burn the house down and you with it."

"What do I care? Let me go."

"If you make velvet paws. Besides, you need these pictures. So long as we have them, Rico will keep his mouth shut."

"We?" she said.

"I'm keeping them."

"No!"

"You asked for my help. This is it. I can keep Rico quiet, and you can't."

"Who will keep you quiet?"

"You will. By being a good girl and doing what I say."

"I don't trust you. I don't trust any man."

"Women, on the other hand, are extremely trust-worthy."

"All right," she said after a while. "You win."

"Good girl." I released her hands. "Who is this Rico?"

"I don't know much about him. His real name is Enrico Murratti, I think he's from Chicago. He did some work for my husband, when they put two-way radios in the cabs."

"And your husband?"

"Let's just talk about human beings for now."

"There are things I want to know about him."

"Not from me." Her mouth set firmly.

"Reavis, then."

"Who's he?"

"You were with him in the Hunt Club."

"Oh," she said. "Pat Ryan." And bit her lip.

"Do you know where he's gone?"

"No. I know where he'll go eventually, and I'll dance at his funeral."

"You're close-mouthed for a woman."

"I have things to be close-mouthed about."

"One more question. Where are we? It feels like Glendale to me."

"It's Glendale." She managed a smile. "You know, I like you. You're kind of sharp."

"Yeah," I said. "I always use my brains to save my brawn. That's how I got this bump on the cerebel-lum."

His long minutes in the dark had aged and mel-lowed Rico. The knuckle-taut youthfulness had sagged out of his face. He looked like what he was: an insecure middle-aged man sweating with fear and discomfort.

I pulled him under the hall light and talked down at him: "You said something a while ago about mak-ing trouble for my client." I nodded at the woman by

the door. "Any trouble you make will be for yourself.
You're going to forget you saw her tonight. You're not
going to tell her husband or anybody else that she
was here. Nobody. And she's not going to set eyes on
your pan for the rest of her natural life."

"You can cut the spiel," he said tiredly. "I know
where I stand."

I took the can of film out of my pocket, tossed it in
the air and caught it a couple of times. His eye
followed it up and down. He licked his lips and
sighed.

"Flat on your back," I said. "But I'm going to give
you a break. I'm not going to beat you, though that
would give me pleasure. I'm not going to turn you
and the film over to the D.A., though that is what you
deserve."

"It wouldn't do Mrs. Kilbourne a lot of good."

"Worry about yourself, Rico. This film is solid evidence of blackmail. Mrs. Kilbourne would never have
to take the stand."

"Blackmail, crap! I never took no money from Mrs.
Kilbourne." He rolled his eyes, seeking the woman's
glance, but she was fixedly watching the film in my
hand. I put it back in my pocket.

"No judge or jury would ever believe it," I said.
"You're in a box. You want me to nail down the lid?"

He lay still for fifteen or twenty seconds, his lean
brown forehead corrugated by thought. "A box is
right," he admitted finally. "What do you want me to
do?"

"Nothing. Nothing at all. Just keep your nose clean
and stay away from my client. A young boy like you
deserves a second chance, after all."

He showed vari-colored teeth in a shamed grin: so
far gone that he was smiling at my jokes. I unwound
the wire from his wrists and let him stand up. All his
joints were stiff.

"You're letting him off easy," the woman said.

"What do you want to do to him?"

She turned her eyes on him, gray and lethal under
the heavy curtains of her lashes. Instinctively he

moved away from her, keeping his back to the wall. He looked willing to be put back into the closet.

"Nothing," she said at last. It was one of her favorite words. But on the way to the door she stepped on the black hairpiece and ground it under her gold heel. The last I saw of Rico, he had his right hand flat on top of his scalp, utter humiliation on his face.

We walked in silence to the nearest boulevard and caught a cruising cab. She told the driver to take her to The Flamenco.

"Why there?" I said, when the cab was under way. "It's closed by now."

"Not for me. I have to go back there anyway. I borrowed taxi-fare from the powder-room girl, and left her my bag for security."

"That's quite a situation you have there. A diamond-studded bag, and nothing in it."

"Tell it to my husband."

"I'd be glad to."

"Oh no!" She moved against me. "You wouldn't really?"

"He's got you frightened out of your wits. Why?"

"You won't ask me any questions, will you? I'm so tired. This business has taken more out of me than you think."

Her head touched my shoulder tentatively, and rested there. I leaned sideways, looking down into her face. Her gray eyes were crepuscular. The lashes came down over them like sudden night. Her mouth was dark and glistening. I kissed her, felt her toe press on my instep, her hand move on my body. I drew back from the whirling vortex that had opened, the drowning pool. She wriggled and sighed, and went to sleep in my arms.

I dropped her half a block from The Flamenco, and asked the driver to take me to Graham Court. He needed directions. It was all I could do to give them to him. My brain and body had gone into a champagne hangover. Through the long ride back, the wearing business of retrieving my car, driving it home, opening and shutting the garage, unlocking the door of my house and locking it behind me, I stayed awake with difficulty. I told my brain to tell my body to do what had to be done, and watched my body do it.

It was twenty after four by the electric alarm on the table beside my bed. Taking off my jacket, I felt for the can of film in the pocket. It was gone. I sat on the edge of the bed and shivered for two minutes by the clock. That made it four-twenty-two.

I said: "Goodnight to you, Mavis." Rolled over in my clothes, and went to sleep.

CHAPTER 13

The alarm made a noise which reminded me of dentists, which reminded me of optometrists, which reminded me of thick-lensed spectacles, which reminded me of Morris Cramm: the man I had been trying to think about when I woke up.

Hilda met me on the third-floor landing with her finger to her lips. "Be quiet now, Morris is sleeping, and he had a hard night." She was blonde and fat and doe-eyed, radiating through her housecoat the warmth and gentleness of Jewish women who are happily married.

"Wake him up for me, will you? Just a minute?"

"No, I couldn't do that." She looked at me more closely. The only light came from a burlap-curtained french door that opened on a fire escape at the end of the hall. "What happened to you, Lew? You look God-awful."

"You look swell. It's wonderful to see nice people again."

"Where have you been?"

"To hell and back. Glendale, that is. But I'll never leave you again." I kissed her on the cheek, which smelt of Palmolive soap.

She gave me a friendly little push that almost sent me backwards over the rail. "Don't do that. Morris might hear you, and he's awful jealous. Anyway, I'm not nice people. I'm a sloppy housekeeper, and I haven't done my nails for two whole weeks. Why? Because I'm lazy."

"I'm crazy about your nails. They never scratch."

"They will if you don't quiet down. And don't think you're going to flatter me into waking him up. Morris needs his sleep."

Morris Cramm was night legman for a columnist, and worked the graveyard shift. He knew everybody worth knowing in the metropolitan area, and enough about them to set up a blackmailing syndicate bigger than Sears Roebuck. To Morris, that idea would never have occurred.

"Look at it this way, Hilda. I am searching for the long-lost son of a wealthy English nobleman. The bereaved father is offering a fantastic reward for the prodigal's Los Angeles address. With Morris, I go halves. If he can give me the address, it will entitle him to this valuable gift certificate, bearing an engraved portrait of Alexander Hamilton and personally autographed by the Secretary of the Treasury." I took a ten-dollar bill out of my wallet.

"You sound like a radio program. A *couple* of radio programs, all mixed up."

"For five minutes of his personal sleeping time, I offer ten dollars in cash. Two dollars a minute, a hundred and twenty dollars an hour. Show me the movie star that gets nine hundred and sixty dollars for an eight-hour day."

"Well," she said dubiously, "if there's money involved. They're selling Beethoven quartets fifty per cent off down at the record shop— Only what if Morris doesn't know the answer?"

"He knows all the answers, doesn't he?"

She turned with her hand on the doorknob and said quite seriously: "Sometimes I think he does. He knows so much it saps the energy right out of him."

Hilda adjusted the blind and let a little light into the bedroom-sittingroom. The floor was covered with newspapers, the walls with shelves of books and record albums. A large Capehart dominated the room and the lives of the two people who lived in it. Morris was sleeping on an uncovered studio bed opposite the window, a small dark man in candy-striped pyjamas. He rolled over and sat up blinking. His eyes looked huge and emotional without his glasses.

He stared at me blindly. "What time is it? Who is it?"

"Nearly nine o'clock, dear. Lew came to ask you a question." She handed him his glasses from a shelf above the bed.

"My God, so early?" He refused to look at me. He put his hands on opposite shoulders and rocked himself and groaned.

"I'm sorry, Morris. It will only take a minute. Can you give me Walter Kilbourne's address? He isn't in the phone book. I have his car license, but this is a personal matter."

"Never heard of him."

"For ten dollars, darling," Hilda said very gently.

"If you don't know where Kilbourne lives, admit it. He looks like money to me, and he's married to the most beautiful woman in town."

"Ten million dollars, more or less," he said resentfully. "As for Mrs. Kilbourne, I don't go for ash blondes myself. My aesthetic taste demands a ruddier coloration." He smiled with frank admiration at his wife.

"Fool." She sat down beside him and ruffled his black wire hair.

"If Mavis Kilbourne was as beautiful as all that, she'd have got on in pictures, wouldn't she? But no, she married Kilbourne."

"Kilbourne or the ten million?"

"More than ten million, come to think of it. Fifty-one per cent of Pacific Refining Company, current quotation 26-⅜, figure it out for yourself."

"Pacific Refining Company," I said slowly and distinctly, thinking of the woman who was drowned. "I thought he was in the taxi business."

"He has some over in Glendale. His finger's in several pies, but Pareco's his plum. They got in early on the Nopal Valley strike." He yawned, and leaned his head against his wife's plump shoulder. "This bores me, Lew."

"Go on. You are cooking electronically. Where does he live?"

"In the Valley." His eyes were closed, and Hilda stroked with maternal awe the forehead that enclosed the filing-cabinet brain. "Staffordshire Estates, one of those private communities you need a special visa to get in. I was out there for a Fourth of July party. They had a Senator for guest of honor."

"U.S. or State?"

"U.S. Senator, what do you think? State Senators are a dime a dozen."

"Democratic or Republican?"

"What's the difference? Haven't I earned my ten dollars, brain-picker? Sweat-shopper?"

"One more question, asphalt intellectual. Where did the money come from in the first place?"

"Am I the Bureau of Internal Revenue?" He started to shrug, but found it required too much effort. "I am not."

"You know things they don't know."

"I know nothing. All I hear is rumors. You are inciting me to commit a libel."

"Spill it," I said.

"Storm-trooper."

"Now that isn't nice to call anybody," Hilda said soothingly.

I reminded him of the question: "The money. Where did it come from?"

"It didn't grow on trees," he said, and smothered a yawn. "I heard that Kilbourne made a fine thing out of black-market cars in Detroit during the war. Then he rushed down here to invest his money legitimately before somebody took it away from him. Now he's grand old California stock and politicians go to his parties. Don't quote me, it's only a rumor. He might have spread it himself to cover up something worse, now that I come to think of it."

Morris looked around the room with a dreaming smile and went to sleep sitting up. Removing his glasses, Hilda laid the limp boyish body out on the bed. I handed her the ten and moved to the door.

She followed me. "Come round in the daytime, Lew, we got the new Strauss from Paris."

"I will when I have some time. I'm on my way to Nevada at the moment."

"Seriously?"

"It looks like it."

"That's where Sue's living, isn't she?" Her round fat face lit up. "You're going to have a reconciliation!"

"Not a chance. This is business."

"I know you'll come back together. Wait and see."

"The bottom dropped out. All the king's horses couldn't put it back in for us."

"Oh, Lew." She looked ready to cry. "You made such a nice couple together."

I patted her arm. "You are lovely and good, Hilda." Morris groaned in his sleep. I went.

CHAPTER 14

From the highway the Staffordshire Estates were a discreet brass marker bolted to a stone arch, through which a new blacktop turned off the public road. A metal sign on one side of the arch informed me further that they were PROTECTED BY PRIVATE PATROL. The rustic redwood gates stood open, and I drove through them. Morning haze was drifting slowly up the canyon ahead, a translucent curtain between the outside world and the privately patrolled world I was entering. There were trees along the road, tall cypresses and elms, and small birds singing in them. Behind adobe walls and thick square-cut hedges, sprinklers were whirling lariats of spray. The houses, massive and low and bright among banks of flowers set in billiard-table lawns, were spaced out of sight of each other, so that no one but the owners could enjoy them. In this corner of the San Fernando Valley, property had become a fine art that was an end in itself. There were no people in sight, and I had a queer feeling that the beautiful squatting houses had taken over the canyon for their own purposes.

Valmy, Arbuthnot, Romanovsky, the mailboxes announced as I drove by them: Lewisohn, Tappingham, Wood, Farrington, Von Esch. WALTER J. KILBOURNE was neatly stenciled on the ninth mailbox and I turned up the drive beside it. The house was built of pink brick and glass, with a flat jutting redwood roof. The drive was lined with twenty shades of begonia. I parked in the gravelled loop that went past the front door, and pressed the button beside it. Chimes echoed through the house. The place was as noisy as a funeral parlor at midnight, and I liked it almost as well.

The door was opened silently by a small Japanese whose footsteps made no sound. "You wish something, sir?" His lips were very careful with the sibilants. Over his white linen shoulder I could see an entrance loggia containing a white grand piano and a white-upholstered Hepplewhite sofa. A pool beyond the white-columned windows threw rippling sapphire shadows on the white walls.

"Mr. Kilbourne," I said. "He told me he'd be home."

"But he is not. I am sorry, sir."

"It has to do with an oil lease. I need his signature."

"He is not at home, sir. Do you wish to leave a message?"

There was no way to tell if he was lying. His black eyes were unblinking and opaque. "If you can tell me where he is—?"

"I do not know, sir. He has gone for a cruise. Perhaps if you were to try his office, sir. They have direct telephone communication with the yacht."

"Thanks. May I call the office from here?"

"I am sorry, sir. Mr. Kilbourne has not authorized me to admit unknown persons to his home." He ducked his bootbrush hair at me in a token bow, and shut the door in my face.

I climbed into my car, closing the door very gently so as not to start an avalanche of money. The loop in the drive took me past the garages. They contained an Austin, a jeep, and a white roadster, but no black limousine.

The limousine met me halfway back to the highway. I held the middle of the road and showed three fingers of my left hand. The black car braked to a stop a few feet short of my bumpers, and the chauffeur got out. His scarred eyes blinked in the brightening sun.

"What's the trouble, mac? You give me the sign."

I hitched the gun from my shoulder-holster as I stepped out of the car, and showed it to him. He raised his hands to shoulder level and smiled. "You're screwy to try it, punk. I got nothing worth taking. I'm an old con myself but I got wise. Get wise like me and put away the iron." The smile sat strangely, like a crooked Santa Claus mask, on his battered face.

"Save it for Wednesday night meeting." I moved up to him, not too close. He was old, but strong and fast, and I didn't want to shoot him.

He recognized me then. His face was expressive, like a concrete block. "I thought you was in the refrigerator." The large hands closed and opened.

"Keep them up. What did you do with Reavis? Refrigerate him, too?"

"Reavis?" he said with laborious foxiness. "Who's Reavis? I don't know any Reavis."

"You will, when they take you down to the morgue to look at him." I improvised: "The Highway Patrol found him by the road outside of Quinto this morning. His throat was cut."

"Uh?" The air issued from his mouth and nostrils as if I'd body-punched him.

"Let me see your knife," I said, to keep his fifty points of I.Q. occupied.

"I got no knife. I had nothing to do with it. I dropped him over the Nevada line. He couldn't come back that fast."

"You came back that fast."

His face worked with the terrible effort of thought. "You're feeding me a sucker's line," he said. "He never went back to Quinto, they never found him."

"Where is he now, then?"

"I ain't talking," the concrete block announced. "You might as well put your iron away and lam."

We were in a dark-green valley walled with close-set laurel on both sides. The only sound was the hum of our idling cars. "You have a deceptive face," I said. "If I didn't know better, I'd think it was alive. You want it gun-whipped."

"Try it on," he said stolidly. "See where it gets you."

I wanted to hurt him, but the memory of the night was ugly in my mind. There had to be a difference between me and the opposition, or I'd have to take the mirror out of my bathroom. It was the only mirror in the house, and I needed it for shaving.

"Run along, quiz kid." I slanted the gun at the road. He went back to his car.

"Punk," he shouted in his thick, expressionless voice as he swerved in the ditch to pass me. His wrap-around bumper nicked the left rear fender of my car, and he blasted my ears with his horn to show it was deliberate. The roar of his accelerating motor rose like a sound of triumph.

I put mine in gear. All the way across the desert I scanned the side of the road for blind cripples and old ladies that I could help across and minister to with potions of camomile tea.

CHAPTER 15

It was late afternoon when I crossed the great level pass. The shadow of my car was running ahead in fleet silence, and slowly increasing its lead. The sun was yellow on the arid slopes, the air so clear that the mountains lacked perspective. They looked like surrealist symbols painted on the shallow desert sky. The heat, which had touched 110 at one, was slackening off, but my hood was still hot enough to fry the insects that splattered it.

The Rush Apartments occupied a two-story frame building on the east side of Las Vegas. Jaundiced with yellow paint, it stood tiredly between a parking lot and a chain grocery store. An outside wooden staircase with a single sagging rail led up to a narrow veranda on which the second-floor apartments opened. An old man was sitting in a kitchen chair tipped back against the wall under the stairs. He had a faded bandana handkerchief around his scrawny neck, and was sucking on a corncob pipe. A week's beard grew on his folded cheeks like the dusty gray plush in old-fashioned railway coaches.

I asked him where Mrs. Schneider lived.

"She lives right here," he mumbled.

"Is she in now?"

He removed his empty pipe from his mouth and

spat on the cement floor. "How do you expect me to know? I don't keep track of women's comings and goings."

I laid a fifty-cent piece on the bony knee. "Buy yourself a bag of tobacco."

He picked it up sulkily, and slipped it into a pocket of his food-crusted vest. "I s'pose her husband sent you? At least she *says* he's her husband, looks more like her bully to me. Anyway, you're out of luck now, slicker. She went out a while ago."

"You wouldn't know where?"

"To the den of iniquity, what do you think? Where she spends all her time." He tipped his chair forward and pointed far down the street. "You see that green sign? You can't make it out from here, but it says 'Green Dragon' on it. That's the den of iniquity. And you want me to tell you the name of this town? Sodom and Gonorrhea." He laughed an old man's laugh, high-pitched and unamused.

"Is that Elaine Schneider?"

"I dont know any other Mrs. Schneiders."

"What does she look like?" I said. "I never saw her."

"She looks like Jezebel." His watery eyes glittered like melting ice. "She looks like what she is, the whore of Babylon rolling her eyes and shaking her privates at Christian young men. Are you a Christian, son?"

I backed away thanking him and crossed the street, leaving my car at the curb. I walked the two blocks to the Green Dragon and worked some of the stiffness out of my legs. It was another seedy-looking bar. Signs in the dirty half-curtained windows advertised LIQUOR, BEER, HOT and COLD SANDWICHES and SHORT ORDERS. I pulled the screen door open and went in. A semi-circular bar with a door to the kitchen behind it took up the rear of the shallow room. The other three walls were lined with slot machines. Kitchen smells, the smell of stale spilled beer, the sick-sour smell of small-time gamblers' sweat, were slowly mixed by a four-bladed fan suspended from the fly-specked ceiling.

There was only one customer at the bar, a thin boy with uncombed red hair hunched desolately over a short beer. The bartender sat on a stool in a corner, as far away from the desolate youth as possible. His greased black head leaned against a table radio. "Three nothing," he announced to anyone who cared. "Top of the seventh." No sign of Jezebel.

I took a seat beside the redheaded boy, ordered a ham and cheese sandwich and a bottle of beer. The bartender went out reluctantly through the swinging door to the kitchen.

"Look at me, eh," the man beside me said. The words twisted his mouth as if they hurt. "How do you like me?"

His thin unshaven face looked dirty. His eyes had blue hollows under them and red rims around them. One of his ears was caked with dry blood.

"I like you very much," I said. "You have that beaten look that everybody admires."

It took the raw edge off his mood of self-pity. He even managed a smile which made him look five years younger, hardly more than a kid. "Well, I asked for it."

"Any time," I said, "any time."

"I asked for it in more ways than one, I guess. I should know better than to go on a bat in Las Vegas, but I guess I'll never learn."

"You have a few more years before you die. What happened to your ear?"

He looked sheepish. "I don't even know. I met a guy in a bar last night and he roped me into a game in a poker-parlor on the other side of town. All I remember, I lost my money and my car. I had three aces when I lost my car, and somebody started an argument: I guess it was me. I woke up in a parking lot."

"Hungry?"

"Naw. Thanks, though. I had a little change. The hell of it is I got to get back to L.A., and I got no car."

The bartender brought my food and drink. "Stick around," I told the young Dostoevsky. "I'll give you a lift if I can."

While I was eating, a woman came through a door at the end of the bar. She was tall and big-boned, with more than flesh enough to cover her bones. The skirt of her cheap black suit was wrinkled where her hips and thighs bulged out. Her feet and ankles spilled over the tops of very tight black pumps. Her north end was decorated with a single gray fox, a double strand of imitation pearls approximately the same color, and enough paint to preserve a battleship. Her chest was like a battleship's prow, massive and sharp and uninviting. She gave me a long hard searchlight look, her heavy mouth held loose, all ready to smile. I took a bite of my sandwich and munched at her. The searchlights clicked off, almost audibly.

She turned to the bar and snapped open a shiny black plastic bag. The yellow hair which she wore in a braided coronet was dark at the roots, obviously dyed. Turn it back to brown, take off a few years and a few more pounds, chip the paint off her face, and she could be Reavis's twin. They had the same eyes, the same thick handsome features.

The bartender clinched it: "Something for you, Elaine?"

She tossed a bill on the pitted woodstone surface. "Twenty quarters," she growled in a whisky voice that wasn't unpleasant. "For a change."

"Your luck is bound to change." He smiled insincerely. "The one you been playing is loaded to pay anytime."

"What the hell," she said, deadpan. "Easy come, easy go."

"Especially easy go," the boy beside me said to the beer-foam in the bottom of his glass.

Mechanically, without excitement or any sign of interest, she fed the quarters one by one into a machine near the door. Somebody phoning long-distance to somebody else who had been dead for years. Some twos and fours, a single twelve, stretched her money out. They went back in as a matter of course. She played the machine as if it was a toneless instrument made to express despair. When the jackpot came in a jangling rush of metal, I thought the machine had simply broken down. Then the slugs and quarters overflowed the bowl and rolled on the floor.

"I told you," the bartender said. "I said she was set to pay."

Paying no attention to her winnings, she crossed to the bar and took the seat beside me. He gave her a double whisky in a shot-glass without being asked.

"*You* pick it up, Simmie." Her voice had a trace of weary coquetry. "I'm wearing a girdle."

"Sure, but I don't need to count them. I'll give you the twenty-five."

"I put thirty-five in." The double shot went down like water down a drain.

"That's the percentage, kid. You got to pay something for all the fun you get."

"Yeah, fun." She folded the twenty and the five he gave her, and tucked them away in her bag.

A newsboy came in with an armful of *Evening Review-Journal*'s and I bought one. The third page carried the story I was looking for, under the heading: EX-MARINE SOUGHT IN NOPAL VALLEY DEATH. It gave no information I didn't have, except that the police were maintaining an open mind as to the cause of death. Accompanying the story was a picture of Reavis, smiling incongruously over the caption: WANTED FOR QUESTIONING.

I folded the paper open at the third page and laid it on the bar between me and the big synthetic blonde. She didn't notice it for a minute or two; she was watching the bartender gather up her jackpot. Then her gaze strayed back to the bar and saw the picture, took hold of it. The breath wheezed asthmatically in her nostrils, and stopped entirely for a period of seconds. She took a pair of spectacles from her bag. With them on her face, she looked oddly like a schoolteacher gone astray.

"You mind if I look at your paper?" she asked me huskily. There was more south in her voice than there had been before.

"Go ahead."

The bartender looked up from sorting the slugs and quarters on the bar. "Say, I didn't know you wore glasses, Elaine. Very becoming."

She didn't hear him. With the aid of a scarlet-tipped finger moving slowly from word to word, she was spelling out the newspaper story to herself. When the slow finger reached the final period, she was silent and still for an instant. Then she said aloud: "Well I'll be ——!"

She flung the paper down, its edges crumpled by the moist pressure of her hands, and went to the street door. Her hips rolled angrily, her high heels spiked the floor. The screen door slammed behind her.

I waited thirty seconds and went after her. Rotating on his stool, the desolate youth followed me with his eyes, like a stray dog I had befriended and betrayed.

"Stick around," I told him over my shoulder.

The woman was already halfway up the block. Though they were hobbled by her skirt, her legs were moving like pistons. The gray foxtail hung down her back, fluttering nervously. I followed her more slowly when I saw where she was going. She went up the outside stairs of the Rush Apartments, unlocked the second door, and went in, leaving it open. I crossed the street and slid behind the wheel of my car.

She came out immediately. Something metallic in her hand caught a ray of sunlight. She pushed it into her bag as she came down the stairs. The forgotten glasses on her face gave it a purposeful air. I hid my face behind a road map.

She crossed the parking lot to an old Chevrolet sedan. Its original blue paint had faded to brownish green. The fenders were crumpled and dirty like paper napkins on a restaurant table. The starter jammed, the exhaust came out in spasms of dark blue smoke. I followed the pillar of smoke to the main highway junction in the middle of town, where it turned south towards Boulder City. I let it get well ahead as we passed out of town onto the open highway.

Between Boulder City and the dam an asphalt road turned off to the left toward Lake Mead, skirting the public beaches along the shore. Children were playing on the gravel below the road, splashing in the shallow waveless water. Further out a fast red hydroplane was skittering back and forth like a waterbug, describing esses on the paper-flat, paper-gray surface.

The Chevrolet turned off the blacktop, to the left again, up a gravel road which wound through low scrub oak. The brush and the innumerable branching lanes made an accidental maze. I had to move up on the woman to keep her in sight. She was too busy holding her car on the road to notice me. Her smooth old tires skidded and ground among the loose stones as she came out of one curve only to enter another.

We passed a public camping-ground where families were eating in the open among parked cars, tents, tear-drop trailers. A few hundred yards further on, the Chevrolet left the gravel road, turning up a brush-crowded lane which was no more than two ruts in the earth. Seconds later, I heard its motor stop.

I left my car where it was and went up the lane on foot. The Chevrolet was parked in front of a small cabin faced with peeled saplings. The woman tried the screen door, found it locked, pounded it with her fist.

"What gives?" It was Reavis's voice, coming from inside the cabin.

I crouched behind a scrub-oak, feeling as if I should be wearing a coonskin cap.

Reavis unhooked the door and stepped outside. His hounds-tooth suit was dusty, and creased in all the wrong places. His hair curled down in his eyes. He pushed it back with an irritable hand. "What's the trouble, sis?"

"You tell me, you lying little crumb." He overshadowed her by half a head, but her passionate energy made him look helpless. "You told me you were having woman trouble, so I said I'd hide you out. You didn't tell me that the woman was dead."

He stalled for time to think: "I don't know what you're talking about, Elaine. Who's dead? This dame I was talking about isn't dead. She's perfectly okay only she says she's missed two months in a row and I don't want any part of it. She was cherry."

"Yeah, a grandmother and cherry." Her voice rasped with ugly irony. "This is one thing you can't lie out of, sprout. You're in too deep for me to try and help you. I wouldn't help you even if I could. You can go to the gas chamber and I wouldn't lift a finger to save your neck. Your neck ain't worth the trouble to me or to anybody else."

Reavis whined and whimpered: "What the hell are you talking about, Elaine. I didn't do nothing wrong. Are the police after me?"

"You know damn well they are. This time you're going to get it, sonny boy. And I want no part of it unnerstan'? I want no part of you from now on."

"Come on now, Elaine, settle down. That's no kind of talk to use on your little brother." He forced his voice into an ingratiating rhythm and put one hand on her shoulder. She shook it off and held her purse in both hands.

"You can save it. You've talked me into too much trouble in my life. Ever since you stole that dollar bill from maw's purse and tried to shift it onto me, I knew you were heading for a bad end."

"You've done real good for yourself, Elaine. Selling it for two-bits in town on Saturday night before you was out of pigtails. You still charging for it, or do you pay them?"

The concussion of her palm against his cheek cracked like a twenty-two among the trees. His fist answered the blow, thudding into her neck. She staggered, and her sharp heels gouged holes in the sandy earth. When she recovered her balance, the gun was in her hand.

Reavis looked at it uncomprehendingly, and took a step toward her. "You don't have to go off your rocker. I'm sorry I hit you, Elaine. Hell, you hit me first."

Her whole body was leaning and focused on the gun: the handle of a door that had always resisted her efforts, and still resisted. "Stay away from me." Her low whisper buzzed like a rattler's tail. "I'll put you on the Salt Lake highway and I never want to see you again in my life. You're a big boy now, Pat, big enough to kill people. Well, I'm a big enough girl."

"You got me all wrong, sis." But he stayed where he was, his hands loose and futile at his sides. "I didn't do nothing wrong."

"You lie. You'd kill *me* for the gold in my teeth. I seen you going through my purse this afternoon."

He laughed shortly. "You're crazy. I'm loaded, sis, I could put you on easy street." He reached for his left hip pocket.

"Keep your hands where I can see them," she said.

"Don't be crazy, I want to show you—"

The safety clicked. The door that had resisted her was about to open. Her whole body bent tensely over the gun. Reavis's hands rose from his side of their own accord, like huge brown butterflies. He looked sullen and stupid in the face of death.

"Are you coming?" she said. "Or do you want to die? You're wanted by the cops, they wouldn't even touch me if I killed you. What loss would it be to anybody? You never gave nothing but misery to a single soul since you got out of the cradle."

"I'll go along, Elaine." His nerve had broken, suddenly and easily. "But you'll be sorry, I warn you. You don't know what you're doing. Anyway, you can put away that gun."

I wasn't likely to get a better cue. I stepped from behind my tree with my gun ready. "A good idea. Drop the gun, Mrs. Schneider. You, Reavis, keep up your hands."

Her whole body jerked. "Augh!" she said viciously. The small bright automatic fell from her hand, rustled and gleamed in the leaves in front of her feet.

Reavis glanced at me, the color mounting floridly in his face. "Archer?"

I said: "The name is Leatherstocking."

He turned on his sister: "So you had to bring a cop along, you had to wreck everything?"

"What if I did?" she growled.

"Hold it, Reavis." I picked up the woman's gun. "And you, Mrs. Schneider, go away."

"Are you a cop?"

"This isn't question period. I could haul you in for accessory. Now go away, before I change my mind."

I kept my gun on Reavis, dropped hers into the pocket of my jacket. She turned awkwardly on her heels and went to the Chevrolet, her hard face kneaded by the first indications of regret at what she had done.

CHAPTER 16

When she was gone, I told Reavis to turn his back. Terror yanked at his mouth and pulled it open. "You ain't going to shoot me?"

"Not if you stand still."

He turned slowly, reluctantly, trying to watch me over his shoulder. He carried no gun. A rectangular package bulged in his right hip pocket. He started when I unbuttoned the pocket, then held himself tense and still as I drew out the package. It was wrapped in brown paper. A melancholy sigh of pain and loss came out of him, as if I had removed a vital organ. I tore one end of the paper with my teeth, and saw the corner of a thousand-dollar bill.

"You don't have to bother to count it," Reavis said thickly. "It's ten grand. Can I turn around now?"

I stepped back, slipping the torn package into the inside breast pocket of my jacket. "Turn around slowly, hands on the head. And tell me who'd pay you ten thousand dollars for bumping off an old lady with a weak heart."

He turned, his blank face twisting, trying to get the feel of a story to tell. His fingers scratched unconsciously in his hair. "You got me wrong, I wouldn't hurt a fly."

"If it was big enough to bite back, you wouldn't."

"I never had nothing to do with that death. It must of been an accident."

"And it was pure coincidence you were on the spot when it happened."

"Yeah, pure coincidence." He seemed grateful for the phrase. "I just went out to say goodbye to Cathy, I thought she might come along with me, even."

"Be glad she didn't. You'd be facing a Mann Act charge as well as a murder rap."

"Murder rap, hell. They can't pin murder on an innocent man. She'll give me a alibi. I was with her before you picked me up."

"Where were you with her?"

"Out in front of the house, in one of the cars." It sounded to me as if he was telling the truth: Cathy had been sitting in my car when I went out. "We used to sit out there and talk," he added.

"About your adventures on Guadalcanal?"

"Go to hell."

"All right, so that's your story. She wouldn't go along with you, but she gave you ten grand as a souvenir of your friendship."

"I didn't say she gave it to me. It's my own money."

"Chauffeurs make big money nowadays. Or is Gretchen just one of a string that pays you a percentage?"

He studied me with narrowed eyes, obviously shaken by my knowledge of him. "It's my own money," he repeated stubbornly. "It's clean money, nothing illegal about it."

"Maybe it was clean before you touched it. It's dirty money now."

"Money is money, isn't it? I'll tell you what I'll do. I'll give you two grand. Twenty per cent, that's a good percentage."

"You're very generous. But I happen to have it all, a hundred per cent."

"All right, five grand then. It's my money, don't forget, I promoted it myself."

"You tell me how you did it, then maybe I'll cut you in. But the story has to be a good one."

He thought that over for a while, and finally made up his mind. "I'm not talking."

"We're wasting time, then. Let's get moving."

"Where you think you're taking me?"

"Back to Nopal Valley. The Chief of Police wants some of your conversation."

"We're in Nevada," he said. "You got to extradite me and you got no evidence."

"You're coming to California for your health. Voluntarily." I raised the barrel of my gun and let him look into the muzzle.

It frightened him, but he wasn't too frightened to talk. "You think you're riding high, and you think you're going to keep my money. All you're gonna do is get caught in a big machine, man."

His face was moist and pallid with malevolence. For less than a day he had been rich and free. I'd tumbled him back into the small time, perhaps into the shadow of the gas chamber.

"You're going to take a ride in a little one. And don't try for a break, Reavis, or you'll limp the rest of your life."

He told me to do an impossible thing, but he came along quietly to my car. "You drive," I said. "I haven't had a chance to look at the scenery."

He drove angrily but well. We passed his sister just out of Boulder City. Nobody waved at anybody. We lost her in no time at all.

Back in Las Vegas, I directed him to the Green Dragon. He looked at me questioningly as he pulled up to the curb.

"We're picking up a friend of mine. You come in, too."

I slid out under the wheel, on his side, and crowded him with the gun in my pocket as we crossed the sidewalk to the screen door. I couldn't trust Reavis to drive across the desert without an accident. I couldn't risk driving myself.

The place looked more cheerful with the lights on,

more people at the bar. The redheaded boy was sitting on the same stool, probably with the same empty beer glass in front of him, as desolate as ever.

I called him to the door. He said hello with a surprised inflection, and heaved up a feeble smile from the bottom of his stomach.

"Can you drive fast?"

"The fastest crate I ever drove would only go ninety, downhill."

"That's fast enough. I'll give you ten dollars to drive me back to the coast. Me and my friend. I'm Archer."

"To L.A.?" He said it as if there were really angels there.

"Nopal Valley. We go back over the mountains. From there you can take a bus."

"Swell. My name is Bud Musselman, by the way." He turned to Reavis with his hand outstretched. Reavis suggested what he should do with it.

"Pay no attention to him," I told the boy. "He suffered a very heavy financial loss."

Musselman took the wheel, with Reavis beside him. I sat in the back of the convertible, my gun on my knees. The downtown streets were brightening into tunnels of colored light under the darkening sky. Its quick nightly tumescence was turning Las Vegas into a city again. Far behind to the east a slice of moon floated low in the twilit sky.

I caught glimpses of it over my shoulder, over the shoulders of mountains, as it slowly rose in the sky, dissolving smaller. The boy drove fast and hard, and no car passed us. I stopped him at a gas station in the middle of the desert. A battered sign advertised Free Zoo: Real live rattlesnakes.

"You still got a third of a tank," he told me eagerly. "We're making good mileage, considering the speed."

"I have a phone call to make."

Reavis had wedged himself in the corner by the door and gone to sleep. One arm was over his face, the fist clenched tight. I reached across him and pushed the hand away from his wet forehead. He sobbed in his sleep, then opened his eyes, blinking in the light of the dash.

"We there already?" he asked me sullenly.

"Not yet. I'm going to phone Knudson. Come along."

Getting out of the car, he walked on loose knees around the gas pumps toward the open glaring door of the office. He looked round at the desert, chiaroscuroed with moon shadows; stole a glance at me, and tensed for movement halfway between the gas pumps and the door. A hunted man in a bad movie, about to risk his two-dimensional life.

I said: "I'm right behind you. My gun is pointed at your hambone."

His knees went loose again. I got change from the attendant and put in a call to the Nopal Valley police station. Reavis leaned beside the wall telephone, yawning wih frustration, so close to me I could smell him. His odor was a foolish hope gone sour.

A metallic voice rasped in my left ear: "Nopal Valley police."

"Chief Knudson, please."

"He ain't here."

"Can you tell me where to reach him?"

"Can't do that. Who's speaking?"

"Lewis Archer. Knudson asked me to report to him."

"Archer. Oh, yeah." A pause. "You got anything to report?"

"Yes. To Knudson."

"He ain't here, I tell you. This is the desk. You can report to me, and we'll take care of it."

"All right," I said reluctantly. "Get in touch with Knudson, tell him I'm coming into town tonight with a prisoner. What time is it now?"

"Five to nine. You on the Slocum case?"

"Yes. We should be there by midnight. We're in the desert now. Tell the Chief, he'll want to know."

"Okay, Mr. Archer." The rasping mechanical voice took on a personal note of curiosity. "You take this Reavis?"

"Keep it to yourself."

"Sure thing. You want a car to meet you?"

"Not necessary. He couldn't fight his way out of a wet paper bag."

I hung up, to meet Reavis's sullen glare. Back in the car, he went to sleep again.

"Your friend seems very unhappy," the boy Musselman said. "Is that a gun you're carrying?"

"It's a gun."

"You wouldn't be a mobster or something, Mr. Archer? I wouldn't want—" He thought better of the sentence.

"Something," I said. "You wouldn't want—?"

"Augh, nothing." He didn't speak to me again for three hours. But he did his job, driving as if he loved it, pushing the long white headlights across the dry-sea floor. The road unrolled like ticker-tape under the wheels.

It was just after midnight when we crossed the second mountain ridge and saw the distant lights of Nopal Valley. Our headlamps flashed on a black and yellow road-sign: Dangerous Grade: Trucks Use Lower Gear. We coasted down.

"Feels like I'm landing a plane," the boy said over his shoulder. Then he was silent, remembering his distrust of me and my gun.

I leaned forward in my seat. Reavis had slipped far down, his arms and shoulders sprawled on the seat, his legs cramped under the dash against the floorboards. His body had given up, and he looked dead. For an instant I was afraid that he was dead, that all his life had run out through the wound in his ego. I couldn't bear the thought, after the trouble I'd gone to.

"Reavis," I said. "Wake up. We're almost there."

He moaned and grumbled, raised his heavy head, painfully uncoiled his long sluggish body. Suddenly the boy applied the brakes, throwing him against the windshield.

I braced myself on the seat. "Watch it."

Then I saw the truck parked across the road near

the foot of the slope. We traveled a couple of hundred feet with brakes screeching, and came to a jarring halt. The truck was lightless, driverless.

"What do they think they're doing?" the boy said.

On one side the bank rose sharply, studded with boulders, and fell away on the other. No room to pass. A spotlight beam shot out from the side of the truck, wavered and found my windshield.

"Back up," I told the boy.

"I can't. I stalled her." His entire body labored with the starter. The motor roared.

"Douse the glim," somebody yelled. "It's him." The spotlight winked out.

The car shuddered backward a few feet and stalled again. "Christ, the brake!" the boy said to himself.

A knot of men waded into our headlight beam: six or seven gunmen carrying their tools. I pushed Reavis aside and got out to meet them. They had handkerchiefs tied over their mouths. "What is this, the great stage robbery?"

One of the handkerchiefs waggled: "Put your gun down, Jack. We want your prisoner is all."

"You'll have to take him."

"Don't be foolish, Jack."

I shot his gun arm, aiming for the elbow. Things were silent. The echo of the shot repeated itself in the narrow valley like a long low titter of despair.

I said to Reavis, without looking at him: "Better run for it, Pat."

His feet scraped on the road behind me. The man I had shot sat down in the road with his gun between his legs. He watched the blood drip off his hand in the moonlight. The other men looked from him to me and back in a quick tense rhythm.

"There are six of us, Archer," one of them said uncertainly.

"My gun holds seven rounds," I said. "Go home."

Reavis was still behind me, uncomfortably still. "Beat it, Pat, I can hold them."

"The hell," he said.

His arm came around my neck and jerked me backwards. The faceless men came forward in a wave. I turned to grapple with Reavis. His face was a blur in the moonlight, but it seemed to me that the eyes and mouth were wet with satisfaction. I struck at them. His fist came into my face. "I warned you, man," he said aloud.

A blow on the back of the neck chilled me down to the toes. I broke away from Reavis and swung my gun at the front man. Its muzzle raked his cheek and tore the handkerchief loose from his face. He doubled over. The others moved into his place.

"Hold your fire," the man on the ground called out. "We only want the one."

Another blow fell from behind, where Reavis was, and I was out before I hit the road.

I came back to consciousness unwillingly, as if I knew already what I would see. The boy was on his knees, a praying figure between me and the stars. The stars were in the same place in the sky, but they looked old and stale. I felt coeval with them.

Musselman jumped like a rabbit when I sat up. He rose to his feet and leaned over me. "They killed him, Mr. Archer." His voice was broken.

I got up painfully, feeling dwarfed and despised by the mountains. "What did they do to him?"

"They shot him, a dozen times or more. Then they poured gasoline on him and threw him down the bank and a match down after him. Was he really a murderer, like they said?"

"I don't know," I said. "Where is he?"

"Down there."

I followed him around the car and switched my spotlight on. The charred leavings of a man lay ten feet below the road in a circle of blackened sage-brush. I went to the other side of the road to be sick. The thin scrap of moon hung in a gap of the mountains, like lemon rind in a tall dark drink of Lethe. I brought up nothing but a bitter taste.

CHAPTER 17

The man behind the wire partition was speaking into a hand mike in a cheerless monotone: "Car sixteen investigate reported assault corner Padilla and Flower. Car sixteen corner Padilla and Flower."

He switched off the microphone and drew on a wet cigarette. "Yes sir?" He leaned forward to look at me through his wicket. "You have an accident?"

"It was no accident. Where's the Chief?"

"He's out on a case. What's the trouble?"

"I called you around nine. Did Knudson get my message?"

"Not me you didn't call. I just come on at midnight." He took another puff and scanned me impassively through the smoke. "What was this here message about?"

"It should be logged. I called at five to nine."

He turned back the top sheet on his board and glanced at the one underneath. "You must of made a mistake. There's nothing here between 8:45, a drunk on State, and 9:25, prowler over on Vista. Unless it was that prowler trouble?"

I shook my head.

"It wasn't the sheriff's branch office you called?"

"I called here. Who was on the desk?"

"Franks."

"He's a detective. He wouldn't be doing desk duty."

"He was filling in for Carmody. Carmody's wife is going to have a baby. Now what about this call? Name?"

"Archer. I'll talk to Knudson."

"You the private dick in the Slocum case?"

I nodded.

"He's out there now. I can call him."

"Don't bother. I'll drive out. Is Franks around?"

"Naw, he went home." He leaned forward confidentially, crushing out his cigarette. "You want my honest opinion, Franks ain't fit to handle this man's job. He dropped the ball before now. Was the call important?"

I didn't say. An ugly shape was taking form in the dreary, austere room, hanging almost tangibly over my head. It dragged on me, slowing my footsteps as I went out to the car. Anger and fear took over when I got my hands on the wheel. I ran through two red lights on the way out of town.

"We're not going back there?" the boy said shakily.

"Not yet. I have to see the Chief of Police."

"I don't understand what's happening. It's terrible. You tried to save him and he turned on you."

"He was stupid. He thought they were his friends. He didn't have any friends."

"It's terrible," he said again, to himself.

The veranda lights of the Slocum house were on, illuminating the massive walls, the clipped funereal lawn. It was a mausoleum banked with flowers and lit for company. The black police car at the foot of the terraces was fit for death to ride in, quietly and fast. I left the boy in the car and started up the walk. Knudson and Maude Slocum came to the front door together. They moved apart perceptibly when they recognized me. Mrs. Slocum stepped through the door alone, with her hand outstretched.

"Mr. Archer! Police headquarters phoned that you were coming. Where in the world have you been?"

"Too far. I could use a drink."

"Of course, come in." She opened the door and held

it for me. "You'll make him a drink, won't you, Ralph?"

He glanced at her warningly—the hard and practiced glance of an old enemy, an old lover. "Glad to, Mrs. Slocum. What's the good word, Archer?" His manner was cumbersome with a false friendliness.

"The word is all bad."

I gave it to them over my drink, in the sitting-room where the Slocums had quarreled the night before and then made up. Mrs. Slocum had a bruise on her cheekbone, barely visible under a heavy coating of suntan powder. She wore a green wool dress which emphasized the luxury of her figure. Her eyes and mouth and temples were haggard, as if the rich hungry body had been draining them of blood. Knudson sat beside her on a chintz-covered settee. Unconsciously, as I talked, her crossed knees tilted toward him.

"I caught up with Reavis in Las Vegas—"

"Who told you he was there?" Knudson asked softly.

"Legwork. I started back with him between six and seven, with a kid I hired to drive. At nine I called your headquarters from a gas stop in the desert, and told the desk to tell you I was coming."

"I didn't get it. Let's see, who was on the desk?"

"Franks. He didn't even bother to log the call. But he leaked the information to somebody else. Seven men stopped me on the Notch Trail, less than an hour ago. They used a truck for a roadblock. I shot one. Reavis thought the men were there to spring him, and he took me from behind. They knocked me out. Then they ventilated Reavis with a dozen slugs and gave him a gasoline barbecue."

"Please," Maude Slocum said, her face closed like a death mask. "How horrible."

Knudson's teeth tore at his thick lower lip. "A dirty lynching, eh? In twenty years in police work I never had a lynching to cope with."

"Save it for your memoirs, Knudson. This is murder. The boy in my car is a witness. I want to know what you're going to do about it."

He stood up. Beneath his surface show of excitement, he seemed to be taking the thing much too easily. "I'll do what I can. Notch Trail is out of my territory. I'll call the sheriff's office."

"Franks is your boy."

"Don't worry, I'll get to the bottom of that. Can you give me a description of these men?"

"They were masked with handkerchiefs. They looked to me like local products, ranchhands or oilfield hoods. One of them has a bullet hole in the inside right elbow. I'd know two voices if I heard them again. The boy might tell you more."

"I'll let the sheriff talk to him."

I stood up facing him. "You don't sound very eager."

He saw my intention of forcing a showdown, decided to stall it off. "These outbreaks of mob violence are hard to deal with, you know that. Even if the sheriff does get hold of the men, which isn't very likely, we'll never get a jury to convict them. Mrs. Slocum was one of the town's most respected citizens: you've got to expect some pretty raw feeling over her murder."

"I see. Mrs. Slocum's death is murder now. And Reavis's death is vigilante stuff, popular justice. You're not that stupid, Knudson, and neither am I. I know a mob when I see one. Those killers were hired. Amateurs maybe, but they didn't do it for fun."

"We won't get personal," he said in a heavy tone of warning. "After all, Reavis got what was coming to him. Amateur or not, the men that lynched him saved the state some money."

"You think he killed Mrs. Slocum."

"There isn't any doubt of it in my mind. The medical examiner found marks on her back, subcutaneous hemorrhages where somebody pushed her. And the somebody seems to be Reavis. We found his cap about fifty feet from the pool, behind the trees that mask the filter system. That proves that he was there.

He'd just lost his job: motive enough for a psycho. And immediately after the crime he skipped out."

"He skipped out, yes, but publicly and slowly. He thumbed a ride from me outside the gate, and stopped off at a bar for a couple of drinks."

"Maybe he needed a couple of drinks. Killers often do."

Knudson had the red and stubborn look of a man who had closed his mind. It was time to play the card I had been saving: "The timing is wrong. The earliest possible time that Marvell heard the splashing was twenty after eight. It was 8:23 exactly when I picked Reavis up, and it's a mile or more from the pool to the gate."

Knudson showed his teeth. A faint reflection of the grimace passed over Maude Slocum's face, which was intent on his. "Marvell is a very imaginative type," he said. "I took another statement from him today, after he calmed down a bit. He couldn't be certain when he heard the splash, or even if he heard a splash at all. It's possible that Mrs. Slocum was murdered a full hour before he found her. There's no way of establishing how long she was in the water."

"Still, I don't think Reavis did it."

"What you don't think isn't evidence. I've given you the evidence, and it's firm. Incidentally, it's a little late for you to be telling me when you picked Reavis up, and going to bat for him. What happened, Archer, did he sell himself to you? I understand he was a very convincing guy."

I held my anger. "There are other things. They can wait till you've done your phoning."

With arrogant slowness, he took a cigar from his side pocket, asked the woman's permission, bit off the end and dropped it in an ashtray, lit the cigar, blew out the match, puffed smoke in my direction. "When I need a door-knocker to tell me how to conduct my official work, I'll send you a special-delivery letter." He left the room, trailing cigar smoke; and came back from the hall immediately, holding Cathy Slocum by the arm. She twisted in his grasp. "Let me go, Mr. Knudson."

He dropped her arm as if she had struck him. "I'm sorry, Cathy. I didn't mean to be rough."

She turned her back on him and moved toward the door, her low-heeled white fur slippers scuffing the rug. Wrapped in a pink quilted robe, with her gleaming hair brushed down her back, she looked like a child. Knudson watched her with a curious, helpless expression.

"Wait a minute, darling," her mother said. "What are you doing up so late?"

Cathy stopped inside the door, but refused to turn. Her satin-covered shoulders were stiff and obstinate. "I was talking to father."

"Is he still awake?"

"He couldn't sleep, and I couldn't either. We heard voices, and he sent me down to see who it was. Now may I go back to bed, please?"

"Of course you may, dear."

"I'd like to ask Cathy a question," I said. "Do you object, Mrs. Slocum?"

She raised her hand in a maternal gesture. "The poor girl's had to answer so many questions. Can't it wait until morning?"

"All it needs is a yes-or-no answer, and it's a crucial question. Pat Reavis claimed her as an alibi."

The girl turned in the doorway. "I'm not a child, mother. Of course I can answer a question." She stood with her feet apart, her fists thrust deep into the pockets of her robe.

"All right, dear. As you wish." I got the impression that the mother was the one who usually gave in.

I said to her: "Reavis claimed he came out here to see you last night. Was he with you before I found you in my car?"

"No. I haven't seen him since that trouble in Quinto."

"Is that all?" Knudson said.

"That's all."

"Come and kiss your mother goodnight," Maude Slocum said.

The girl crossed the room with an unwilling awkwardness and kissed her mother on the cheek. The older woman's arms moved up around her. The girl stepped out of them quickly, and away.

Knudson watched them as if he was unaware of the tension between them. He seemed to take a simple delight in the forced, loveless transaction of the kiss. He followed Cathy out of the room with a set smile on his face, the glowing cigar held cockily in the middle of the smile.

I sat down on the settee beside Maude Slocum: "Reavis is sewed up tight. I see what Knudson meant."

"Are you still unsatisfied?" she asked me earnestly.

"Understand me, Reavis means nothing to me. It's the total picture that bothers me: there are big gaps in it. For example. Do you know a man by the name of Walter Kilbourne?"

"More questions, Mr. Archer?" She reached for a silver cigarette box on the table beside her. Her hand, badly controlled, knocked the box to the floor. The cigarettes spilled out, and I started to pick them up.

"Don't bother," she said, "please don't bother. It doesn't matter. Things in general seem to be going to pieces. A few cigarettes on the floor are the least of my worries."

I went on picking up the cigarettes. "What is the greatest of your worries? Is it still that letter you gave me?"

"You ask so many questions. I wonder what it is that keeps you asking them. A passion for justice, a passion for truth? You see, I've turned the tables on you."

"I don't know why you should bother to." I set the full box on the table, lit her cigarette and one for myself.

She drew on it gratefully. Her answer was visible, written in smoke on the air: "Because I don't understand you. You have mind and presence enough for a better job, certainly one with more standing."

"Like your friend Knudson's? I worked in a municipal police department for five years, and then I quit. There were too many cases where the official version clashed with the facts I knew."

"Ralph is honest. He's been a policeman all his life, but he still has a decent conscience."

"Two of them, probably. Most good policemen have a public conscience and a private conscience. I just have the private conscience; a poor thing, but my own."

"I was right about you. You do have a passion for justice." The deep eyes focused on mine and probed them, as if a passion for justice was something she could see and remember the shape of. Or a strange growth in a man that could be X-rayed out.

"I don't know what justice is," I said. "Truth interests me, though. Not general truth if there is any, but the truth of particular things. Who did what when why. Especially why. I wonder, for example, why you care whether I'm interested in justice. It could be an indirect way of asking me to drop out of this case."

She was silent for a time. "No. It isn't that. I have some regard for truth myself. I suppose it's a woman's regard: I want the truth if it doesn't hurt too much. And I suppose I'm a little afraid of a man who cares strongly about something. You really care, don't you, whether Reavis is innocent or guilty?"

"Doesn't Knudson and his decent conscience?"

"He did, but I don't know if he still does. There are a lot of things going on that I don't understand." That made two of us. "My esteemed husband, for instance, has retired to his room and refuses to emerge. He claims that he'll spend the rest of his life in his room, like Marcel Proust." Hatred flashed in the ocean-colored eyes and disappeared, like a shark-fin.

I crushed out my cigarette, which tasted acrid on an empty stomach. "This Marcel something-or-other, is he a friend of yours?"

"So now you're going to play dumb again?"

"I might as well. It seems to be all the rage in this *ménage*. You're perfectly willing to talk about abstractions like truth and justice. But you haven't told me a single damned fact that might help to find the person that wrote the letter, or the person that killed your mother-in-law."

"Ah, the letter. We're back at the letter again."

"Mrs. Slocum," I said, "the letter wasn't written about me. It was written about you. You hired me to find out who wrote it, remember?"

"So much has happened since, hasn't it? It seems unimportant now."

"Now that she's dead?"

"Yes," she answered calmly. "Now that she's dead."

"Has it occurred to you that the letter-writer and the murderer may be the same person?"

"It hadn't. I can't see any connection."

"Neither can I. With co-operation, I might; if you'd tell me what you know about the relations between the people in this house."

She raised her shoulders and let them fall in a gesture of weary resignation. "I can't claim immunity to questioning on the grounds of extreme youth, like Cathy. I *am* most frightfully tired. What do you want to know?"

"How long you've known Knudson, and how well."

She gave me a second slow and probing look. "Just the last year or so, not at all intimately."

"Yesterday you mentioned a friend of yours, by the name of Mildred Fleming. She might be able to tell me a different story. Or don't you confide in your friends, either?"

She answered coldly: "I think you're being insolent, Mr. Archer."

"Very good, ma'am. We'll play the game according to the formal rules. Unless you want to call it on account of insolence."

"I haven't decided about that. I'll tell you one thing, though, I do know Walter Kilbourne. In fact, I saw him tonight."

Knudson's heavy feet came down the hall, his

sloping shoulders filled the doorway. "I finally routed the sheriff out of bed. He'll meet us at the Notch."

"You," I said, "not me. Mrs. Slocum has just been kind enough to offer me another drink, and I need it. I'll give the sheriff a statement in the morning. Take the kid along. His name is Musselman and he's in my car, probably sleeping by now.—You should get some good tread-marks where the truck pulled onto the shoulder to turn around."

"Thank you very much for the masterly suggestion." His tone was ironic, but he seemed to be relieved that I wasn't going along. He and the sheriff could putter around the scene of the crime, gather up the remains and drive them back to town. Nothing was going to be done.

"See that the kid has a decent place to sleep, will you? And give him this for me, I owe it to him." I handed him a ten-dollar bill.

"Whatever you say. Goodnight, Mrs. Slocum. I appreciate your co-operation."

"It was a pleasure."

Old lovers, I thought again, playing with double entendres. Knudson went out. My initial liking for him had changed to something quite different. Still, he was a man, and a policeman. He wouldn't push his way to what he wanted over an old lady's dead body. He'd choose a harder way.

Maude Slocum rose and took my empty glass. "Do you really want a drink?"

"A short one, please, with water."

"I think I'll join you."

She poured me two fingers of whisky from the decanter, four fingers for herself. She took it at a gulp.

I sipped at mine. "What I really want is the dope on Kilbourne. I'll take that straight."

"God-damned truthoholic," she said surprisingly. The idea of the whisky had hit her before it had time to work. She sat down beside me heavily and loosely. "I don't know anything about Walter Kilbourne, nothing against him I mean."

"That makes you unique, I guess. Where did you see him tonight?"

"At the Boardwalk restaurant in Quinto. I thought Cathy deserved a change after the dreary day she'd had with the police and—her father. Anyway, I drove her over to Quinto to have dinner, and I saw Walter Kilbourne in the restaurant. He was with a blonde young creature, a really lovely girl."

"His wife. Did you have any conversation with him?"

"No. He didn't recognize me, and I'd never particularly liked him. I did ask the headwaiter what he was doing here. Apparently his yacht is in the harbor."

It was what I needed. Tiredness had drained my body of energy and begun to attack my will. I'd been chinning myself on the present moment, too exhausted to see beyond it. Now I could see myself crossing the pass to Quinto.

But there were more questions to ask. "How did you happen to know him in the first place?"

"He was here a couple of years ago. He made a business arrangement with my mother-in-law, to test for oil on her ranch. This was when they'd made a big strike on the other side of the valley, before they'd touched this side. A crew of men came out with Kilbourne and spent several weeks on our property, drilling holes and setting off explosive charges—I forget the technical name for it."

"Seismographing?"

"Seismographing. They found the oil all right, but nothing came of it. Mother"—her lips moved round the word as if it tasted strange—"Mother decided that oil derricks would obstruct her precious view, and broke off relations with Kilbourne. There was more to it than that, of course: she didn't like the man, and I don't think she trusted him. So we've continued to live in genteel poverty."

"Weren't other companies interested? Oil's getting pretty scarce in this part of the world."

"She didn't really want to lease to anyone. Besides, there was something in the original contract for the exploration; it gave Kilbourne's company first refusal."

"Naturally, it would."

Her erratic hand reached blindly for a cigarette. I took one out of the box, put it between her fingers, lit it for her. She sucked on it uncontrolledly like a child. The whisky had combined with her fatigue and given her nervous system a hard one-two. Her face, her muscles, her voice, were rapidly going to pieces.

So I asked her the question that would hurt, and carefully watched her face for its effect: "You won't be living in genteel poverty much longer, will you? I suppose that you and your husband will be getting in touch with Kilbourne. Or is that why he's up here now?"

"It hadn't occurred to me," she said. "I imagine, though, that that's just what we'll do. I must talk to James about it."

She closed her eyes. From the places where it was pinned to the durable bone, the flesh of her face fell in thin slack folds. The folds made dark lines slanting downward from the corners of her closed eyes, the wings of her nose, the edges of her jaw, deep charcoal shadows cartooning dissolution.

I said goodnight and left her.

CHAPTER 18

There was only one light in the lower part of the house, a shaded wall-lamp in the hall midway between the front door and the kitchen. It cast a brownish glow into the alcove under the stairs where the telephone was. A copy of the Quinto-Nopal Valley telephone directory lay on the low table beside the telephone. I flipped through it to the F's. Only one Franks was listed, a Simeon J. residing at 467 Tanner Terrace. I called his number and listened to half-a-dozen rings at the other end. Then a voice answered, harsh and surly:

"Franks speaking. That the station?"

I had opinions to express, but I kept them to myself.

"Hello," he said, "this is Franks."

I hung up. And heard the soft susurrus of feet descending the stairs above my head, a whispering amplified by the sounding-board of the stairs and my keyed-up senses. A face like a pale moon against a cloud of hair leaned over the banister.

"Who is it?" the girl said.

"Archer." I moved out into the hall where she could see me plainly. "Aren't you in bed yet, Cathy?"

"I daren't close my eyes. I keep seeing Grandma's face." Both of her hands clung to the oaken rail, as if she needed a grip on solid reality. "What are *you* doing?"

"Telephoning. I'm finished now."

"I heard Mr. Knudson telephoning before. Is it **true** that Pat is dead?"

"Yes. You liked him?"

"Sometimes, when he was nice. He was a lot of fun. He taught me how to dance, but don't tell father. He didn't really kill Grandma, did he?"

"I don't know. I don't think so."

"Neither do I." She glanced furtively down the hall, which was choked with shadows. "Where are the others?"

"Knudson has gone. Your mother's in the sitting-room. I think she's asleep."

She drew her hand back further into the soft folds of her robe. "I'm glad that *he's* gone anyway."

"I have to go now, too. Will you be all right?"

"Yes, I'll be all right." She came down the rest of the way, her forearm sliding on the banister. "I'd better wake mother up and send her to bed."

"Maybe you'd better."

She followed me to the door. "Goodnight, Mr. Archer. I'm sorry I was rude to you last night. I must have felt that something was going to happen. I'm very sensitive, you know, at least that's what people tell me. I'm like a dog that howls at the moon when there's trouble in the air."

"But you didn't see Reavis last night."

"No. I was kind of afraid that he might come—I hate emotional scenes—but he didn't." Her finger described a cross on her silken breast. "Cross my heart and hope to die." She giggled in sudden strained mirth: "What a ghastly thing to say: 'hope to die'."

I said: "Goodnight, Cathy."

Number 467 Tanner Terrace was a white frame bungalow in one of the cheaper suburbs, standing among a dozen houses like it. They all had slanting roofs, useless green shutters on the two front windows, and the rootless temporary air of a row of trailers in a vacant lot. You told them apart by the

numbers stenciled on the curb. Also, Sergeant
Franks's house contained light. It leaked around the
edges of the closed venetian blinds in the front windows and sprinkled the struggling lawn.

I drove on past, U-turned at the first intersection
and parked a hundred feet short of the house. Franks
was a policeman. In his own territory he could make
trouble for me. I wasn't the one I wanted trouble to
be made for. I turned off engine and lights, slid down
in the seat, dozed off with my consciousness slightly
ajar. The sound of a nearing motor woke me a moment before bright headlights swept the street.

They straightened out and came to rest in front of
Franks's bungalow. There were three blue taxi-lights
above the windshield. A man climbed awkwardly out
of the back seat and started up the walk. His gait was
a little lopsided; in the dim light I thought he was a
cripple. The front door opened before he reached the
low concrete stoop. He moved forward into the light, a
short thick man in a brown horsehide windbreaker.
Its right side bulged, and its right sleeve dangled
empty. The front door closed on him.

The taxi turned in a driveway and rolled back to
the curb in front of the house. Its lights winked out. I
waited for a minute or two and left my car without
slamming the door. The taxi-driver was stretched out
in his seat, waiting for sleep.

I asked him: "Are you busy?"

He answered me with his eyes half-closed: "Sorry.
I'm on a return trip."

"To where?"

"Quinto."

"That's where I'm going."

"Sorry, mister. This is a Quinto cab. I can't take
Nopal fares."

"You can if you don't charge me."

"Then what's the percentage?" He sat up straight,
and his eyes snapped all the way open. They were
blue and bulging in a hollow face. "Listen, what goes
on?"

I showed him a ten-dollar bill. "Your percentage," I said.

The bill crackled in my fingers, as if it was taking fire under the intensity of his gaze. "Okay, I guess it's okay, if the other guy don't object." He leaned back to open the door for me.

I got in. "He shouldn't object. Where is he going in Quinto?"

"I don't know, where I picked him up, I guess. Down by the boardwalk."

"Ever see him before?"

It was one question too many. He turned in his seat and looked me over. "You're a cop?"

"It didn't used to show."

"Look'it here, I didn't take your money. I didn't say for sure I would take your money. Matter of fact, I wouldn't touch your money. So how about just getting out and leaving me be. I'm trying to make an honest living, for gosh sakes."

"All right. I'll get out, and you beat it back to Quinto."

"For gosh sakes, have a heart. This is a seven-dollar run."

"Take it out of this." I held out the ten-dollar bill.

He shied from it wall-eyed. "Uh-uh. No thanks."

"Then beat it fast. There's going to be trouble here, and you don't want to wait for it."

Before I got out, I tucked the bill between the cushions and the back of the seat, where taxi-drivers had a habit of looking. The forward motion of the cab closed the door. I went back to my car and waited. The man with the bulky right side and the empty sleeve came out almost immediately. He said good-night to someone and turned toward the street. He was on the sidewalk before he noticed that the cab was gone.

He looked up and down the road, and I slid lower in my seat. His left hand pantomimed disgust in an outward-pushing gesture. His voice announced clearly that he would be fornicated with. I recognized his voice. When he turned to look at the house, the lights were gone. Shrugging lopsidedly, he started to walk in the direction of the highway. I let him walk a block before I started my motor, and pulled even with him as he reached the second corner. My gun was on the seat beside me.

"You want a lift?" I blurred my voice.

"I sure could use one, Jack." He stepped off the curb into the road, within the circle of light from the streetlamp overhead. An oil-stained fedora cast a shadow over his dark broad face, from which the eye-whites gleamed.

"Quinto?"

"This is my lucky—" He recognized me or my car, and the sentence was never finished. His left hand dropped to the leather-flapped pocket of his windbreaker.

I swung the door wide open and waved my gun. His fingers were twisting at the leather button that held the flap over the pocket.

"Get in," I said. "You don't want it to happen to the other arm? I have a passion for symmetry."

He got in. I drove left-handed in low to a dark lacuna between streetlights, and parked at the curb. I shifted the gun to my left hand and held it low to his body. The gun I took from his pocket was a heavy revolver which smelt of fresh oil. I added it to the arsenal in my glove compartment and said: "Well."

The man beside me was breathing like a bull. "You won't get far with this, Archer. Better get back to your hunting-grounds before it happens to you."

I told him I liked it where I was. My right hand found the wallet in his left hip-pocket, flipped it open under the dashlights. His driver's license bore the name Oscar Ferdinand Schmidt.

I said: "Oscar Ferdinand Schmidt is a very euphonious name. It will go well in a murder indictment."

He advised me to commit sodomy. I held my impulse to hurt him. Next to the driver's license, an envelope of transparent celluloid held a small blue card which identified Oscar F. Schmidt as a Special Officer of the Company Police of the Pacific Refining

Company. There were bills in the folding-money compartment, but nothing bigger than a twenty. I tucked the bills in his pocket, and the wallet in mine.

"I want my wallet back," he said, "or I slap a charge on you."

"You're going to be busy fighting one of your own. The sheriff is going to find your wallet in the brush by the Notch Trail."

He was silent for a minute, except that the horsehide jacket creaked like a bellows with his breathing. "The sheriff will give it back to me, without no questions asked. How do you think the sheriff gets elected?"

"I know now, Oscar. But it happens the FBI is interested in lynchings. Do you have an in with the Justice Department, too?"

His husky voice had changed when he answered. It had sick and frightened overtones. "You're crazy if you try to buck us, Archer."

I prodded him hard with the gun, so that he grunted. "You'll sit in the cyanide room before I reserve a bed at Camarillo. Meanwhile I want you to talk. How much did you give Franks for the information, and who gave you the money?"

His brain worked cumbrously. I could almost hear it turn over and stall, turn over slowly again. "You let me go if I tell you?"

"For the present. I couldn't be bothered with you."

"And give me back the wallet?"

"I keep the wallet, and the gun."

"I never fired the gun."

"You never will."

His brain turned over again. He was sweating, and starting to smell. I wanted him out of the car.

"Kilbourne gave me the money," he said finally. "Five C's, I think it was. You're crazy if you buck him."

I said: "Get out of my car."

Where Tanner Terrace met the highway, I turned left back into Nopal Valley, instead of right to Quinto. The case was breaking faster than I had expected, faster than I could handle by myself. From where I sat, it looked as if Kilbourne had sparked a double play that would never be recorded on the sports pages: paid Reavis to dispose of Mrs. Slocum, then paid to have Reavis disposed of before he could talk. I didn't like this theory: it explained the more obvious things, the deaths and the money, and gave no clue to the rest, but it was the best I had to go on. In any case, I couldn't act on it without consulting my client. James Slocum's wife was not above suspicion, but she hadn't called me in to tie a noose around her handsome neck.

It was after closing-time, and the main street was almost deserted. A few late drunks were cruising the sidewalks, unwilling to end the night and face the morning. Some had female companions to assure them that fun was still to be had, that there were still doors in the dark walls that would open on romance for a nominal payment. The women were the kind that seldom appear in daylight and look dead when they do. Two plain-clothes men were trying doors on opposite sides of the street.

Passing Antonio's place, I saw a small light behind the bar, half eclipsed by a man's head. I braked the car and nosed in to the curb. I had ten thousand dollars in my breast pocket, which would be hard to explain if I was shaken down by the cops, harder to survive if anyone else found it on me. I wrapped the torn brown package in a piece of newspaper and tied it with friction tape. I'd talked to Antonio once, and didn't know his last name, but he was the man I trusted in Nopal Valley.

He came to the blinded door when I rapped on the plate glass, opened it four inches on a chain. "Who is it, please?" His face was in the shadow.

I showed him mine.

"I am very sorry, I cannot sell after hours."

"I don't want a drink, I want you to do me a favor."

"What kind of a favor?"

"Keep this in your safe until tomorrow." I pushed one end of the package through the narrow opening.

He looked at it without touching it. "What is in the parcel?"

"Money. A lot of money."

"Who is the owner of the money?"

"I'm trying to find out. Will you keep it?"

"You should take it to the police."

"I don't trust the police."

"Yet you trust me?"

"Apparently."

He took the package from my hands and said: "I will keep it for you. Also, I must apologize for what happened in my bar last night."

I told him to forget it.

CHAPTER 19

The house on the mesa was dark and silent. Nothing stirred, inside or out, but the shrill sighing of the cicadas rising and falling in the empty fields. I knocked on the front door and waited, shivering in my clothes. There was no wind, but the night was cold. The insect cry sounded like wind in autumn trees.

I tried the door. It was locked. I knocked on it again. After a long time a light appeared in the hall, footsteps dragged themselves toward the door. The porch light over my head was switched on, and the door opened, inch by inch. It was Mrs. Strang, the housekeeper, her time-bleached hair in double braids, her eyes puffed and reddened from sleep.

The old eyes peered at me: "Is it Mr. Archer?"

"Yes. I have to see Mrs. Slocum."

Her hands plucked at the collar of her blue rayon wrapper. A pink-flowered flannel nightgown showed beneath it. "Mrs. Slocum is dead," she said with a frown of grief.

"Not Maude Slocum. I saw her less than two hours ago."

"Oh, you mean *young* Mrs. Slocum. She's in bed, I guess. Which is where you should be. This is no hour of the night—"

"I know. I have to see her. Will you wake her for me?"

"I don't know whether I ought to. She'll be displeased."

"I'll wake her myself if you don't."

"Gracious, no." She moved as if to bar the door against me, then changed her mind: "Is it as important as all that?"

"A matter of life and death." I didn't know whose life, or whose death.

"Very well, come in. I'll ask her to come down."

She left me in the sitting-room and shuffled out. The twin braids down her back looked stiff and dry, like flowers pressed in an old forgotten book.

When she returned her face and body were sagging with anxiety. "Her door is locked. She doesn't answer."

I moved toward her, hurried her with me into the hall and along it to the stairs. "Do you have a key?"

"There is no key for that door." She was panting. "It's bolted on the inside."

"Show me."

She toiled up the stairs ahead of me and led me down the upstairs hall to the last door. It was made of heavy oak panels. I set my shoulder against it and failed to move it.

The housekeeper took my place at the door and cried out, "Mrs. Slocum!" on a cracked note of despair.

"You're sure she's in there," I said.

"She must be in there. The door is bolted."

"I'll have to break it down. Do you have a crowbar or a pinchbar? Anything."

"I'll go and see. There are tools in the back kitchen."

I switched off the light in the hall and saw that there was light behind the door. I leaned against it again and listened. No snore, no sound of drunken breathing, no sound of any kind. Maude Slocum was sleeping very soundly.

Mrs. Strang came back, her body moving like a lumpy bundle of terror and compunction. Her veined hands held a short steel bar with one flat end, the kind that is used to open packing cases. I took it from her and inserted the flat end between the door and the frame. Something cracked and gave when I pulled on it. I shifted the bar and pulled hard once again. Wood tore, and the door sprang open.

There was a triple-mirrored dressing-table against the wall to my right, an oversize Hollywood bed, its chenille surface uncrumpled, to my left beside the windows. Maude Slocum lay between them. Her face was dark gray shaded with blue, like a Van Gogh portrait at its maddest. The fine white teeth glaring in rictus between the purple lips gave it a grotesque blackface touch. I kneeled beside her, felt for pulse and heartbeat. She was dead.

I stood up and turned to the housekeeper. She was advancing into the room slowly against great pressure. "Has something happened?" she whimpered, knowing the answer.

"The lady is dead. Call the police, and try to contact Knudson."

"Augh!" She turned away, and the pressure of death drove her scuttling to the door.

Cathy Slocum passed her coming in. I moved to shield the corpse with my body. Something in my face stopped the girl in her tracks. She stood facing me, slim and soft in a white silk nightgown. Her eyes were dark and accusing.

"What is it?" she demanded.

"Your mother is dead. Go back to your room."

All her muscles tightened, drawing her body erect. Her face was a white tragic mask. "I have a right to stay."

"You're getting out of here." I took a step toward her.

She caught a glimpse of the thing that lay behind me. The white mask crumbled like plaster suddenly. She spread one hand across her blind face. "How can she be dead? I—" Grief took her by the throat and choked her into silence.

I laid an arm across her shuddering back, turned

her toward the door, propelled her out. "Look, Cathy, I can't do anything for you. Go and get your father, why don't you?"

She blubbered between sobs: "He won't get out of bed—he says he can't."

"Well, get into bed with him then."

It wasn't the right thing to say, but her reaction shocked me. Both of her small fists exploded against my face and sent me off balance. "How dare you say a dirty thing like that?" She followed it up with every Anglo-Saxon word that every schoolgirl knows.

I retreated into the room where the silent woman lay, and shut the door on Cathy. The heavy iron bolt hung loose and useless in its socket; the screws that held it had been torn out of the moulding, but the latch still worked. It clicked, and I heard the girl's bare feet go down the hall. I went to the windows, which stood in a row of three above the bed. They were steel-framed casements, opening outward above the tiled roof of the veranda, and all of them were open. But there were copper screens inside the glass set in metal frames and fastened firmly with screws. No one could have entered the room or left it after the door was bolted.

I returned to the woman on the floor. A lambswool rug was wadded under one shoulder, as if she had crumpled it up in a convulsion. She had on the same dress I had seen her in, pulled high up on her dingy-colored thighs. I had an impulse to pull it down, to cover the sprawling legs I had admired. My training wouldn't let me. Maude Slocum belonged to strychnine and policemen and black death.

The light in the room came from a double-barreled fluorescent desk-lamp on a writing-table opposite the door. A portable typewriter stood uncovered directly under the lamp, a sheet of plain white paper curling from the roller. There were a few lines of typing on the paper. I stepped around the body to read them.

Dear Heart: I know I am being a coward. There are some things I cannot face, I cannot live with them.

*Believe me love it is for the best for all. I have had
my share of living anyway.*

*It is strychnine sulphate I think it is from Olivia
Slocum's prescription. I won't be pretty I know but
maybe now you know they won't have to cut me up
I can feel it I can't write anymore my hands zre*

That was all.

A small green medicine bottle stood open by the
typewriter, its black metal cap beside it. The label
bore a red skull-and-crossbones. It stated that the
prescription, ordered by Dr. Sanders for Mrs. Olivia
Slocum, had been made up by the Nopal Valley
Pharmacy on May 4 of that year, and was to be taken
as directed. I looked into the bottle without touching
it and saw that it was empty.

There was nothing else on the top of the table, but
there was a wide drawer in its front. I pushed a chair
out of the way, and using a handkerchief to cover my
fingers, pulled the drawer halfway out. It contained
some sharpened pencils, a used lipstick, hairpins and
paperclips, a scrambled mass of papers. Most of these
were receipted bills from shops and doctors. A book
from a Nopal Valley bank showed a balance of three
hundred and thirty-six dollars and some cents, after a
withdrawal of two hundred dollars two days before.
Flipping through the papers with the point of a broken pencil, I found one personal letter, typed on a
single sheet with a Warner Brothers letterhead.

It started out with a bang:

Hi there Maudie-girl:

*It seems like a coon's age (as old massuh used to
say before they put him in the cold cold ground and
a darned good thing it was too I never liked the old
bastid) since I've heard from you. Break out the
word-making machine and let down the back hair,
girl-friend. How goes the latest campaign against the
Slocum clan, and also what about Him? The news
from this end is all good. Mr. Big has raised me to
one-twenty and last week he told Don Farjeon who
told his secretary who told me that I never make a*

*mistake (except in matters of the heart, that is, ha
ha, but what am I laughing at?) But the biggest news
is guess what and keep it under your hat if you ever
wear one. England, my sweet. Mr. Big is making a
picture in England starting next month, and he's going to take me along!!! So you better duck out from
under the trials and tribs of the vie domestique one
of these fine days soon, and we'll have a big lunch
at Musso's to celebrate. You know where to get me.*

*Meantime, my love to Cathy and you know what I
think of the rest of the Slocum caboodle. See you
soon.*

The letter was undated, and was signed "Millie." I
looked at the woman on the floor, and wondered if
she had ever had that lunch. I also wondered if
Mildred Fleming had left for England yet, and how
much she knew about "Him." "Him" sounded more like
Knudson than the deity. And Knudson would soon be
here.

I pulled the drawer out further. A folded newspaper clipping, stuck in the crack between the bottom
of the drawer and the back, had slipped down almost
out of sight. I pulled it out, unfolded it under the
light. It was a long newspaper column headed by a
two-column picture of two men. One was Knudson,
the other a dark young man in a torn white shirt.
"Captor and Escapee," the caption said. "Lieutenant
of Detectives Ralph Knudson, of the Chicago police,
holds Charles "Cappie" Mariano, convicted slayer of
three, who escaped from Joliet Penitentiary last Monday. Lieutenant Knudson tracked him down in Chicago's Skid Row, and took him into custody the follow-
ing day." The news story gave details of the exploit,
and I read it slowly and carefully. The dateline was
April 12, but there was no indication of the year. I
folded the clipping again, put it back where I found
it, and closed the drawer.

The message in the typewriter drew me back.
There was something funny about it I couldn't name,
something that needed explaining. Without a clear
idea of what I was doing, I took the letter Maude

Slocum had given me out of my inside pocket, and spread it out on the table beside the typewriter. "Dear Mr. Slocum." It was like a memory of something I had heard a long time ago, way back before the war. "Lilies that fester smell far worse than weeds." The woman on the floor would fester soon; the letter didn't matter now.

My attention fastened on the first word of the salutation, "Dear;" shifted to the note in the typewriter, "Dear Heart;" came back to the letter on the table. The two "Dears" were identical: the initial D of each was slightly out of line, and the 'a' had a barely perceptible break in the middle of the curve. Though I was no typewriter expert, it looked to me as if Maude Slocum's suicide note and the letter to her husband had been typed on the same machine.

I was trying to make sense of it when heavy footsteps sounded in the hall. The door opened and Knudson came into the room. I stood and watched him like a vivisectionist studying an animal under the knife. But his reaction was a man's. When he saw the darkened face on the floor, his entire body buckled. He almost went down, but caught himself and leaned upright against the door-frame. A uniformed policeman looked over his shoulder into the room. Knudson shut the door on the questioning face.

He turned to me. His bloodless skin was a dirty yellow and his eyes glared. "Maude is dead?" The big voice came out small and furred with pain.

"She's dead. Strychnine takes them fast."

"How do you know it's strychnine?"

"It shows on her. And there's a note in the typewriter. I think it was meant for you."

He looked at the woman on the floor between us, and flinched. "Give me the note." His shoulder stayed against the door-frame. He would not walk over or past her.

I pulled the sheet from the roller and brought it to him.

He read it over and over to himself, his heavy lips

forming the syllables. Sweat came out on his face and gathered in its crevices like tears.

"Why did she want to kill herself?" The effort of speaking wrenched his mouth sideways and left it that way.

"You tell me. You knew her better than I did."

"I loved her. I guess she didn't love me. Not enough."

Grief worked on him like truth serum. He had forgotten that I was there, or who I was. Perhaps he had forgotten who he was.

Slowly he remembered. His forces regrouped themselves around a stony core of ego. I could see hard masculine pride come into his face, straightening the mouth and jaw, masking the hurt eyes. He folded the suicide note with large and gentle fingers, thrust it away in a pocket.

"I just got here," he said. "Nothing was said. You didn't find this paper." He patted the pocket.

"And you are George the Sixth, the King of England. Not ex-Lieutenant Knudson of the Chicago police."

His right hand reached for me, took hold of the front of my coat and tried to shake me. "You'll do as I say."

I struck the hand down. The letter I had been holding tore from my fingers and slid to the floor. He stooped and had it in a single movement. "What's this?"

"The letter I was hired to investigate. It was written on the same typewriter as the suicide note. Think about that. When you've finished thinking about that, think about this. Your boy Franks got paid five hundred for the information that I was on my way here with Reavis. Walter Kilbourne paid him. I can identify the leader of the lynching party as one of Kilbourne's men."

"You talk too much." He read the letter, grunting impatiently, then crushed it into a ball and put it away with the other.

"You're destroying evidence, Knudson."

"I said you talk too much. I'm the judge of what's evidence around here."

"You won't be for long. You can take that as a threat if you want to."

He leaned toward me with his teeth bared. "Who's threatening who? I've had enough from you. Now you can get out of town."

"I'm staying."

He leaned closer. His breath was fetid and hot like a carnivore's. "You're getting out of town tonight, now, and you're not coming back. I can send you up for a long time, Archer. You brought Reavis across a state line under duress. You know what that is in the law."

He had me. I'd tied myself up and handed myself to him. Bitter water squeezed from my eyes and burned on my face.

His right hand moved under his coat, loosening the gun in his shoulder holster. "Are you going, or are you staying to take the rap?"

I didn't answer.

He opened the door and I went out past the policeman in the hall. Times and places went through my head in a red rush. There had to be another time and place for me and Knudson.

CHAPTER 20

Mrs. Strang met me at the foot of the stairs. "Mr Archer, somebody wants to speak to you on the telephone. A woman. She's been on the line for some time but I didn't like to interrupt when you were talking to the Chief of Police."

"No," I said. "That would be *lèse majesté.*"

She looked at me strangely. "At least I *hope* she's still on the line. She said she'd wait. Are you all right, Mr. Archer?"

"I feel fine." There was a roaring hollowness in my head, a tight sour ball at the bottom of my stomach. My case had been taken away from me just as it started to break. I felt fine.

I said, "This is Archer," into the telephone.

"Well, you needn't bite my head off. Were you sleeping?" The voice was sweet and lingering, like a fragrance: Mavis Kilbourne in a melting mood.

"Yeah, I was having nightmares. About a fancy broad who turned out to be a pickpocket whose surname was Trouble."

She laughed: a mountain stream just below the snowline. "I'm not really a pickpocket, or even a broad. After all, I took what was mine. You're not in a very pleasant mood, are you?"

"Improve it for me if you can. Tell me how you knew I was here."

"I didn't. I called your house and office in Los Angeles. Your answering service gave me the number. I don't even know where you are, except that it's Nopal Valley. I'm in Quinto."

The operator cut in and asked for another ten cents please. The bell on the pay telephone sounded clearly over the line.

"I'm running out of dimes," Mavis said. "Will you come to Quinto and talk to me?"

"Why the sudden interest at three in the morning? There's nothing in my pocket but a gun."

"It's three-thirty." Her yawn rustled in the mouthpiece. "I'm dead."

"You're not the only one."

"Anyway, I'm glad you have a gun. You may need it."

"For what?"

"I can't tell you over the phone. I need you to do something for me. Will you accept me as a client?" The siren note again, like distant violins at a fine feast.

"I already have a client," I lied.

"Couldn't you work for both of us? I'm not proud."

"I am."

She lowered her voice. "I know it was a dirty trick to play on you. I had to do it, though. I burned the film, and it didn't explode like you said."

"Forget that. The trouble is that this could be another dirty trick."

"It isn't. I really need you. I may not sound afraid, but I actually am."

"Of what?"

"I said I can't tell you. Come to Quinto and I will. *Please* come." We were talking in circles.

"Where are you in Quinto?"

"In a lunchroom by the beach, but I better not meet you here. You know the big pier by the yacht basin?"

"Yeah," I said. "A perfect setup for an ambush."

"Don't be like that. I'll be out at the end of the pier. There's nobody there at this time of night. Will you come?"

"Give me half an hour."

Quinto was any small seaport at four o'clock in the morning. Dark and empty streets slanted down to the dark and empty ocean. The air was fairly clear but droplets of water formed on my windshield and a sea smell, bitter and fresh, invaded the unpeopled town. At night it was an outpost of the sea, filled by cold tidal winds and shifting submarine blackness.

The reflection of a stop-light made a long red smudge on the asphalt where 101 Alternate crossed the foot of the town. Four or five heavy trucks had gathered at the truckstop on the corner like buffalo at a waterhole. As I turned right onto the freeway, I could see the drivers bent over early breakfast, and a thin-browed, pug-faced waitress smoking a cigarette by the kitchen door. It would have been very pleasant to stop and eat three eggs and talk a while and then go back to bed in the motel. I cut my wheels sharp left at the next crossing, and the tires whined in self-pity: so late, so weary. I said aloud, to myself and the whining tires: "Get it over with."

The Quinto pier was a continuation of the street, carrying the blacktop road two hundred yards beyond the concrete sea wall. Below the pier the long white surges mumbled the sand, lapped at the ancient pilings that supported it, in a work of slow sure destruction. My brights lit up the white railings along the sides. They were bare from end to end, and the road was naked between them. Toward the outer end a group of small buildings huddled against the night: a bait-and-tackle booth, a hot-dog stand, a seashell-souvenir store, a ship's carpenter shop, all closed and lightless. I parked on their landward side, by a ten-cent public telescope, and walked on. The polished wooden butt of my automatic was wet-cold in my palm.

The smell of the sea, of kelp and fish and bitter moving water, rose stronger in my nostrils. It flooded my consciousness like an ancestral memory. The swells rose sluggishly and fell away, casting up dismal gleams between the boards of the pier. And the whole pier rose and fell in stiff and creaking mimicry, dancing its long slow dance of dissolution. I reached the end and saw no one, heard nothing but my footsteps and the creak of the beams, the slap of waves on the pilings. It was a fifteen-foot drop to the dim water. The nearest land ahead of me was Hawaii.

I turned my back on Hawaii and started for shore. Mavis had changed her mind and stood me up. A final goodbye to Mavis, my cold brain chattered; she was unaccountable no-account not-to-be-counted-on. Or had her mind been changed for her. My feet dragged on the planking. Too late, too old, too tired, the deep surge at the back of my mind was sighing.

False dawn was spreading like spilt milk in the sky above the mountains. At their foot the streets of Quinto lay like an unseen cobweb beaded with lights. The highballing trucks from San Francisco and Portland and Seattle went south on 101 like shooting stars. To my right the long arc of the breakwater curved toward the pier. A light on a tower at its end flashed on and off, stroking the narrow channel with intermittent stripes of grayish green. Forty or fifty vessels, of high and low degree, lay in the sheltered basin behind the breakwater. There were swans and ugly ducklings, arrowy racing sloops and broad-beamed Monterey fishing-boats, cabin cruisers and flatties, Star-boats and dinghies. One or two of the fishing-boats showed early-morning lights.

Another light went on as I watched, bringing a triple window into sharp yellow contrast with a low dark cabin. The long hull below it had lines of movement even though it was anchored and dead in the water. It was painted so white that it seemed to shine with its own luminescence. From a quarter mile away it looked like a small neat cruiser. But comparing it with the other boats I guessed it was seventy feet long: except for the purse-seiners, the biggest boat in the harbor. Kilbourne would choose that kind of coracle to ride in.

The light went out, as if by telepathy. I strained my eyes, trying to guess what went on behind the three oblong windows that I could no longer see. A hand from nowhere plucked at my trousers leg. I stepped out of reach, jerked my gun out, snapped a cartridge into the chamber. The wind whistled in my throat.

A head appeared above the planking at the edge of the pier. Light hair frothed out from under a beret. A light voice whispered: "It's me."

"Don't play hiding-games." I snarled, because she'd unnerved me. "A forty-five slug would play hell with your constitution."

She stood up and showed herself, a dark slim shape in sweater and slacks against the dark gray water. With racing lines for a long fast voyage by night, and a sweet full spinnaker bosom. "I like my constitution the way it is." She half-turned into another pose, held it like a model. "Don't you, Archer?"

"You'll get by," I said, and lied in my teeth: "You fascinate me as a source of income solely."

"Very well, sir. We'd better go below. We'll be seen up here." She held out her hand for mine. It was as cold as a fish.

She was standing on a railed gangway which slanted down to the water below the pier. We descended to a floating platform at the edge of the forest of pilings. A little plywood boat was tied to a rusty iron ring at the edge of the platform. Boat and platform rose and fell together with the waves.

"Whose boat?"

"It's a tender from the yacht. I came ashore in it."

"Why?"

"The water-taxis make so much commotion, and besides they'd know where I went."

"I see. Now I know everything."

"Please don't be nasty, Archer. What's your first name, anyway?"

"Lew. You can call me Archer."

"I'm sorry if I frightened you, Lew," in that small, contrite, aphrodisiac voice. "I didn't really mean to. I had to be sure it was you."

"Who else were you expecting?"

"Well. It might have been Melliotes."

"Who in hell," I said, "is Melliotes? Or did you invent the name?"

"If you think Melliotes is a figment, come out to the boat and meet him."

"Is that the family boat?" I pointed to the long white hull on the other side of the basin.

"It is." She thumbed her nose at it. "Some family. Take my husband's dear good friend Melliotes, for example. Last night my dear good husband held me down in my bunk while dear good Dr. Melliotes gave me a shot of morphine to put me to sleep."

I offered her a cigarette, which she took automatically. Lighting it for her, I looked into her eyes. The dark gray pupils were as tiny as a bird's.

"You see," she said, "I'm no liar. Feel my heart." Her hand pressed mine against her ribs below the left breast. There was a pounding in the tips of my fingers, but it was my own heart I felt. "You see?"

"Why aren't you still asleep?"

"I didn't go to sleep. Morphine just stimulates me, I'm like a cat. I feel the hangover now, though. I think I'd better sit down." Still with her hand on my wrist, she sat on the foot of the gangway and drew me down beside her. "I could show you the mark of the needle but that wouldn't be ladylike, would it?"

"Always the lady," I said. "Who are you, Mavis?"

She yawned and stretched herself. I didn't look at her, and she subsided. "A working girl. Used to be, anyway. I wish I still was. Only I was going to tell you about Dr. Melliotes. He was driving the car when Rico brought you home."

I remembered the man I had fought with in Reavis's shack. "He didn't look like a medical man to me."

"He calls himself a doctor, but Folsom's his alma mater if he has one. He's some kind of hydrotherapist, and he runs a sanitarium in Venice. Walter has a spastic colon and he's been going to Melliotes for years. He even brings him along on cruises, which is very convenient when he wants me put to sleep. I fooled them tonight, though. I didn't go to sleep, and I heard what went on.

"I heard my husband conspiring to murder a man. Pat Ryan, the man you asked me about. Walter gave orders to a man called Schmidt to have Pat Ryan killed. A couple of hours later Schmidt came aboard again and said that it was done." She peered into my face. "Doesn't that mean anything to you at all?"

"Plenty. Did anybody say why Reavis had to be shot?"

"Nobody said why, but I know why." She tilted her head toward me, her soft lower lip protruding. "You haven't promised me you'd go to work for me."

"You haven't told me what you want done. I'm not a hired gun like Schmidt."

"I only want justice done. I want you to pin Pat's murder on Schmidt, and on my husband."

"You'll have to tell me why."

"I'll tell you everything if it will help. I want my husband dead or put away, and I haven't nerve enough to do it myself."

"I'm afraid he's too big for me to take alone, but we might get at him through Schmidt. One thing I don't understand, how Kilbourne got you buffaloed. You're frightened to death of him."

"I was. Not any more. I wouldn't be here if I was frightened, would I?" But her voice was light and tinny, and she glanced towards the yacht across the water. A Monterey seiner moved in a semi-circle and nosed towards the channel. Thin shreds of light like metal foil were falling on the water and dissolving.

"Give me the straight story, Mavis. We don't have time to argue."

"Yes. The straight story." Her mouth closed over the words. Her face and body were tense, fighting off sleep. "I feel like a junkie, Archer. The morphine's getting me."

"Let's walk."

"No. We'll stay here. I have to get back to the boat soon. They don't know I'm gone."

I remembered the light that had gone on and off, and wondered.

But she had begun to talk in a steady flow of words, like a pentothal subject:

"I'm partly to blame for what happened. I did a sluttish thing, I suppose, and anyway I wasn't naïve when I married him. I'd been living on the fringes for too long, taking what I could get, waiting on tables, doing extra work and trying for a bit part. I met him at a party in Bel-Air last year. I was doing some modeling at the time, and I was paid to be at the party, but Kilbourne didn't know that, at least I don't think he did. Anyway, he took to me, and he was loaded with money, and I had lost my nerve, and I took to him. He wanted a hostess and a clothes-horse and a bed-companion and he bought me the way he'd buy a filly for his stable. We did the town for ten nights running and married in Palm Springs. We found out over the weekend that we didn't like each other at all. I asked him why he married me and he said that it was cheaper in the end. So I tortured his vanity: Kilbourne's colossally vain. I'd have let him alone if I'd known how nasty he could get.

"I found out later. In the meantime I had new toys to play with and no real kick coming. Then Patrick Ryan turned up last winter. He'd dated me during the war a couple of times, and I liked the guy. I met him at Ciro's one night. We ditched Kilbourne and I went home with Ryan. His place was horribly crummy, but he was good. He reminded me that even sex could be good, and I guess I fell in love with him in an unguarded moment." Her voice was breathless and dry. Her shoulder moved against me restlessly. "You asked for the straight story. It doesn't make me look nice."

"Nobody's straight story ever does. Go on."

"Yes." She leaned against me lightly, and I held her across the shoulders. Her bones were small and sharp in the rounded flesh. "We needed a chauffeur at the time; our old one had been picked up for violating parole. Kilbourne has a weakness for ex-convicts: he says they make faithful servants. I talked him into hiring Pat Ryan so I could have him around. I needed someone, and Pat said he loved me. We were going to run away together and start a new life somewhere. I guess where men are concerned I'm a lousy picker. I haven't told you about the pre-Kilbourne ones, and I don't intend to. Anyway, Kilbourne found out about us. Pat may have told him himself, to curry a little favor. So Kilbourne got me drunk one day and left me alone with Pat and hired a man to take pictures of us together. They were very pretty pictures. He ran them for me the next night, with running commentary, and I haven't got over it yet. I never will."

"But the pictures are gone now?"

"Yes. I destroyed them last night."

"He doesn't need the film to get a divorce."

"You don't understand," she said. "Divorce is not what he wants. I've begged him for a divorce every day for the last six months. He wanted to keep me under his fat thumb for the rest of his life, and that was his way of doing it. If I stepped out of line just once, he was going to let Rico sell the film for distribution. They'd be showing it for years at stag parties and conventions and after-hours nightclubs. My face is known. What could I do?"

"What you did. Does he know the film is gone?"

"I haven't told him. I don't know how he'll react. He could do anything."

"Then leave him. He can't touch you any more, if you're sure there was only one copy."

"There was only one copy. I made up to Rico one night and got that much out of him. But I'm afraid of Kilbourne." She didn't notice the contradiction: her feeling was too real.

"It's a bad habit you have."

"You don't know Kilbourne," she flared. "There's nothing he won't do, and he has the money and men to do it. He killed Pat last night—"

"Not over you, Mavis, though that might have helped. Maybe Kilbourne couldn't forget the pictures, either, but he had more reasons than that. Pat was working for Kilbourne, did you know that? Taking his money up to the day he died."

"No!"

"You still cared for Pat?"

"Not after he ran out on me. But he didn't deserve to die."

"Neither do you. You married one wrong one, and went to bed with another. Why don't you take yourself out of circulation for a while?"

"Stay with you?" She half-turned toward me and her right breast trembled against my arm.

"That's not what I mean. You wouldn't be safe with me. I have some friends in Mexico who are safe, and I'll put you on a plane."

"I don't know. I don't know what to do." Her voice wandered in the scale. Her skin in the growing light was blanched by fatigue. Her eyes moved uncertainly, huge and heavy and dark, with morphine dragging down hard on the lids.

She couldn't make a decision. I made it for her, hoisting her to her feet with my hands in her armpits. "You're going to Mexico. I'll stay at the airport with you till you can get a plane."

"You're nice, you're good to me." She lolled against me, clutching at my arms and sliding down my chest.

The first explosions of a choked motor barked and spluttered on the other side of the basin. The spluttering settled into a steady roar, and a speedboat rounded the stern of the yacht and headed for the pier. Its dark sharp prow cut like shears through the metal water. A man in the cockpit was watching me through binoculars. They made him look like a large goggle-eyed toad.

Mavis hung limp across my arm. I jerked her upright and shook her. "Mavis! We have to run for it." Her eyes came partly open, but showed only white.

I lifted her in both arms and took her up the gangway. A man in a striped linen suit and a washable linen hat was squatting on the pier near the top of the gangway. It was Melliotes. He straightened up, moved quickly to bar my way. He was built like a grand piano, low and wide, but his movements were light as a dancer's. Black eyes peered brightly from the gargoyle face.

I said: "Get out of my way."

"I don't think so. You turn around and go back down."

The girl in my arms sighed and stirred at the sound of his voice. I hated her as a man sometimes hates his wife, or a con his handcuffs. It was too late to run. The man in the linen suit had his right fist in his pocket, with something more than a fist pointed at me.

"Back down," he said.

The motor of the speedboat died behind me. I looked down and saw it coasting in to the landing platform. A blank-faced sailor turned from the wheel and jumped ashore with the painter. Kilbourne sat in the cockpit, looking complacent. A pair of binoculars hung on a strap around his thick neck, and a double-barreled shotgun lay across his knees.

I carried Mavis Kilbourne down to her waiting husband.

CHAPTER 21

The yacht's main cabin was dim and chilly. The early-morning light oozed weakly through the curtained ports and lay in glimmering pools on the built-in mahogany furniture. One bulkhead was almost covered by a photomural of the Acapulco cliffs, the Kilbourne yacht riding below them. Our feet were soundless as undertakers' on the thickly carpeted floor. Kilbourne went to the head of the table that occupied the center of the cabin, and sat down facing me.

"Sit down, Mr. Archer, sit down. Let me offer you some breakfast." He tried a genial smile, but the mouth and eyes were too small to carry it. The voice that issued from the great pink face was little and peevish and worried.

"I'd have to be hungrier than I am," I said.

"Well, if you'll excuse me, I'll have a bite myself." He glanced at the man in the linen suit, who was leaning against the hatch with a gun in his hand. "Melliotes, tell the steward I'll have breakfast. And let's have some light on the subject. I haven't had a good chance to look at our friend's face."

Melliotes switched on an overhead light, then leaned out through the hatch to talk to someone at the head of the ladder. I thought of making a break, and my knees tensed with the thought. But without a gun it was hopeless. And Mavis was lying unconscious in a berth just forward of the cabin. I couldn't run out on her: I hadn't been able to when I had a better chance. Anyway, this was where I wanted to be. Kilbourne was the man I had to talk to. I said it over to myself: this was where I wanted to be. If I said it often enough, maybe I could believe it.

There was a sharp thud at the other end of the table. Kilbourne had drawn my gun and placed it on the polished mahogany surface within reach of his hand. Tiny fingernails glistened like slivers of mica in the tips of his thick white fingers.

"You'll pardon this show of weapons, I hope. I'm very much a pacifist myself, but I understand you're quite the man of violence. I do hope you won't force us to use these ridiculous guns. Physical violence has always unsettled my stomach."

"You're lucky," I said. "Not everybody can afford to have his killings done for him."

Melliotes turned sharply and looked at me three-eyed. His own two eyes were dark and glowing. I preferred the gun's single eye. I couldn't stare it down, but it bore no malice.

"Please, Mr. Archer." Kilbourne raised his hand, dead white as a policeman's in a policeman's gesture. "You mustn't leap to rash conclusions before you know the truth of things. The truth is simpler than you suppose and really not at all sinister. I've had to take one or two extra-legal shortcuts, I admit, in order to protect my interests. If a man won't act to protect his own interests, he can't expect anyone else to. That's one of the home truths I learned when I was a two-for-a-quarter car salesman in Ypsilanti. I came up from small beginnings, you see. I don't propose to return to them."

"Your reminiscences fascinate me. May I take notes?"

"Please," he said again. "We share a mutual distrust, of course, but there's nothing more than distrust standing between us. If we could be perfectly frank with each other—"

"I'll be frank with you. It looks to me as if you hired Reavis to kill the elder Mrs. Slocum, then hired somebody else to kill off Reavis. If that's so, I'm not going to let you get by with it."

"The decision is out of your hands, isn't it?"

I noticed that the table, which was fastened to the deck, was trembling slightly under my forearms. Somewhere aft, the diesels were turning over. Forward, a rattling winch was reeling in the anchor. The screw turned in the water, and the whole craft shuddered.

"After murder," I said, "kidnapping comes easy." But I remembered what I had done to Reavis, and felt a twinge of hypocrisy. Remorse and fear mixed in my veins, and made a bitter blend.

"The correct term is 'shanghaied,'" Kilbourne said, with his first real smile. It was a close-mouthed smile of complacence. Like other self-educated men, he was vain of his vocabulary. "But let's get back to your allegations. You are less than half right. I had nothing whatever to do with the old lady's death. Ryan conceived the plan by himself, and executed it unaided."

"He was in your pay, and you stood to profit by her death."

"Precisely." His fingers clasped each other like mating worms. "You do understand the situation after all. Innocent as I was, I couldn't afford to have Ryan caught and questioned. I gave him money to escape. To that extent I confess I was an accessory to the crime. If Ryan had been brought to trial, I'd have been dragged in willy-nilly."

"So you had to have him silenced."

"Before the District Attorney could take a statement from him. Precisely. You see, in an atmosphere of candor, we *can* have a meeting of minds."

"There's one place we haven't met at all. You haven't explained the important thing: why Reavis wanted to kill her. What was he doing in Nopal Valley in the first place?"

"Let me sketch in the background." He leaned across the table with his hands still clasped in each other. I couldn't understand his eagerness to explain, but while it lasted I could use the explanations. "Ryan had been in my employ less than a year. He was my chauffeur, as a matter of fact, and did one or two other small tasks for me." The shrewd little eyes went blank and imbecile for a moment, as they surveyed the past and Ryan's part in it. In the alcove out of sight, his wife was snoring gently and rhythmically.

A fine American marriage, I said to myself. There wasn't much doubt that Kilbourne himself had hired Pat to make love to his wife.

"Early this year," he continued, "it became inconvenient, for various reasons, to have Ryan as a member of my household. Still, I didn't want to lose touch with him entirely. I have enemies, of course, and Ryan might have become their willing tool. I put him on the company payroll and cast about for a place to use him. As you probably know, I'd had business dealings with the late Mrs. Slocum. You may not know, however, that before the deal broke down I spent nearly a hundred thousand dollars in the exploration of her property. It occurred to me that it might be desirable to have a representative in her home as a partial protection for my investment. If other groups that are interested in the valley made overtures to her, I'd be in a position to know. So I arranged for Ryan's employment by the Slocums as their chauffeur. I had no idea he'd take his responsibilities so very seriously." He raised both hands and smacked them flat on the table. Beneath the sleeves of his blue flannel jacket, the flesh on his forearms quivered for some time.

"Are you sure you had no idea?" I said. "You must have known he was a psychopath, capable of anything."

"No, I did not. I believed him to be harmless." His voice was earnest. "Now don't misunderstand me. I'm not pretending to be free from blame. In a moral sense I know I'm responsible for her death. There may even have been an occasion when, thinking out loud in Ryan's presence, I voiced a wish for her death. I believe there was an occasion of that sort a few weeks ago. In any case, Ryan knew that her continued presence on the scene was costing me hundreds of dollars a day."

"Why split hairs? He was working for you. You wanted her killed. He killed her."

"But I did not incite him to murder. Never, at any time. If I were planning a murder, Ryan is the last man I'd choose as my agent. He was a talker, and I didn't trust him."

That made sense to me. His whole story made sense, in a crazy way. Against my will and my better judgment, I caught myself half believing it.

"If you didn't tell him to kill her, why did he do it?"

"I'll tell you why." He leaned toward me again and narrowed his eyes. The upper eyelids hung in thick overlapping folds. The eyes themselves were of indeterminate color, dull and opaque as unpolished stones. "Ryan saw an opportunity to tap me for a very great deal of money. What seemed to him, at least, a very great deal. By killing Mrs. Slocum he placed me in jeopardy along with himself. His jeopardy was also mine. I had to help him out of it, and he knew it. Now he didn't admit as much when he came to me the night before last, but that certainly was in his mind. He asked for ten thousand dollars, and I had to give it to him. When he was careless enough to allow himself to be captured, I had to take other measures. I'd have been wiser to have him shot in the first place, but my humane impulses deterred me. In the end my hand was forced. So while I can't claim that my motives in this sorry business were wholly pure, neither have they been entirely black."

"Sometimes," I said, "I like a good solid black better than mottled gray."

"You don't have my responsibilities, Mr. Archer. A great company depends on me. A single misstep on my part can destroy the livelihood of thousands of people."

"I wonder if you're that important," I said. "I think life would go on without you."

"That isn't the point at issue." He smiled as if he'd uttered a witticism. "The point is whether life can go on without *you*. I've gone to a good deal of trouble to explain my position. I've hoped that if you understood it, you'd take a somewhat different attitude toward me. You're an intelligent man, Mr. Archer, and, to be frank, I like you. Also, I abhor killing, as I've told you. There's the further fact that my wife seems to admire you, and if I were to have you put away she'd certainly be aware of it and perhaps even try to make trouble. I can deal with her, of course. I can even endure the thought of another death, if you prove its necessity to me. But I'd so much rather handle this thing in a rational, urbane way. Wouldn't you?"

"I'll listen. How much?"

"Good. Fine." The little mouth curled upwards like a cherub's. "I believe you have ten thousand dollars of mine. I don't know for sure, but it stands to reason, doesn't it? If you were to admit that you have it, it would be very valuable proof of your good faith."

"I have it," I said, "out of your reach."

"Keep it. It's yours." He waved his hand in a fat and royal gesture.

"What do I do for it?"

"Nothing. Nothing whatever. I'll put you ashore at San Pedro and you can simply forget that I ever existed at all. Take up your own affairs again, or go for a long vacation and enjoy yourself."

"I have the money now."

"But not the means to enjoy it. That is still in my gift."

The yacht was beginning to pitch and roll in the open sea. I glanced at the man in the linen suit, still stationed by the door with his three eyes on me. His legs were wide and braced against the vessel's movement. The gun was steady. While my glance was on it, he shifted it from one hand to the other.

"You can relax, Melliotes," Kilbourne said. "We're well away from shore." He turned back to me: "Well, Mr. Archer, will you accept the gift of freedom on those terms?"

"I'll think about it."

"I have no wish to hurry you. Your decision is an important one, to both of us." Then his face lit up like a man's who has heard his sweetheart's footsteps: "My breakfast, I do believe."

It came on a silver tray that was almost too wide for the hatchway. The white-jacketed mulatto steward was sweating under its weight. Kilbourne greeted each dish separately as the metal covers were lifted. Next to Walter Kilbourne, food was his one true love.

He ate with a gobbling passion. A piece of ham and four eggs, six pieces of toast; a kidney and a pair of mountain trout; eight pancakes with eight small sausages; a quart of raspberries, a pint of cream, a quart of coffee. I watched him the way you watch the animals at the zoo, hoping he'd choke to death and settle things for both of us.

He leaned back in his chair at last and told the steward to take the empty dishes away.

"Well, Mr. Archer?" The white fingers crawled through his thin pink curls. "What is your decision?"

"I haven't thought it through yet. One thing, how do you know you can trust me?"

"I don't know that I can. Rather than have your blood on my hands, I'm willing to take a certain amount of risk. But I do think I can recognize an honest man when I see one. That ability is the foundation of my success, to be perfectly frank." His voice was still thick with the passion of eating.

"There's a contradiction in your thinking," I said. "If I took your dirty money, you wouldn't be able to trust my honesty."

"But you have my dirty money now, Mr. Archer. You secured it through your own alert efforts. No further effort on your part is required, except that I presume you'll scour it thoroughly before you spend it. Of course I realize how foolish I would be to place my whole dependence on your honesty, or any man's. I'd naturally expect you to sign a receipt for it, indicating the nature of the services rendered."

"Which were?"

"Exactly what you did. A simple notation, 'For capture and delivery of Pat Ryan,' will suffice. That will kill two birds with one stone. It will cancel out my payment to Ryan, which is the only real evidence against me in Mrs. Slocum's death. And more important, it will protect me in case your honesty should ever falter, and the murder of Pat Ryan come to trial."

"I'll be an accessory before the fact."

"A very active one. Precisely. You and I will be in the position of having to co-operate with each other."

I caught the implication. I watched it grow in my mind into a picture of myself five years, ten years later, doing dirty errands for Walter Kilbourne and not being able to say no. My gorge rose.

But I answered him very reasonably: "I can't stick my neck out that far. There were half a dozen men involved in Ryan's death. If any of them talks, that tears it open."

"Not at all. Only one of them had any connection with me."

"Schmidt."

The eyebrows ascended his forehead like surprised pink caterpillars. "You know Schmidt? You are active indeed."

"I know him well enough to stay clear of his company. If the police put a finger on him, and they will, he'll break down and spill everything."

"I am aware of that." The cherub mouth smiled soothingly. "Fortunately, you can set your mind at rest. Oscar Schmidt went out with the tide this morning. Melliotes took care of him for all of us."

The man in the linen suit was sitting on the leather bench that lined the after bulkhead. He showed his

teeth in a white and happy smile and stroked the
fluted barrel of his gun.

"Remarkable," I said. "Ryan takes care of Mrs. Slocum. Schmidt takes care of Ryan. Melliotes takes care
of Schmidt. That's quite a system you have."

"I'm very pleased that you like it."

"But who takes care of Melliotes?"

Kilbourne looked from me to the gunman, whose
mouth was expressionless again, and back to me. For
the first time our interests formed a triangle, which
relieved me of some pressure.

"You ask very searching questions," he replied. "I
owe it to your intelligence to inform you that Melliotes took care of himself several years ago. A young
girl of my acquaintance, one of my employees to be
exact, disappeared in Detroit. Her body turned up in
the Detroit River a few days later. A certain un-
licensed medical practitioner who shall be nameless
was wanted for questioning. I was on my way to
California at the time, and I offered him a lift in my
private plane. Does that answer your question?"

"It does. I wanted to know exactly what I was
being offered a piece of. Now that I know, I don't
want it."

He looked at me incredulously. "You don't seriously
mean that you want to die?"

"I expect to outlive you," I said. "You're a little too
smart to have me bumped before you recover your
thousand-dollar bills. That money really worries you,
doesn't it?"

"The money means nothing to me. Look, Mr. Archer, I am prepared to double the amount." He brought
a gold-cornered wallet out of an inside pocket and
dealt ten bills onto the table. "But twenty thousand is
my absolute limit."

"Put your money away. I don't want it."

"I warn you," he said more sharply, "your bargain-
ing position is weak. One reaches a point of diminish-
ing returns, where it would be cheaper and more
convenient to have you killed."

I looked at Melliotes. His glowing eyes were on

Kilbourne. He hefted the gun in his hand, and asked a question with his knitted black eyebrows.

"No," Kilbourne said to him. "What is it that you want, if not money, Mr. Archer? Women perhaps, or power, or security? I could find a place in my organization for a man that I can trust. I wouldn't waste my words on you, frankly, if I didn't happen to like you."

"You can't trust me," I said, though the fear of death had dried my lips and tightened the muscles of my throat.

"That's precisely what I like about you. You have a certain stubborn honesty—"

"I don't like you," I said. Or maybe I croaked it.

Kilbourne's face was expressionless, but his white fingers plucked petulantly at each other. "Melliotes. We'll give Mr. Archer a little longer to make up his mind. Do you have your pacifier?"

The man in the linen suit stood up in eager haste. His brown hand flicked into a pocket and came out dangling a polished leather thing like an elongated pear. It moved in the air too fast for me to avoid it.

CHAPTER 22

I was walking in the gravel bed of a dry river. Gravel-voiced parrots cawed and flew in the stiff painted air. A girl went by me on silent feet, her golden hair blown out behind by her movement. I stumbled after her on my knees and she looked back and laughed. She had Mavis's face, but her laugh cawed like the parrots. She entered a dark cave in the bank of the dry river. I followed her gleaming hair into the darkness.

When she turned for a second laughing look, her face was Gretchen Keck's, and her mouth was stained with blood. We were in a hotel corridor as interminable as time. Little puffs of dust rose from her feet as she moved. The dust stank of death in my nostrils.

I picked my way after her through the debris that littered the threadbare carpet. Old photographs and newspaper clippings and black-edged funeral announcements, used condoms and love letters tied with pink ribbon, ashes and cigarette butts brown and white, empty whisky bottles, dried sickness and dried blood, cold half-eaten meals on greasy plates. Behind the numbered doors there were shrieks and groans and giggles, and howls of ecstasy and howls of pain. I looked straight ahead, hoping none of the doors would open.

The girl paused at the final door and turned again: it was Cathy Slocum, beckoning me. I followed her into the jasmine-scented room. The woman lay on the bed under a black police tarp. I drew it back from her face and saw the foam.

Someone fumbled at the door behind me. I crossed the room to the casement window and flung it open. The doorlatch clicked. I looked back over my shoulder at the charred featureless face. I said I didn't do it. The calcined man walked towards me, his footsteps soft as ashes. I leaned far out of the window and looked down: far down in the street, the cars marched in antlike procession. I let myself go, fell into wakefulness.

The blood was pounding in my brain like heavy surf on a deserted beach. I was lying on my back on something neither hard nor soft. I raised my head, and a lightning flash of pain blazed in my eyeballs. I tried to move my hands; they wouldn't move. My fingers were in contact with something coarse and damp and insentient. I lay still for a while, hoping the coarse numb surface wasn't my own skin. Cold sweat tickled the sides of my face.

There was yellow light in the room, which came from a high wire-netted window in the canvas-covered wall. I looked down at my immobilized arms and saw that they were bound in a brown canvas straitjacket. My legs were free; not even trousers covered them, but I still had my shoes on. I drew them up and rocked myself to a sitting position on the edge of the cot. A bolt snapped back, and I stood up facing the leather-padded door as it swung open.

Melliotes came into the room. A tiny gray-haired woman loitered behind him. He was wearing white duck trousers and a white Mediterranean smile. Black curling hair like persian lamb covered his naked torso from collarbone to navel. The insteps of his bare feet had a growth of thick black fur.

"Well, well. Good morning again. I hope you enjoyed your rest." His grimace parodied the genial host.

"Your accommodations are lousy. Take this off." I

was ashamed of my voice, which came out thin and dry.

"It wouldn't be very modest to take it off." He looked down at the little woman. "He should have *something* on in the presence of ladies. Isn't that right, Miss Macon?"

She wore a white nurse's uniform. The top of her gray cropped head came just above his waist. Her owlish eyes smiled up into his glowing black ones, and she giggled.

I aimed my head at the hairy abdomen, and rushed him. His feet skipped lightly aside like a matador's. His knee caught the side of my head and caromed me against the padded wall. I sat down on the floor and got up again. The little woman giggled:

"He's violent, doctor. Acts like a mental all right, don't he?"

"We know how to deal with him, Miss Macon." To me he said: "We know how to deal with you."

I said: "Take this off." When I closed my mouth, my back teeth ground together of their own accord.

"I don't see how I can. You're in a disturbed condition. It's my responsibility to keep you out of mischief for a while, until you grow calmer."

She leaned against his thigh, twisting her miniature hand in his canvas belt and looking up admiringly at the source of such fine talk.

"I've killed one man," I said. "I think you'll be the second."

"Listen to him," she simpered. "He's homicidal all right."

"I'll tell you what I think," Melliotes said. "I think a hydro treatment would do him a world of good. Shall we give him one, Miss Macon?"

"Let's."

"We'll give you a hydro treatment," he said between the smile.

I stood where I was, my back against the wall.

He took a bunch of keys from the keyhole and struck me with them sharply across the face.

"You'll be the second," I said.

He swung the keys again. I lost the beat of time in their harsh jangling. The lightning blazed ferociously in my head. A drop of blood crawled down my face, leaving a wet snail track.

"Come along," he said, "while you can see to come along."

I went along. To a room like a burial vault, white-tiled, windowless and cold. The morning light fell through a skylight in the twelve-foot ceiling and gleamed on a row of chromium faucets and nozzles along one wall. He held me by the shoulders while the woman unbuckled the straps across my back. I tried to bite his hands. He jangled the keys.

He pulled the jacket off me and tossed it to the woman. She caught it, rolled it up and stood against the door with the bundle clasped in her arms. There was a gleeful little waiting smile on her face, the smile of a baby that had not been born.

I looked down at my arms. White and shrunken, they were unbending slowly like snakes in the early spring. A ram of water hit me, flung me onto the tiled floor and rolled me against the wall. I sat up gasping. Above the roar of the water, the woman let out a laugh of childish pleasure.

Melliotes was leaning easily against the opposite wall. Waterdrops glistened like dew in his personal thicket. One of his hands held a nozzle attached to a white rubber hose. The other rested on a chromium wheel in the wall. Cold water gushed in my face.

I moved toward him on hands and knees, sideways, with my face averted. Water rushed under me and laid me on my back. I twisted onto my feet and jumped for him, was stopped in midair and dropped, forced back to the wall. I stood up again.

He took another nozzle from its hook, sighted along it like a sharpshooter. "Look at this one," he said. "My prettiest fountain."

A tiny stream of water sprang across the room and stung my chest. When I looked down, a six-inch letter M was printed in red on my skin, oozing droplets of blood.

"Speaking of killing, as you were," he said, "this little fountain will kill."

I moved across the room and got one hand on his throat. He shook me off and I staggered, almost too weak to stand. The heavier stream of water pounded me back to the wall.

"It will kill," he said. "It will blind."

"Do it to him," Macon said, with girlish whinny-ings.

"I'd like to. But remember we have to stay on the right side of the law." He said it seriously.

The water took my legs from under me, rapped my head on the wall. I lay where I fell until the door slammed shut and the key turned in the lock. Then I sat up. My chest and stomach were covered with red welts turning blue. And I was wearing his monogram.

The door was made of white enameled steel tightly fitted into the frame. It opened outwards but was knobless on my side. I hit it twice with my shoulder and gave up.

The skylight was frosted glass reinforced with wire netting. But it was a good twelve feet off the floor, beyond the reach of any human leap. I tried climbing the wall by way of the taps and nozzles. All that got me was a shower-bath I didn't need. I closed the tap I had accidentally opened and watched the water with loathing. It ran into a central depression in the floor, where it was caught by a drain. The drain was covered by a circular metal screen. The screen lifted out when I got my fingernails under it. I squatted over the four-inch pipe which was the only way out, and wished I was a sewer rat. A soggy idea moved in my head like a half-drowned animal.

There was another way out of the white room. It was hermetically sealed, built to hold water. If I could fill it with water, I might be able to float myself up to the skylight. A dangerous experiment, but not so dangerous as staying where I was, waiting for Melliotes to think of other games. The first thing I had to do was plug the drain.

I took off my shoes and socks and crammed the toe

of one shoe into the opening, wadding the socks around it. Then I turned all the taps on full. Water hissed and gushed and splattered from the wall. I dodged it as well as I could; Melliotes had given me a bad case of hydrophobia. Standing in the furthest corner, I watched the water creep up over my ankles, up to my knees, all the way up to my waist. In fifteen or twenty minutes I was afloat.

It was pleasantly warm, and I gradually lost my fear of it. I lay on my back and waited for the ceiling to come closer. When I raised my head, I could hear the trapped air hissing out through the cracks around the skylight. After a long time, during which I rose surely and imperceptibly with the water, I was close enough to the ceiling to reach it with my hand.

I trod water and swung a fist at the skylight. Without intending to I pulled the punch; if my fist went through I knew I'd mangle my hand. The blow cracked the reinforced glass but rebounded ineffectually.

I took some deep breaths and dove for one of my shoes. The water was clear and still except where the incoming streams bubbled and tumbled from the nozzles in the wall. A shaft of sun angled down from the skylight and turned the liquid mass to a cube of pale green light. I stroked along the floor and got my hands on the extra shoe. My ears were aching from the pressure of tons of water above me.

There was a sudden movement in the water, a tremor and vibration that turned my stomach over. Something I hadn't counted on was happening to my plan; it looked as if I'd cleverly arranged to die like a rat in a well. I started for the taps to turn them off. But first my lungs needed air and there wasn't much left at the top. With the shoe in my hand I gathered my legs for the upward push.

Another tremor shook the water and me. A metallic crackling sounded from the direction of the door. It had been built to hold water, but not an entire roomful of the stuff. As I turned in swimmer's slow-motion the white door bellied out like a sail and disappeared

in a churning rush and welter. The released weight of
the water pushed me after it. My free hand reached
for something to hold on to, and closed on liquid
nothing.

I was swept through the empty doorway, banged
against the opposite wall of the corridor, somersaulted
along it. I caught a door-frame with one hand and
held on while the water tore at me. The current
slowed almost as suddenly as it had begun, and the
level of the water subsided. I found the floor and
braced myself in the doorway.

Melliotes was in the room with the woman. She
was struggling in the water, splashing with arms and
legs. He bent over her and lifted her in his arms. She
clambered on him, a hairless pink monkey gibbering
piteously. My shoe was still in my hand; it was a
Scotch walking shoe with an iron-shod heel, and I
used it on the back of Melliotes' head. He fell in the
shallow water with the woman clinging to him. Father chimpanzee and child.

I looked around the room. The woman's white uniform, an up-ended wastebasket, a scattered bunch of
flowers, papers and oddments of clothing, floated in
the ebbing tide. There was a white oak desk, a leather
armchair and couch, all marked by the water. A piece
of office stationery on the desk bore the letterhead: ANGEL OF MERCY NURSING HOME. HYDROTHERAPY
AND COLONIC IRRIGATION. PRIVATE ROOMS FOR PATIENTS.
DR. G. M. MELLIOTES, PROPRIETOR. A Venice address
and phone number.

The heavy red drapes at the window dragged sod-
denly. Through the slats of the Venetian blind I could
see a sunlit lawn bright with flowerbeds and
deckchairs. A thin old man in tropical cotton was
walking from one chair to another, if you could call it
walking. He moved erratically, in several directions at
once, as if the terminals of his nervous system had
been cut. Fortunately he was in good hands. The
Angel of Mercy Nursing Home could give him a permanent cure.

Something small and clammy and furious scratched

at my legs. I moved away from her. I didn't like to touch her.

"He's drowning," she cried. "I can't turn him over."

Melliotes was spreadeagled on the wet-dark carpet, his face in a puddle of water. I looked at the bloody back of his head and felt no pain. I took him by an arm and leg and flipped him over. The whites of his eyes were showing, threaded with red. His chest was heaving like a tired dog's.

The woman minced around the desk and opened a drawer. She came back toward me holding Melliotes' gun in both her hands. I didn't intend to die in that company, and I slapped it down. She growled in the back of her throat and hugged her meager breast with pipestem arms.

"I want my clothes," I said. "And put something on yourself. I can't stand the sight of you."

Her mouth opened and closed, opened and closed like a fish's. I picked up the gun and she did as she was told. She opened a closet door and pulled a cotton dress on over her head. My clothes were scrambled on the floor of the closet.

I waved the gun at the woman. "Now go away."

She went, with a backward look at the man on the floor. The pathos of their parting plucked at my heartstrings. I put on my clothes.

CHAPTER 23

The gun was a .38 calibre S. and W. revolver with a six-inch blue steel barrel, serial number 58237. I shoved it into the pocket of my jacket. Melliotes' striped linen coat was draped over a hanger in the closet. In its inside pocket, I found both my automatic and my wallet. I put them where they belonged and made for the door. Melliotes' breathing had slowed down, but he was still sleeping the sleep of the sapped.

My shoes squished on the floor of the corridor. There were heavy doors on either side, all of them closed and locked. The hallway was as dim and ugly as the one in my dream. The only light came from a curtained door at the far end. I had it open and one foot on the porch when someone cried out behind me. It was a woman's cry, muffled by thick sound-proofed walls. I went back into the building.

"Let me out." The consonants were blurred and only the vowels came through: "Lemmeow," like a hurt cat's yowling. "Pleaslemmeow."

The cry was louder at one door than at the others. When I shook that door, the woman said: "Who is it? Let me out." Mavis again. My heart sank into my boots and bounced back into my throat. The burnt child can't stay away from the fire.

I said under my breath, "To hell with you, Mavis," but these were only words.

What I did was go back to Melliotes and take his keys and try them on the door till I found the one that opened it. Mavis stood back and looked at me, then moved into my arms with a little tearing sigh. "Archer. You came."

"I've been here for some time. I seem to be fairy-godfather-in-residence."

"Anyway, you're here."

She walked backward into the room and sat down weakly on the cot. It was a cell much the same as the one that I had occupied, complete with wire-screened window and padded walls. The angels of mercy took good care of their patients.

"What kind of a clientele does Melliotes have? The wet-sheet set?"

Pale and distraught, she looked a little mental herself. She moved her head back and forth, and her eyes swung back and forth as if by their own great weight. "I've never been here before." And in the same tone, quiet and forlorn: "I'm going to kill him." There were flakes of dried blood on her lower lip where she had bitten it.

"There's been too much killing already. Buck up, Mavis. This time you're going to Mexico for sure."

She leaned forward blindly, her small head against my thigh. Her hair parted at the nape and fell forward around her face like two bright wings. From that hiding place she whispered: "If you'll go with me."

We were back where we had left off. The yacht and the water-chamber, Kilbourne and Melliotes, were characters and scenes in a morphine dream. I remembered the fire-blunted features of Pat Reavis, and backed away from her. "I'll go as far as the airport with you. I'll even buy you a ticket, one-way."

"I'm afraid to go by myself." Her voice was a wisp, but her eyes were bright behind the web of hair.

I said that I was afraid to go along. She stood up suddenly and stamped one high-arched foot on the hard composition floor. "What's the matter, Archer, have you got a girl somewhere?"

She was a very bad actress, and I was embarrassed. "I wish I had."

She stood in front of me with her arms akimbo and accused me of *impotentia coeundi*. Those weren't the words she used.

I said: "Men have been spoiling you since grade school, haven't they? But there's no percentage in standing here calling names. In just two minutes I'm walking out of here. You can come along if you like. As far as the airport."

"As far as the airport," she mimicked me. "I thought you liked me."

"I like you. But I have two good reasons for staying clear. One, what happened to Reavis. Two, the case on my hands."

"I thought you were working for me?"

"I work for myself."

"Anyway, aren't I the best part of the case?"

I said: "The whole is always greater than the parts."

But I didn't hear the sound of my own voice. A car door slammed somewhere, and footsteps scraped on concrete, growing louder. Somebody heavy and fast was coming up the walk. She heard the sounds and froze: a nymph on an urn.

I drew my gun and sighted down the corridor. The curtained front door was standing slightly ajar the way I had left it. A shadow rose on the curtain, the screen door creaked. I stepped back into the room and examined the clip of my automatic. It was full, and the cartridge was still in the chamber. The footsteps approached the open doorway of the room we were in, lagging slower each time.

Mavis's fingers bit into my shoulder. "Who is it?"

"Be quiet."

But the heavy feet had stopped. They moved indecisively, and retreated. I stepped out into the corridor. Kilbourne was waddling rapidly toward the open front door.

I said, "Stand," and shot at the wall beside him. The bullet tore a six-inch gash in the plaster, and halted him in his tracks.

He turned slowly, his hands ascending under hydraulic pressure. He was wearing a Homburg and a fresh dark suit with a mottled pink carnation in the lapel. His face was the same mottled pink. "Melliotes was right," he said. "I shouldn't have let you live."

"You've made a lot of mistakes. There are hundreds of people still living—"

The car door closed again, almost inaudibly. I handed the blue revolver to the woman behind me. "Can you use it?"

"Yes."

"Take him into the room and keep him there."

"Yes."

I elbowed Kilbourne out of my way, ran for the front door and slid behind it. A man ran up to the porch, the breath in his ruined nose like a fanfare of trumpets. When Kilbourne's chauffeur came through the door I hooked his shins with my toe. He went down heavily on hands and knees, and I poleaxed him with the butt of my forty-five. The screen door slammed.

Its echo came back to me from the far end of the corridor, amplified to a heavy gun's explosion.

She met me in the doorway, empty-handed. "I had to do it," she chattered. "He tried to take it away from me. He would have shot us both."

"Leave me out of it."

"It's true, he was going to kill me." The parrot screech of hysteria drowned out Mavis. She looked at her hands as if they were evil white birds. A wicked magician named Kilbourne had attached them to her by witchcraft.

Kilbourne was reclining on the floor, one heavy shoulder propped against the cot. A mound of flesh expensively dressed for death, with a single flower which he had bought for himself. A darker carnation blossomed in one eye-socket. Melliotes' gun lay across his lap.

"Will you take me to the airport?" she said. "Now?"

"Not now." I was feeling the flaccid puffed wrist. "You always do the wrong thing, beautiful."

"Is he dead?"

"Everybody is dying."

"I'm glad. But take me away from here. He's horrible."

"You should have thought of that a minute ago."

"Don't uncle me, for God's sake. Take me away."

I looked at her and thought of Acapulco. The fine warm fishing waters and the high sea-cliffs and the long slow tequila nights. Ten million dollars and Mavis, and all I had to do was a little fixing.

It went past the secret eye of my mind like a movie that had been made a long time ago. All I had to do was take it out of the can and dub in dialogue. Not even dialogue was necessary. The chauffeur had been knocked out before the shot. Melliotes was unconscious. And the slug in Kilbourne's brain was from his gun. Mavis and I could walk out of there and wait for the will to be probated.

I took a long hard look at her full body and her empty face. I left it in the can.

She saw my intention before I spoke. "You're not going to help me, are you?"

"You're pretty good at helping yourself," I said. "Not good enough, though. I could cover up for you, but you'd let something slip when the men from the District Attorney's office came around. It would be first degree then, and I'd be in it."

"You're worried about your own damned scrawny neck."

"I only have the one."

She changed the approach. "My husband didn't make a will. Do you know how much money he has? Had."

"Better than you do, probably. You can't spend it when you're dead or in the pen."

"No, you can't. But you're willing to send me there." Her mouth drooped in self-pity.

"Not for long, probably not at all. You can cop a

manslaughter plea, or stick to self-defense. With the kind of lawyers you can buy, you won't spend a night in jail."

"You're lying to me."

"No." I stood up facing her. "I wish you well."

"If you really wished me well, you'd take me out of here. We could go away together. Anywhere."

"I've thought of that, too. No go."

"Don't you want me?" She was distressed and puzzled. "You said I was beautiful. I could make you happy, Lew."

"Not for the rest of my life."

"You don't know," she said, "you haven't tried me."

I felt ashamed for her. Ashamed for myself. The Acapulco movie stirred like a brilliant snake at the back of my mind.

"There's a phone in Melliotes' office," I said. "You call the police. It's better, if you're going to plead self-defense."

She burst into tears, stood sobbing violently with her mouth open and her eyes tight closed. Her wild urchin grief was more touching than any of her poses. When she groped for something to cry on, I gave her my shoulder. And eased her down the corridor to the telephone.

CHAPTER 24

The studio guard was a big ex-cop wrapped in crisp cellophane refinement. He leaned toward the hole in his plate-glass window. "Who was that you wanted to see?"

"Mildred Fleming. She's secretary to one of the producers or directors."

"Oh yes. Miss Fleming. One moment if you please." He talked into the phone at his elbow, looked up with question-mark eyebrows: "Miss Fleming wants to know who it is."

"Lewis Archer. Tell her Maude Slocum sent me."

"Who sent you?"

"Maude Slocum." The name had unexpected reverberations in my interior.

He talked into the telephone again and came up smiling. "Miss Fleming will be with you shortly. Have a seat, Mr. Armature."

I took a chromium chair in a far corner of the big, airy lobby. I was the only living person on the secular side of the plate glass, but the walls were populated by giant photographs. The studio's stars and featured players looked down on me from a lofty unreal world where everyone was young and hugely gay. One of the bright-haired fillies reminded me of Mavis; one of the dark young stallions could have been Pat Ryan thoroughly groomed and equipped with porcelain teeth. But Pat was huddled somewhere on a slab. Mavis was at the Hall of Justice talking to her lawyers about bail bond. The happy endings and the biggest oranges were the ones that California saved for export.

A short woman in a flame-colored blouse came through a plate-glass door that shut and locked itself behind her. Her short bobbed hair was blue-black and fitted her small head like a coat of Chinese lacquer. Her eyes, dark brown and experienced, carried a little luggage underneath.

I stood up and met her as she came toward me, her girdle-sheathed body moving with quick nervous energy. "Miss Fleming? I'm Archer."

"Hello." She gave me a firm cold hand. "I thought Al said your name was Armature."

"He did."

"I'm glad it isn't. We had an assistant director called Mr. Organic once, but nobody could take him seriously. He changed his name to Goldfarb and did right well for himself." Her rate of speech was a hundred words a minute, timed to the typewriter in her head. "Al also said Maude sent you, or is that another of his famous blunders?"

"He said that, but it isn't exactly true."

The smiling crinkle left her eyes, and they raked me up and down in a hard once-over. I was glad I'd changed to a fresh suit on the way from the Hall of Justice. In five or ten years she'd still remember the pattern of my tie, be able to pick my picture from a rogues' gallery.

"Well," she said with hostility, "you tell me what you're selling and I'll tell you how much I don't want whatever it is. I'm busy, brother, you shouldn't *do* these things."

"I sell my services."

"Oh, no, not that!" She was a natural clown.

"I'm a private detective. I worked for Mrs. Slocum until last night."

"Doing what?"

"Investigating. A certain matter."

"It's funny she didn't tell me." She was interested again. "I saw her at lunch the day before yesterday. What happened last night, she fire you?"

"No. She resigned."

"I don't get you." But she understood the finality of my tone. Emotion flowed into her eyes as dark as ink.

"She committed suicide last night," I said.

Mildred Fleming sat down suddenly, perched stiffly on the edge of a green plastic settee. "You're kidding."

"She's dead all right."

"Why in God's name?" Some tears spilled out of her eyes and coursed down her cheeks, eroding the heavy makeup. She wiped them with a ball of crumpled kleenex. "Excuse me. I happened to be pretty fond of the girl. Ever since high school."

"I liked her too. It's why I want to talk to you."

She moved like a hummingbird, toward the outside door. "Come on across the street. I'll buy you a coffee."

The drugstore on the opposite corner contained everything a drugstore should except a pharmacy. Newspapers and magazines, motion picture projectors and pogo sticks, sunglasses and cosmetics and bathing suits, and twenty assorted specimens of human flotsam watching the door for a familiar face. There was a lunch bar at the rear, with booths along the wall, most of them empty in the afternoon lull.

Mildred Fleming slipped into one of the booths and held up two fingers to the waitress behind the counter. The waitress came running with two heavy mugs, and fussed over my companion.

"Silly girl," she said when the waitress had bounced away. "She thinks I've got a pull. Nobody's got a pull any more." She leaned across the scarred table, sipping at her coffee. "Now tell me about poor Maude. Without coffee, I couldn't take it."

I had come to her for information, but first I told her what I thought was fit for her to know. What water had done to Olivia Slocum, what fire had done to Ryan, what strychnine had done to Maude. I left out Kilbourne and Mavis, and what they had done to each other.

She took it calmly, except that toward the end she needed her makeup more. She didn't say a word, till I mentioned Knudson and the fact that he had run me out ot town.

"You shouldn't pay too much attention to what he said. I can imagine how he feels. I don't know whether I should tell you this—"

"You don't have to tell me. Knudson loved her, it was pretty obvious."

I was probing for a gap in her defenses. Most good secretaries had an occupational weakness: they gathered inside information and after they had gathered it they had to tell it to somebody.

She was piqued. "If you know the whole story already, why come to me?"

"I know damn little. I don't know who drowned Olivia Slocum or why Maude Slocum took strychnine. I came to you because you're her closest friend. I figured you had a right to know what happened and that you'd want to help me get to the bottom of it."

She was gratified. "I *do* want to help you. I've always been in Maude's confidence, and I can tell you she's had a tragic life." She called for more coffee, and turned back to me: "As far as her mother-in-law is concerned, didn't you say that this man Pat Ryan killed her?"

"That's Knudson's theory, and most of the evidence supports it. I've taken an option on it, but I haven't bought it yet."

"You don't think Maude—?" Her eyes shone blackly in the dim booth.

"I do not."

"I'm glad you don't. Anyone that knew her would tell you she couldn't hurt anyone. She was a gentle creature, in spite of everything."

"Everything?"

"Her whole damned messy life. Everything that made her want to suicide."

"You know why she did it then?"

"I guess I do, at that. She was crucified for fifteen years. She's the one woman I've ever known that wanted to do the right thing and couldn't make it. Everything about Maude was right except her life. She made a couple of mistakes that she couldn't wipe out. I'll tell you on one condition. Do you have a word of honor?"

"I have a word. I was an officer in the war, but the gentleman part didn't take."

The stern sharp glance raked me again. "I think I'd trust you as far as I would myself, no further. Give me your word that Cathy will never hear this, and that it won't affect Cathy in any way."

I guessed what she was going to tell me. "I can't do that if other people know it."

"Nobody but me," she said. "And Knudson, of course, and maybe Knudson's wife."

"So Knudson has a wife."

"He hasn't lived with her for fifteen or sixteen years, but they're still married, for keeps. She'll never divorce him, no matter what he does. She hates him. I guess she hates everyone in the world. She's going to be glad to hear that Maude killed herself."

"You know the woman, do you?"

"Do I know her! I lived in her house for nearly a year, and I know her better than I want to. Eleanor Knudson is one of these hard righteous women who wouldn't donate two pennies to close a dead man's eyes. Maude lived there too, we were room-mates: that's how the whole thing started. We were in our sophomore year at Berkeley."

"Mrs. Knudson ran a boarding house in Berkeley?"

"A rooming house for girls. Her husband was a sergeant with the Oakland police. She was older than he was; I never figured out how she managed to hook him. Probably the usual landlady-roomer business: propinquity and maternal care and more propinquity. She had brains and she wasn't bad-looking if you like the cold-steel type. Anyway, she and Ralph Knudson had been married for several years when we moved in."

"You and Maude, you mean?"

"Yes. We'd taken our freshman year in the Teachers' College in Santa Barbara, but we couldn't stay there. We both had to work our way through school, and there wasn't enough work in Santa Barbara. Maude's father was a rancher in Ventura—that's where we went to high school, in Ventura—but the depression had wiped him out. My father was dead and my mother couldn't help me. She was having a hard enough time supporting herself in 'thirty-two. So Maudie and I moved on to the big city. We both knew typing and shorthand and we made a go of it, doing public stenography and typing dissertations. Living was cheap in those days. We paid Mrs. Knudson ten dollars a month for our room, and did our own cooking. We even managed to get to some of our classes."

"I was around in those days," I said.

She supped the dregs of her coffee and lit a cigarette, regarding me somberly through the smoke. "They were wonderful sad days. There were lines a mile long at the mission soup-kitchens in San Francisco and Oakland, but we were going to be career girls and set the Bay on fire. I've realized since then that it was all my idea. Maudie just went along because I needed her. She had more brains than me, and more goodness. The pure female type, you know? All she really wanted was a husband and a home and a chance to raise some decent kids like herself. So she got herself tangled up with a man who could never marry her as long as he lived. As long as Eleanor Knudson lived, anyway. I watched it happen and couldn't do a thing to stop it. They were made for each other, Maudie and Ralph, like in the love stories. He was all man and she was all woman and his wife was a frigid bitch. They couldn't live in the same house without falling in love with each other."

"And making music together?"

"Damn your eyes!" she spat out suddenly. "You've

got a lousy attitude. It was the real thing, see. She was twenty and proud, she'd never gone with a man. He was the man for her and she was the woman for him. They were like Adam and Eve; it wasn't Maudie's fault he was married already. She went into it blind as a baby, and so did he. It just happened. And it was real," she insisted. "Look how it lasted."

"I have been looking."

She stirred uncomfortably, shredding her cigarette butt in her small hard fingers. "I don't know why I'm telling you these things. What do they mean to you? Is somebody paying you?"

"Maude gave me two hundred dollars; that's all gone by now. But once I'm in a case I sort of like to stay through to the end. It's more than curiosity. She must have died for a reason. I owe it to her or myself to find out the reason, to see the whole thing clear."

"Ralph Knudson knows the reasons. Eleanor Knudson knows: hell, it was her idea in a way. Maude had to spend her good years with a man she didn't love, and I guess she simply got sick of it."

"What do you mean, she had to marry Slocum?"

"You haven't given me your word," she said. "About Cathy."

"You don't have to worry about Cathy. I feel sorry for the girl. I wouldn't touch her."

"I suppose it doesn't matter a hell of a lot after all. James Slocum must have known she wasn't his child. They said she was a seven-months' baby, but Slocum must have known."

"Knudson is Cathy's father then."

"Who else? When he found out Maude was pregnant he begged his wife for a divorce. He offered her everything he had. No soap. So Knudson left his wife and his job and cleared out. He was crazy to take Maudie with him, but she wouldn't go. She was scared, and she was thinking about the baby she was carrying. James Slocum wanted to marry her, and she let him."

"How did he come into the picture?"

"Maude had been typing for him all winter. He was

doing graduate work in drama, and he seemed to be well-heeled. That wasn't really why she married him, though, at least not the only reason. He had a faggot tendency, you know? He claimed he needed her, that she could save him. I don't know whether she did or not. Chances are she didn't."

"She was still trying," I said. "You should be doing my work, Miss Fleming."

"You mean I notice things? Yes, I do. But where Maudie was concerned I didn't have to: we were like sisters. We talked the whole thing out before she gave Slocum her answer. I advised her to marry him. I made a mistake. I often make mistakes." A bitter smile squeezed her mouth and eyes. "I'm not really a Miss, incidentally. My name is Mrs. Mildred Fleming Kraus Peterson Daniels Woodbury. I've been married four times."

"Congratulations four times."

"Yeah," she answered dryly. "As I was saying, I make mistakes. For most of them I take the rap myself. Maude took the rap for this one. She and Slocum left school before the end of the spring semester and went to live with his mother in Nopal Valley. She was determined to be a good wife to him, and a good mother to the kid, and for twelve years she stuck it out. Twelve years.

"In 1946 she came across a picture of Knudson in the *Los Angeles Times*. He was a police lieutenant in Chicago, and he'd run down some ex-con or other. It suddenly hit Maude that she still loved him, and that she was losing her life. She came down here and told me about it and I told her to beat her way to Chicago if she had to hitchhike. She had some money saved, and she went. Knudson was still living by himself. He hasn't been since.

"That fall the Chief of Police in Nopal Valley was fired for bribery. Knudson applied for the job and got it. He wanted to be near Maude, and he wanted to see his daughter. So they finally got together, in a way." She sighed. "I guess Maude couldn't stand the strain of having a lover. She wasn't built for intrigue."

"No. It didn't work out well."

"Maude had enough maturity to see what had to be done, if she could do it. She'd have gone away with Knudson this time. But it was too late. She had Cathy to think about. The hell of it was that Cathy didn't like Knudson. And she was crazy about Slocum."

"Too crazy," I said.

"I know what you mean." The dark sharp eyes veiled themselves, and unveiled. "Of course, she believes Slocum is her father. I think she'd better go on believing that, don't you?"

"It's not my problem."

"Nor mine. I'm glad it isn't. Whatever happens to Cathy, I'm sorry for her. It's a shame, she's a wonderful kid. I think I'll go up and see her over the weekend.—I almost forgot, the funeral. When is the funeral?"

"I wouldn't know. You better call her house."

She stood up quickly, and offered me her hand. "I must be going now—some work to finish up. What time is it?"

I looked at my watch. "Four o'clock."

"Goodbye, Mr. Archer. Thanks for listening to me."

"I should be thanking you."

"No. I had to talk to somebody about it. I felt guilty. I still do."

"Guilty of what?"

"Being alive, I guess." She flashed me a difficult smile, and darted away.

I sat over a third cup of coffee and thought about Maude Slocum. Hers was one of those stories without villains or heroes. There was no one to admire, no one to blame. Everyone had done wrong for himself and others. Everyone had failed. Everyone had suffered.

Perhaps Cathy Slocum had suffered most of all. My sympathies were shifting from the dead woman to the living girl. Cathy had been born into it innocent. She had been weaned on hatred and schooled in a quiet hell where nothing was real but her love for her father. Who wasn't really her father.

CHAPTER 25

The ride to Quinto, on an old bus sardined with weekenders, was long and slow and hot. A girl who exhaled beer fumes and mauve-scented perfume regaled me with stories of her bowling triumphs in the twenty-alley Waikiki Bowl on Figueroa Boulevard. At the Quinto junction I bade her a quick farewell and walked out to the pier.

My car was where I had left it. A parking-ticket was tucked under the windshield wiper. I tore it into eight pieces and tossed them into the ocean one by one. I didn't intend to come back to Quinto if I could help it.

Over the pass again to Nopal Valley. The central street was choked with late afternoon traffic, and parked cars lined the curbs. One of them pulled out ahead of me and I backed into its place. I walked a block to Antonio's and took a seat at the end of the crowded bar. Antonio saw me and nodded in recognition.

Without a word spoken he went to his safe and opened it. When he came to take my order, the clumsy newspaper package was in his hands. I thanked him. He said I was welcome. I asked for a double bourbon, which he brought. I paid him for it.

He lit my cigarette. I drank the bourbon straight and walked out with the money in my pocket.

Gretchen Keck was standing in front of the butane stove just inside the door of her trailer. She was wearing a halter and slacks. Her yellow hair was pulled up into a top-knot, held in place by an elastic band. The egg that she was frying spluttered and popped like a tiny machine gun riddling my guts with hunger.

She didn't notice me until I rapped on the open door. Then she saw who it was. She picked up the frying-pan and brandished it clublike. The egg fell onto the floor and lay there drooling yellow. "Get away from me."

"In a minute."

"You're a dirty bull, ain't you, one of the ones that bumped Pat? I got nothing to say."

"I have."

"Not to me you haven't. I don't know nothing. You can amscray." With the frying-pan upraised, ready to throw, she should have looked ridiculous. There was nothing ridiculous about her.

I talked fast: "Pat gave me something for you before he died—"

"Before you killed him, you mean."

"Shut up and listen to me, girl. I haven't got all day."

"All right, finish your pitch. I know you're lying, copper. You're trying to hook me in, only I don't know nothing. How could I know he was going to murder somebody?"

"Put it down and listen to me. I'm coming in."

"In a pig's eye!"

I stepped across the threshold, wrenched the iron pan from her hand, pushed her down into the solitary chair: "Pat didn't murder anybody, can you understand that?"

"It said he did in the paper. Now I know you're lying." But her voice had lost its passionate conviction. Her soft mouth drooped uncertainly.

"You don't have to believe what you read in the papers. Mrs. Slocum died by accident."

"Why did they kill Pat then if he didn't murder her?"

"Because he claimed he did. Pat heard a policeman tell me she was dead. He went to the man he was working for and convinced him that he killed her."

"Pat wasn't that crazy."

"No. He was crazy like a fox. The big boss gave him ten grand lamster's money. Pat talked himself into getting paid for a murder he didn't do."

"Jesus!" Her eyes were wide with admiration. "I told you he had a brain on him."

"He had a heart, too." That lie left a bile taste on my tongue. "When he saw he wasn't going to make it, he gave me the ten grand to give to you. He told me you were his heir."

"No. He told you that?" The cornflower eyes spilled over. "What else did he say?"

My tongue wagged on: "He said he wanted you to have it on one condition: that you get out of Nopal Valley and go some place where you can live a decent life. He said it would all be worth it if you did that."

"I will!" she cried. "Did you say ten grand? Ten thousand dollars?"

"Right." I handed her the package. "Don't spend it in California or they might try to trace it. Don't tell anybody what I've told you. Go to another state and put it in a bank and buy a house or something. That's what Pat wanted you to do with it."

"Did he say that?" She had torn off the wrappings and crushed the bright bills to her breast.

"Yes. He said that." And I told her what she wanted to hear because there was no reason not to: "He also said that he loved you."

"Yes," she whispered. "I loved him, too."

"I have to go now, Gretchen."

"Wait a minute." She rose, her mouth working awkwardly, trying to frame a question. "Why did you—I mean I guess you really was his friend, like you said.

I'm sorry. I thought you was a copper. And here you just came to bring me the money from Pat."

"Put it away," I said. "Get out of town tonight if you can."

"Yeah. Sure. I'll do just what Pat wanted me to. He really was a swell guy after all."

I turned and went out the door, so that she wouldn't see my face. "Goodbye, Gretchen."

The money wouldn't do her any permanent good. She'd buy a mink coat or a fast car, and find a man to steal one or wreck the other. Another Reavis, probably. Still, it would give her something to remember different from the memories that she had. She had no souvenirs and I had too many. I wanted no mementos of Reavis or Kilbourne.

Mrs. Strang ushered me into James Slocum's bedroom. It was a very manly room, equipped with red leather chairs and solid dark furniture. Prints of old sailing vessels, like portholes opening on a motionless sea, adorned the paneled oak walls. Built-in bookcases, crammed with volumes, covered the length and height of one wall. The kind of room a hopeful mother might furnish for her son.

Olivia Slocum's son was sitting up at the end of the great four-poster bed. His face was bloodless and thin. In the late gray light from the windows he looked like a silver image of a man. Francis Marvell was sitting on his own feet in a chair beside him. Both of them were intent on a chessboard set with black and white ivory pieces that rested on the edge of the bed between them.

Slocum's hand emerged from his scarlet silk sleeve and moved a black knight. "There."

"Jolly good," Marvell said. "Oh, jolly good."

Slocum withdrew his dreaming gaze from the board and turned it on me. "Yes?"

"You said you would see Mr. Archer?" the housekeeper faltered.

"Mr. Archer? Oh. Yes. Come in, Mr. Archer." Slocum's voice was weak and vaguely peevish.

Mrs. Strang left the room. I stood where I was.

Slocum and Marvell projected an atmosphere, a circle of intimacy, which I didn't care to enter. Nor did they want me to enter it. Their heads were turned toward me at the same impatient angle, willing me to be gone. To leave them to the complex chess-play between them.

"I hope that you're recovering, Mr. Slocum." I had nothing better to say.

"I don't know, I have had a perfectly dreadful series of shocks." Self-pity squeaked behind the words like a rat behind the wall. "I have lost my mother, I have lost my wife, my own daughter has turned against me now."

"I'm standing by, dear fellow," Marvell said. "You can count on me, you know." Slocum smiled weakly. His hand moved toward Marvell's, which was resting slack by the chessboard, but paused short of it.

"If you've come about the play," Marvell said to me, "I'm afraid I have to confess we've given it up. After all that's happened, it may be months or years before I can regain the world of imagination. Poor dear James may never act again."

"No great loss to the theatre," Slocum said with quiet pathos. "But Mr. Archer isn't interested in the play, Francis. I'd supposed you knew by now that he's a detective. I imagine that he's looking for his pay."

"I have been paid."

"That's just as well. You'd never have a penny out of me. May I hazard a guess as to who paid you?"

"You needn't. It was your wife."

"Of course it was! And shall I tell you why?" He leaned forward, clutching the bedclothes. His eyes were bright with fever or passion. The silver face was peaked and hollowed like an old man's. "Because you helped her to murder my mother, didn't you? Didn't you?"

Marvell uncoiled his legs and stood up, his face averted in embarrassment.

"No, Francis, please don't go. I want you to hear

this. I want you to know the sort of woman I've had
to spend my life with."

Marvell slumped back into the chair and began to
bite his knuckles.

"Go on," I said. "This is interesting."

"It came to me the night before last. I lay here
thinking the night through, and I saw the whole thing
plainly. She'd always hated my mother, she wanted
her money, she wanted to leave me. But she didn't
dare to murder her without assistance. You were to
lend the professional touch, were you not?"

"And what was my particular contribution?"

His voice was soft and sly: "You provided the scape-
goat, Mr. Archer. No doubt Maude drowned mother
herself; she wouldn't delegate that task, not she. You
were there to make sure that Reavis took the blame.
My suspicion was confirmed yesterday when Reavis's
cap was found in the grove by the pool. I knew that
Reavis didn't leave it there. He'd left it on the front
seat of the car. I saw it in the car myself. I suggest
that you saw it there too, and realized what could be
done with it."

"I'm not very suggestible, Mr. Slocum. But let's
assume that what you say is true. What are you going
to do about it?"

"There is nothing I can do." With his eyes turned
up toward the ceiling, his hands now gripping each
other, he looked like a mad saint. "In order to have
you punished, I should have to trumpet my shame,
my wife's shame, to the world. You can rest easy,
unless you have a conscience. Last night I did my
duty to my dead mother. I told my wife what I have
told you. She killed herself. It was fitting."

Hard words rose in me. I held them back with
clenched teeth. Slocum had retreated from reality. If I
told him that he had driven his wife to suicide for no
good reason, it would only drive him further into the
unreal world.

Maude Slocum hadn't killed herself because she
murdered her mother-in-law. Her husband's story of

the cap had simply told her that Reavis hadn't done it. Which meant that someone else had.

I said to Marvell: "If you care about this man, you'd better get him a damn good doctor."

He batted his eyes at me, and stuttered something incoherent against his knuckles. Slocum's face was still turned to the ceiling, wearing a sad holy smile. I went out. From the hallway I heard him say: "It's your move, Francis."

I went through the house alone, thinking of Maude Slocum and looking for her daughter. The rooms and corridors were empty and still. The tide of violence running in the house had permanently ebbed and drawn the life out with it. The veranda and the loggia and the terraces were empty of life, except for the flowers burning in the fading light. I avoided the pool, which glimmered through the trees like a wicked blade. At the end of the funereal alley of cypresses I came to the old lady's garden.

Cathy was sitting on a stone bench islanded among the lake of flowers. Her face was turned to the west, where a while before the sun had died in glory. Her young look traveled up beyond the fieldstone wall of the garden to the mountains. She was watching their purple masses as if they formed the walls of a great prison where she had been sentenced to live alone forever.

I called to her over the gate: "Cathy. May I come in?"

She turned slowly, the mountains huge and ancient in her eyes. Her voice was flat: "Hello, Mr. Archer. Do come in."

I released the redwood latch and stepped into the garden.

"Don't close it," she said. "You can leave it open."

"What are you doing?"

"Just thinking." She moved aside on the bench, to make room for me. The concrete surface still held the sun's heat.

"What about?"

"Me. I used to think this was all so beautiful, and

now it doesn't mean a thing. Coleridge was right about nature, I guess. You see the beauty there if you have it in your heart. If your heart is desolate, the world is a wilderness. Did you ever read his 'Ode to Dejection'?"

I said I never had.

"I understand it now. I'd kill myself if I had my mother's courage. As it is, I suppose I'll sit around and wait for something to happen to me. Something good or something bad, it doesn't really matter."

I didn't know what to say. I settled for something meaningless and soothing: "All the bad things have happened, haven't they?"

"Except the desolation in the heart." If she hadn't been completely earnest, the phrase would have sounded foolish.

I said: "Talk it out to me."

"What do you mean?"

She met my gaze. For a long moment we looked at each other. Her body narrowed and shrunk, drawing away from me. "I don't know what you mean."

"You killed your grandmother," I said. "You might as well tell me about it."

She bowed her head and shoulders and sat there, dry-eyed and quiet. "Does everybody know?"

"Nobody knows, Cathy. Just me and Ralph Knudson."

"Yes. He talked to me today. Mr. Knudson is my father. Why didn't they tell me sooner? I'd never have sent that letter."

"Why did you send it?" I said.

"I hated my mother. She was cheating on my father—Mr. Slocum. I saw her and Mr. Knudson together one day, and I wanted to make her suffer. And I thought if my father—if Mr. Slocum found out he'd make her leave and we could be together. Don't you see, they were always quarreling or giving each other the silent treatment. I wanted them separated so there would be some peace. But the letter didn't seem to make any difference at all."

For a while she had seemed a woman; more than

that, an ageless sybil speaking from ancient wisdom. She had become a child again, a harried child trying to explain the inexplicable: how one could do a murder with the best intentions in the world.

"So you did it the hard way," I said. "You thought your grandmother's money would blow them apart. Your mother would run off with her lover, and you could live happily ever after with your father."

"Mr. Slocum," she corrected me. "He isn't my father. Yes, I thought that. I am a hideous creature." And she wailed.

A mockingbird in the cypresses took it up. The sobbing howls of the girl and the bird demented the twilight. I laid one arm across Cathy's shuddering back. She said: "I am hideous. I should die."

"No, Cathy. Too many people have died."

"What are you going to do with me? I deserve to die. I really hated Grandma, I wanted to kill her. She twisted my father from the time he was a little boy, she made him what he is. You know what an Oedipus complex is, don't you?"

"Yes. I've also heard of an Electra complex."

She missed that. It was just as well, because I shouldn't have said it. She knew too much already, more than she could bear.

She had given over crying, but the bird still howled from the tree like a disembodied conscience.

I said: "Cathy. I'm not going to do anything to you. I haven't the right."

"Don't be nice to me. I don't deserve anything nice from anybody. From the moment I decided to do it, I've felt as if I was cut off from every human being. I know what they mean by the mark of Cain, I have it." She covered her high fair brow with her hand, as if it might actually be branded.

"I understand how you feel. I was responsible, in a way, for Pat Reavis's death. Once I killed another man with my hands. I did it to save my own life, but his blood is on my hands."

"You are being too good to me, and so was Mr. Knudson. My father." The word sounded remarkable from her lips, as if it stood for something great and mysterious and new. "He blamed himself for everything that happened. Now you're blaming yourself. I'm the one that did it, though. I even intended Pat to take the blame for me. I did see him here that night. I lied to you when I told you that I didn't. He wanted me to run away with him, and I tried to want to, but I couldn't. He was drunk; I sent him away. Then I saw the cap he'd left in the car, and that was when I decided I could do it. It was terrible. Once I saw what I could do, I felt as if I had to do it. You know?"

"I think I know."

"I felt as if I'd sold my soul to the devil, even before it happened—No, I mustn't say it *happened*, because I made it happen. Still I thought if I could get away from here, it wouldn't have to happen. I saw you coming out of the house, and I got into your car. But you wouldn't take me away."

"I'm sorry."

"Don't be sorry, you couldn't help it. What could you have done with me? Anyway, you left me there. I knew Grandma was sitting here in the garden. I couldn't go back into the house until it was done. I went down by the pool and hid Pat's cap in the hedge, then I called her. I told her there was a dead bird in the pool. She came to look and I pushed her in. I went into the house and went to bed. I didn't sleep all night, or last night either. Do you think I can sleep tonight, now that other people know?"

She turned her face to me. It was open and tormented, its flesh gray and almost translucent, like the last falling light in the garden.

"I hope so, Cathy."

Her cold lips moved: "Do you think I'm insane? I've been afraid for years that I was going insane."

"No," I said, though I hadn't any idea.

A man's voice called her name from somewhere out of sight. The bird flew out of the tree and circled to another, where it took up a new cry.

Cathy's head came up like a deer's. "I'm here." And

she added in the same clear voice: "father." The strange and ancient word.

Knudson appeared at the gate. He glowered when he saw me. "I told you to get out and stay out. Leave her alone."

"No," Cathy said. "He's been nice to me, father."

"Come here, Cathy."

"Yes, father." She went to him, her head bowed and watchful.

He spoke to her in a low voice, and she walked away in the direction of the house. She moved uncertainly, a traveler on new ground, and was lost in the cypress shadows.

I went to the gate and faced Knudson in the narrow opening between the fieldstone posts. "What are you going to do with her?"

"That's my business." He was taking off his coat. He was in civilian clothes, and his gunbelt was missing.

"I've made it my business, too."

"You've made a mistake. Several mistakes. You're going to suffer for them." He swung a fist at me.

I stepped out of reach. "Don't be childish, Knudson. Bloodletting won't help either of us. Or Cathy."

He said: "Take off your coat." He draped his over the swinging gate.

I threw mine on top of it. "If you insist."

He backed onto the grass, and I followed him. It was a long hard fight, and a useless one. Still it had to be fought through. He was bigger and heavier than I was, but I was faster. I hit him three times to his one. I knocked him down six times before he stayed, prone on his back with both hands over his face. Both of my thumbs were sprained and swelling tight. My right eye was almost closed by a mouse on the upper lid.

It was full dark when it ended. He sat up after a while and spoke between sobbing breaths. "I had to fight somebody. Slocum was no good to me. You fight well, Archer."

"I was trained by pros. What are you going to do with Cathy?"

Slowly he got to his feet. His face was striped with black blood which dropped from the end of his chin and splattered his torn shirt. He staggered and almost fell. I steadied him with my hand.

"Officially, you mean?" He mumbled, through puffed lips. "I turned in my resignation this afternoon. I didn't tell them why. You're not going to tell them, either."

"No," I said. "She's your baby."

"She knows that she's my baby. She's coming with me, back to Chicago. I'll put her in school there, and try to give her a home. Does that sound impossible to you? I've seen worse cases than Cathy straighten out and grow up into people. Not often, but it happens."

"Cathy will make it if anybody will. What does Slocum say?"

"Slocum can't stop me," he said. "He isn't going to try. Mrs. Strang is coming with me; she and Cathy are fond of each other."

"Good luck, then."

Around us and above us the darkness was immense. Our hands groped for each other and met. I left him there.

ABOUT THE AUTHOR

ROSS MACDONALD was born near San Francisco in 1915. He was educated in Canadian schools, traveled widely in Europe, and acquired advanced degrees and a Phi Beta Kappa key at the University of Michigan. In 1938 he married a Canadian who is now well known as the novelist Margaret Millar. Mr. Macdonald (Kenneth Millar in private life) taught school and later college, and served as communications officer aboard an escort carrier in the Pacific. For over twenty years he has lived in Santa Barbara and written mystery novels about the fascinating and changing society of his native state. Among his leading interests are conservation and politics. He is a past president of the Mystery Writers of America. In 1964 his novel *The Chill* was given a Silver Dagger award by the Crime Writers' Association of Great Britain. Mr. Macdonald's *The Far Side of the Dollar* was named the best crime novel of 1965 by the same organization. Recently, he was presented with the Mystery Writers of America's Grand Master Award. *The Moving Target* was made into the highly successful movie *Harper* (1966). And *The Goodbye Look* (1969), *The Underground Man* (1971), *Sleeping Beauty* (1973), and *The Blue Hammer* (1976) were all national bestsellers.

Ross Macdonald
Lew Archer Novels

"The finest series of detective novels ever written by an American . . . I have been reading him for years and he has yet to disappoint. Classify him how you will, he is one of the best novelists now operating, and all he does is keep on getting better."

—The New York Times

☐ THE BARBAROUS COAST	10207	$1.75
☐ THE DROWNING POOL	10910	$1.75
☐ THE IVORY GRIN	10979	$1.75
☐ THE MOVING TARGET	10982	$1.75
☐ THE FAR SIDE OF THE DOLLAR	10985	$1.75
☐ THE WAY SOME PEOPLE DIE	10987	$1.75
☐ THE GOOD-BYE LOOK	10995	$1.75
☐ THE INSTANT ENEMY	10997	$1.75
☐ THE NAME IS ARCHER	11021	$1.75
☐ THE UNDERGROUND MAN	11240	$1.75